THE SCARLET DOVE

THE SCARLET DOVE

a novel by

Mark Beauregard

A GIANT BOOK

Second Giant Publishing Edition February 2019

Bibliographical Note: This novel is an unabridged reprint of the same
novel published in 2007 under the name Mark Zero. Mark Zero and
Mark Beauregard are both pen names of Beauregard Mark Zero. First
Giant Publishing Edition August 2007.

Library of Congress Control Number: 2019932908

ISBN: 9781933975108

10 9 8 7 6 5 4 3 2

cover photograph © Masterfile.

www.giantpublishing.com

THE FLOOD

The storm began as a concourse of towering black clouds that battered the plains with heavy rain till the arroyos churned with whitewater. Vicious winds thrashed boats into driftwood, wrenched juniper trees up by their roots and washed the bloated bodies of unlucky cows downriver. At first, people thought it merely an extreme instance of the violent squalls that swept across the Menodoc Plateau every afternoon in August: storms that made men cower for an hour but then blew away as swiftly as they came, leaving behind sodden debris and lazy summer sun. But this storm didn't blow over after the usual hour, and it didn't blow over after three days, and after two weeks of constant rain, falling now as nickel-sized drops that welted bare skin, now as a soft fine mist steaming out of the air, the levy above the flats broke and flooded both rivers around Tres Cruces.

The highland from which Tres Cruces surveyed the rivers—Rio Fuerte to the east, Rio Fortuna to the west—became progressively less high, until the town was seated on an island between the rivers, whose channels widened by the day. As the rivers swelled, they seemed to generate rain of their own, seeding the clouds above with the water that had dropped the moment before, in an endless cycle of replenishing depletion, thirst slaked by thirst. The thunder-battles between storm-clouds and the lightning striking trees and barns seemed need-lessly to emphasize what everyone in town already knew from the rain itself: that their property and their plans, their time and their dreams would be consumed, discarded or destroyed by forces that held them in no regard whatsoever.

Jonathan Vega, owner of the Coronado Saloon and Inn, staring through the windows of his tavern: "Even if the rain lets up this second, nobody'll cross the rivers for a week. The ferry on the Fuerte's washed away and the ford across the Fortuna won't exist after these floods. We're lucky if the food holds out."

Diana Clayborn, a prostitute with a room above the Saloon, smoking a cigarette: "Plenty of beans and rice, Jonathan, beans and rice till doomsday. What's gonna run out is tobacco and whisky. And we're lucky if the river don't wash us away just for spite."

Collins, the bank agent from San Luis, sipping bourbon at the upright piano: "Rivers aren't spiteful, Miss Diana. People are spiteful."

Pastor Charles, a Methodist circuit-rider, holding two eights in a game of five-card draw: "According to the Good Book, the rain is a sure sign of the will of God. If I may quote from the Book of Ezra: 'the people are many and it is a time of much rain, and we are not able to stand without, neither is this a work of one day or two: for we are many that have transgressed in this thing.'"

Collins: "So we brought the rain on ourselves, Reverend? Hogwash. If that were true, we could make it stop. So how do we make it stop, Reverend? How do we appease your angry God?"

Jonathan, the saloon owner: "Gentlemen, this is not a place for philosophical arguments. Live and let live and have another round of whisky."

Pastor Charles spread his cards on the table. His pair of eights was trumped by a pair of queens, then by two pair deuces and fours, and then Otis the Frogboy, the farmhand from Rancho Cielito, laid down a full house, sevens over jacks. Otis the Frogboy was incapable of understanding the intricacies of poker, but nevertheless won with astonishing regularity.

As a background to the conversation at the Coronado Saloon, as accompaniment to the plunking on the upright piano, as the impetus of the card games and dice games and memory games played to pass the time: the rain and thunder and the sizzle of lightning close enough to electrify knuckle hairs. The toneless cacophony of drops against tin roofs, wooden roofs and thatch, the thudding arrhythmia of water plummeting against plank sidewalks and sandstone, the effervescent almost-harmonies of rainbeads splashing into puddles and splattering windowpanes and the insistent, maddeningly irregular drip drip drip of leaks unsealing ceilings, swelling soggy floorboards underfoot. The rain washed the back of everyone's minds with the bracken and flotsam of other people's lives, the fodder of useless hours of thought, insisting and then relenting, ebbing and flowing like an aerial tide not just of water, but of longings and frustrations so pervasive to the conscious mind as to seem eternal. The difference between dreams of rain and waking nightmares of rain merged, until distinctions between the dreamer and the dream all but disappeared.

As the storm stretched into its third week and showed no signs of abating, daylight came to mean only a diffuse effulgence coming from everywhere and nowhere at once, and the demarcations between days lost their significance. After one particularly long, dark blast that blacked out the sky, followed by night, followed by more gloomy rain, a fistfight broke out in the Coronado Saloon about the correct day of the week; or, if not exactly about the correct day of the week, then about the need for the existence of days and weeks, and the frustration of having them nullified by the rain.

THE SCARLET DOVE

Insofar as she had a mother, Diana's mother had been a prostitute—a scarlet dove. Beyond that, her ancestry consisted of the whole heaving mass of mankind, humping and sweating and bleeding and somehow muddling through the generation of subsequent generations. As recently as twenty years before, the Coronado Saloon and Inn had been bustling enough to support four scarlet doves all on its own, an enterprise overseen by Jonathan Vega, in that he took their money for himself and (occasionally) complained to the marshal about a cowboy's or miner's or drifter's misuse of the girls. Diana's mother had died in childbirth with Diana, and Diana had become a ward of Jonathan's other painted ladies, where she was doted on and pampered and loved the way bored children love stray kittens, with equal amounts gushing affection and contempt. She became the secret vessel where her prostitute mothers hid their deepest humiliations.

Diana grew up in the bawdy, angry days of Tres Cruces' prosperity, before quiet became negative and empty. As the daughter of a fallen woman in a community of fallen women, she became her surrogate mothers' last best hope, and they scrimped and saved and squirreled money away for Diana, to send her to school, to send her away, to send her into the better life that they could no longer imagine for themselves; but Diana lacked imagination of her own in such abstract matters as the future, and not even her mothers could say clearly what they meant by a better life beyond the idea that it could be something more than shameful. The boys of the town treated Diana worse than chickens treat their runts.

When Diana was fourteen, she fell in love with a man called Pepper who rode through Tres Cruces on his way to Santa Elena, and she rode off with him, giving herself to him body and soul; and when Pepper had had his fill of her body, he sent her soul back to Tres Cruces, where it haunted the Saloon and spent her mothers' money recklessly. Diana's inability to imagine any future besides the past, besides an endless series of humiliations large and small and scrabbling for money and all of life revolving around men and cattle and guns led her by hook and by crook into the trade, until she found the obliteration of selling sex for money almost a relief from the greater despair that she couldn't name, the despair that breathed stale must from under her bed and old sweat from behind her closet door and eyed her through the bedroom window on hot summer nights.

Twenty years had passed and so had Diana's mothers, and so had most of the drifters and miners and speculators who had once spent their money improvidently in Tres Cruces. The ranches were still prosperous, the rancher-barons kept the town's commercial wheels greasy, and the cowhands still came in to Tres Cruces most Sundays, but nobody panned the Fuerte or Fortuna any more. Land speculation had dried up when the railroad went north through San Luis, and traders had stopped bringing Indian jewelry across these flats to Santa Elena. The cattle drive in March, the tardy get-rich-quick schemers who had missed the real boom, the mail riders, local pokes: that was the extent of Diana's trade. None of the respectable people in Tres Cruces had any use for her except as an object of ridicule and religious derision. Only Jonathan, who used Diana as his personal pet, cared whether she lived or died.

Diana was always holding a little money back, sewing it into her petticoats or the ruffled white trim around her maroon and black dress, dreaming of a day when she might know what to use it for. Somehow she had entered her thirties and still she couldn't imagine going anywhere or knowing anything that would make any difference. If she went to San Luis, what would she do there? If she went to Haskell, or Santa Elena, or especially to some seaside port at the mouth of the rivers, what would she do when she got there except fuck men for money, and who knew how even that familiar lubricious grind would be in a port with sailors hard and angry from the masculine quarantine of the sea, from satisfying each other furtively in the dank dark below decks; and who knew the value in a bustling sea port of a thirty-four year old ghost from a ghost town still just a little too prosperous to know it was dead?

When the rains came to Tres Cruces, when the rivers flooded and the telegraph lines snapped, Diana was nonplussed. The rain changed nothing for her: it merely composed a new variation on the theme of her life, trapped in a town unable to communicate with the outside world, with no prospect of help, no knowledge of the future beyond its unpredictable grimness, no hope for anything but damage. The ceaseless wringing of hands, the wringing of necks, the wringing-out of fluids from her own body, now had a counterpart of heroic proportions in the wringing-out of rain from the storm clouds overhead. Diana welcomed the rain, and she hoped the rivers would rise up and wash Tres Cruces a thousand miles away and her with it, leave this land as clean and empty as it once must have been and give it the chance to start over, the chance that she would never have.

Diana, smoking her tenth cigarette of the day, staring out her window into the afternoon twilight of drizzling, creamy white clouds: "Now we're all in the same boat. Collins, the banker, he's no better than Otis the Frogboy as long as we're holed up in this saloon. We're all just waitin' for the trumpets to blow the end of the world. And what if we do run out of food? What if the floods come and take us all away? What good's the pastor's Good Book then? What's the use of Collins's gold?"

Diana and Jonathan and Mr. and Mrs. Mathers, who owned the General Store, were the only people still earning money in Tres Cruces: Jonathan for his rooms at the Inn (at a generous discount, he would say, owing to these unfortunate conditions, and he would smile his glad-handing smile), Diana on her back (beneath the travelers trapped in Tres Cruces by the storm, as they fucked away the money they had saved for tools or transit or even tithes), and the Mathers down at the General Store, who locked shop at night with padlocks and shotguns and fervent prayers that folks didn't get so desperate as to kill and steal. But no one in Tres Cruces was that hungry yet.

Diana: "Ah, hell, another leak in the ceiling."

A knock at her door.

"It's open."

"Pardon me. I was wondering if you were available. . . for. . . service?"

"Service? Is that your idea how to talk? Service?"

Suddenly angry: "I don't need no lip from no whores."

"Relax. It's cute, that's all. Reserved. Ah, I remember, you're that fella all the way from Virginia, is that right? Southern gentleman, that's the idea?"

"That's right."

"Come to dig out the Rodriguez Mine, or the Potter Mine, was it?"

"I don't keep track of such names." He pushed his fat stomach all the way into the room and took off his hat, which looked new but for a layer of sweat now rinsed mostly clean by the rain. Blue denim work shirt, blue jeans, brown boots with a white-stitched design swirled over the pointy toe. Heavy footfalls into the room and the click of the door latch behind him. "My partner, Jerry, he's got a head for maps and figures and such. He knows the mines." The man's face, though hidden by four days' growth, was still young and fresh and confident. Diana took another cigarette from the red wooden box on her nightstand and lit it.

"Jerry knows, huh? This your first time on a little adventure, then? For profit? Ain't no more gold in them mines, you know. Nor in the rivers neither."

"Jerry says people don't know how to read survey maps, they don't know nothin' about geology. He says he knows how to find gold that's right under other people's noses, only they can't see it." Awkwardly holding his hat in front of him. "Anyway. . . so you want my business? Saloon keeper says you'll french me for a dollar."

Exhaling a silver streak of smoke and laughing spitefully: "So you do need lip from a whore, after all, don't you, Mr. Reserved Southern Gentleman? Look, it's early for me, Mr. . . what's your name?"

"Burns. David."

"David. David and Jerry, lookin' for gold. Look, David, why don't you come back later? You don't look so all-fired desperate to me. Come back after dark maybe."

A long pause. "Maybe?" A hint of menace.

"Come back after dark. I'll give you something special. All right?"

David Burns put his hat back on, looked long and hard into Diana's eyes, then turned, walked out the door and shut it a little too hard, for emphasis. Diana cringed and shook her head, bored and perturbed, and took another long drag on her cigarette. She sat down on her bed and stared out at the dusk gathering between steadily plunking silver-headed drops of rain.

LUCK OF THE DRAW

It was late afternoon and hot. Clothing pasted itself to sweaty skin like papier-mâché and everyone in the Coronado Saloon stank of new and old sweat mixing and cheap cigars and sour alcoholic breath. The oil lamps in the black steel chandelier above the poker table guttered smoke to the ceiling, and the sixteen surly rain-numbed denizens of the saloon who weren't involved in the poker game stared out at the rain or scrawled private, mundane thoughts across paper so dampened by humidity that it tore softly like tissue. Jonathan Vega, standing behind the bar, made endless avaricious notes in the margins of his account books, while Collins the banker coaxed Civil War laments from the piano. No one but the five poker players spoke, and only Otis the Frogboy might have been called animated, though his squeals, grunts, and indecent squawks could hardly be called speech.

The only poker player in Tres Cruces with no tells to give away his hand was Otis the Frogboy: he didn't chew his fingernails or pull on his ear lobe or look in one direction or the other or slouch or clear his throat, the way every other gambler revealed the secret of his cards. Otis the Frogboy sometimes drooled on his chips. His eyes rolled in opposite directions. He clapped his hands spontaneously in the middle of a deal, of a call, or while somebody else was collecting his money from the pot, but these were clues only to his larger idiocies, not to the value of his hand. Yet Otis was the best player at the table.

In a man of normal intelligence, his success at cards might have been ascribed to uncanny intuition or mathematical genius or even sophisticated chicanery, but, as everyone in Tres Cruces knew, Otis the Frogboy won or lost on sheer dumb luck. He would discard four and then draw a flush. He would stand pat with six high. In a game of straight poker, he would fold with three queens showing. His behavior was unpremeditated and his sense of the value of money indeterminate, both of which might have made him a gambler's best mark, except that he won far more than he lost, a fact that no one could explain.

The ranch hands at Rancho Cielito had started Otis playing cards as a joke to amuse themselves, but the Frogboy had soon collected all of their money, which rendered the joke unamusing. The ranch hands took their money back. Otis the Frogboy didn't seem to mind one way or the other. Then a cowboy from New Hebron, hired on one summer for roping and branding, spent three straight months teaching Otis about money, until Otis became angry when the ranchers took his winnings away, and the ranchers stopped playing with Otis and ran the cowboy out of town. Now, in the Coronado Saloon, the prisoners of the rain let the Frogboy play for the distraction of it, to prove to themselves that dumb luck couldn't hold over time, that chance would eventually succumb to even modest skill; but, at the moment, Otis the Frogboy was holding a little bit of everybody else's money.

The deal rotated after every hand, so that each player dealt, except Otis the Frogboy never took a turn. Otis had trouble with both the mechanics and the concept of shuffling, and anyway his luck appeared unaffected no matter who the dealer or what the style of cut or shuffle, so that the matter of dealers' strategies, sleight of hand, palming, top or bottom dealing, concealed or marked cards, and other tricks known to gamblers were of no concern to him. Now, the deal went to Jackson.

Jackson was a black man with a thick beard, one of two professional gunmen hired by the banker Collins to escort a shipment of money from Tres Cruces to San Luis. The fact that Collins's money now languished in the safe of the Hidalgo Trust Bank down the street from the saloon concerned Jackson only mildly: by agreement, his pay was insured by the very money he would escort to San Luis once the rain broke, and it didn't matter how long it took to get it there. He kept his hat pulled low over his eyes, to survey the table from the recesses of his shadowed sockets.

Jackson, dealing, staring ambiguously through his own cigar smoke at the ante pile: "Straight poker, three down, three up, money card, jacks are better." Now staring directly across the table at Pastor Charles. "You been doin' some damage to my little nest egg today, Parson. You got God lookin' in on my cards for you?"

Pastor Charles, the Methodist circuit-rider, kept his chips stacked on his Bible and continuously quoted scripture aloud while he contemplated his cards, as if debating the merits of his hand with God himself. "In poker, the Lord helps those who help themselves, no one can doubt it. I take the admonishment in Proverbs chapter ten to heart, when the prophet says 'he becometh poor that dealeth with a slack hand: but the hand of the diligent maketh rich.'"

Ironically: "Didn't know they played poker back in the Bible days, Parson."

"Ah, you're a Bible student, then, Mr. Jackson? I wouldn't have guessed it."

"Mainly I'm studyin' them chips pilin' up on your Bible."

"Study hard, Mr. Jackson, but notice that the Frogboy has more of your money than I do. Jacks are better, you said?"

David Burns, the neophyte miner from Virginia, was gambling to kill time till dark, when he would go to Diana upstairs and not come down again till he got what he wanted. Breathing heavily over his cards: "I bet a nickel."

Hargis, the telegraph clerk, whose occupation had been voided when the storm downed the lines, clicked his chips together rapidly, raining curses and insults on the heads of everyone in the saloon in Morse Code. "I call."

And finally, Otis the Frogboy, in his middle twenties, whose color was an odd olive tan, whose left cheek rode slightly higher than his right, whose head bobbed back and forth and side to side in sharp spasms that made his wild brown hair and wild brown eyes appear even wilder, sat with his legs crossed beneath him in his chair and grunted. Everyone at the table pointed emphatically at Otis, the signal that he was to bet. As if at random, the Frogboy slid two nickel chips from his pile into the middle, and the Parson, with a quick motion, reached out and slid one off the pile back to Otis.

Jackson: "Table calls, everyone takes another." Dealing. "Pair of fives to Mr. Otis."

Everyone again pointed emphatically at the Frogboy, who flung two nickel chips into the center.

"That's ten cents to you, Parson."

David Burns: "Not that it's my business, Parson, but I thought men of the cloth didn't believe in games of chance."

"Games of chance? No. But games, my friend, games."

"Which game don't have odds, Parson?"

"In the book of Job, chapter 24, Job asserts that no man can know his fate, yet in Second Timothy chapter two, we learn that the foundation of God standeth sure, and so does the man who stands on that foundation. I take it from that, gentlemen, that while even the game of life may have its odds, the man who trusts the foundation of God can be assured of the ultimate winning hand. Faith in God eliminates the odds. I see the ten and raise ten."

David Burns: "When I was a boy, in Virginia, they ran a priest out of town for holding dice games in the church on Saturday nights."

"Some parishioners would believe that God himself does not play dice."

A crackle of lightning lit the saloon, followed immediately by a report of thunder so loud and monstrous that a windowpane at the far corner of the room shattered. A man in a rumpled brown suit, who had been hunkered by the window spinning pennies on the sill, cried out as the pane crashed in; he leapt up, knocked over his chair and patted his body for cuts and shards. He quickly picked his change out of the glass and walked in as dignified a manner possible to a table at the other side of the tavern.

Jonathan Vega, angrily collecting a broom and dustpan from behind the bar and striding to the broken window: "Ain't it bad enough that my inn's a goddamn sieve without the goddamn storm punching holes in it?" He used the broom to sweep glass off of the sill and then moved the table out of the corner and swept the floor all around before returning to the bar and depositing the broken glass in a bin. "I bet there ain't a damn sight of glass left in this whole town."

Collins banged out a quick verse of "I'd Choose to be a Gypsy" on the piano, as a blast of wind rattled the tavern doors and rain whipped in through the newly broken window. The crowd in the saloon recovered themselves by cursing at the plague of water and wind.

Pastor Charles, to no one in particular: "Shall we receive good at the hand of God and not receive evil?"

Collins: "What benefit does your God offer if he hands out good and evil equally?"

"God is not for your benefit, Mr. Collins."

Jonathan was fashioning a patch for the broken window out of a frayed square of wallpaper he'd found under the bar. "What did I tell you two about philosophical disagreements in my saloon?"

"Would you prefer gunfire, Mr. Vega?"

Jackson: "Pair of nines to you, Hargis."

As the card players continued to play, people with rooms at the inn would wander upstairs or downstairs, or would leave the saloon to walk down the short streets of Tres Cruces, to visit other denizens holed up in other buildings or simply to avoid going mad staring at the rain by letting the rain drench them. After a stroll through the stormy streets, they would return to the inn to peel off their sopping clothes and relieve their minds paradoxically by soaking themselves in a bath before putting on clean clothes sticky and damp from the humidity and staring out at the rain once again, which would not have changed. No one could tell the difference any more between their own sweat and the air around them, and no matter their attempts to alleviate the pressure of it, the dense tropical heat drenched their minds with apathy and hate.

A man named Moreno, a drifter heading west, sauntered to the bar and bought a bottle of whisky. He asked the number of Diana's room, then clomped upstairs, sneaking looks at the gamblers' hands. David Burns eyed Moreno territorially and thought of Diana kneeling in front of him or lying beneath him.

Jackson called Pastor Charles's hand. As Pastor Charles laid out a heart flush, Jackson made a move under the table and a shot reported across the saloon. The table tottered as Jackson's revolver recoiled up into it and Pastor Charles's chair jerked backwards—his feet flew up, kicking the table with all of its chips and cards six inches into the air. Otis the Frogboy clapped and grunted and David Burns rolled from his chair onto the floor and scuttled toward the bar. At the other end of the tavern, a woman screamed as Jackson jumped up with pistol in hand, looking down at Pastor Charles splayed awkwardly out of his upturned chair. Blood flowed in a rapidly spreading stream from Charles's chest.

A thundercrack overhead masked the hammer click as Jonathan drew his shotgun from under the bar and leveled it at Jackson. "Drop the gun, boy, drop it." Jackson lowered his revolver slowly, eased the hammer down and holstered his weapon.

"Saul, run fetch Doc Drumwright. Now!" Jonathan's nephew Saul grabbed his hat and ran out into the rain as Jonathan came out from behind the bar, keeping the shotgun trained on Jackson, and knelt down to check Pastor Charles. He felt a pulse in his neck.

"What the hell you do that for, boy? You shot an unarmed man and a man of the cloth besides, completely unprovoked, and if I don't take you out back and shoot you right now, we'll hang you sure as you're standing there, providin' we don't think of somethin' worse first. What do you got to say for yourself?"

Jackson wiped his lips with his fingers and moved his head just an inch to the left and right. He saw that those not cowering in the corners had formed a loose ring around him and Vega's shotgun allowed few options. Jackson said loudly and slowly: "I believe, if you'll examine the good reverend, and especially his Bible, you'll find I'm in the right."

Collins, approaching from the piano: "Cheating? Hellfire, man, are you telling me you shot this man because he cheated in a penny-ante poker game?" Otis the Frogboy laughed dementedly and clapped his hands. "You don't kill people for a dollar's worth of pennies."

Jackson, inflamed: "Mr. Collins, with all due respect, sir,

what did you hire me to do? What about that pile of pennies you got sittin' in your bank down the street? What about ridin' shotgun with your pile of pennies to San Luis? I could kill people for that pile of pennies with your blessing, now, couldn't I?"

Vega: "Shut up, both of you. Hargis, open the man's Bible."

Hargis opened Pastor Charles's Bible and found a number of cards, mostly sixes and sevens, of all suits. They examined the reverend's sleeves and pockets and found an eight of every suit.

Jackson: "Like I said. He kept his chips on his Bible and he slid cards from between the pages while he fiddled with his chips. Every hand, he was workin' on a flush."

"That ain't no reason to shoot an unarmed man."

Saul ran back in from the rain with a soaking wet Doc Drumwright, whose breath stank as much as anyone's there from whisky, whose spectacles dripped water into his bushy salt-and-pepper mustache. Drumwright was mostly a barber, but as the only man in Tres Cruces with any knowledge of anatomy and any delicacy with a blade, he had become the doctor by default and now prided himself on keeping up with the latest medical trends. He had been reclining in his own barber chair throwing back shots of whisky reading an old issue of *Harper's* when Saul burst in with the news.

Doc Drumwright knelt down and wrestled Pastor Charles out of his chair before feeling for a pulse in his wrist, then in his neck, and then holding his own spectacles underneath Charles's nose to detect a breath. "Dead. I'd say the bullet clipped an artery or went right into his heart, most likely, all this blood. Did he cry out or talk?"

"No."

"Well, that's good, I reckon. Quick that way. Less painful,

at least. Where's the marshal?"

"Out to Rancho Cielito, remember? Nobody's seen him since the levy gave way."

"I guess we better move the body back to my shop so I can prepare him for burial, though we'd do just as well shippin' him down the river on a barge as wet as the ground'll be. This the fella who shot him?"

"That's right."

"Gonna lock him up?"

Jackson, now plaintive but firm: "Mr. Collins, you know me, you know I ain't no criminal. This man has been proved to be a liar and a thief that was stealing money from everybody at this table."

"But why didn't you just expose him as a cheat, Jackson?"

"I believe I *have* exposed him as a cheat, Mr. Collins."

Vega, still with the shotgun on Jackson: "You're gettin' locked up, boy. In addition to killing a man in cold blood, you wrecked private property and endangered everyone in the bar. If that ricochet had gone another way, you might have killed some perfectly innocent man, more than what you already did. You can't go shootin' off your guns every time you think somebody wrongs you."

Collins, reluctantly, protecting his investment: "I'll vouch for him, Mr. Vega. Give me your guns, Jackson, and mind your business, and we can turn this matter over to the marshal when he returns."

Hargis, the telegraph operator: "Like hell, Collins. What good is your word that this coon won't—"

Jackson: "You said coon?"

"You got a problem with 'coon,' nigger?"

Jackson turned and drew on Hargis, but before he could level his gun Collins hurled himself against Jackson's shoulder and Jackson's revolver discharged into the floorboards. A host of men jumped from all sides on Jackson, wrestled his gun away and subdued him with blows and kicks to the head and body and vigorous twistings of his arms and legs. When Jackson cried out for mercy and lay motionless under the weight of bodies, they kicked him some more.

Jonathan decided that they would use the jail key entrusted to Doc Drumwright to incarcerate Jackson until the marshal returned, or until such a time as they decided amongst themselves that he should be strung up or shot or whipped or all three. Collins and Hargis were selected to carry Jackson's now-unconscious body down to the cells in the marshal's office.

Jerry, the miner from Virginia, and a young merchant named McKinley picked up the dead Pastor Charles like a sack of oats and hefted his body down to the barbershop in the company of Doc Drumwright. Saul got a mop and a bucket and began wiping away the blood, while the temporary residents of the Coronado Saloon expressed their shock and disbelief over the incident in tones ranging from loud indignance to self-pity and calls for the return of slavery.

The rain fell harder now as darkness weaved through the water engulfing the air around Tres Cruces. Though the thunder grew more insistent, the violent events alleviated everyone's boredom and thereby generally lifted everyone's spirits. David Burns helped straighten the tables and chairs and picked up the poker chips, adding all of Jackson's and most of Pastor Charles's chips to the tally owed to him. As Saul sopped up the blood of the former Reverend, Otis the Frogboy hovered around the bucket of bloody water, slowly and seemingly obliviously sticking one finger after another up his nose.

An Improbable Proposition

After the commotion of the shooting had died down and they had had their fill of gawking from the upstairs landing, Diana and Moreno returned to Diana's room and poured fresh glasses of whisky. They stared at one another in the ochre tallow candlelight. Moreno's shadowy reflection in the mirror atop Diana's cheap vanity made him appear even darker than he was. Diana held the lip of her shot glass to her own bottom lip and breathed in the caramel and corn and antiseptic aridness of the whisky before drinking it in sips so small that the alcohol seemed to evaporate as it crossed her tongue.

Moreno sat in Diana's vanity chair, facing her where she sat on her bed, the bottle of whisky between them siphoning off the night. Moreno said he had been a blacksmith's apprentice in La Union, and then a mechanic on a steamer, and then a tanner's apprentice, before deciding to go west to the coast to try his hand in a shipyard. Stranded in Tres Cruces with nothing to do but watch and think, he had decided on a new profession, riskier but more lucrative, and all he needed was a partner.

Diana: "I can't see how a bank robbery could possibly work. Aside from the fact that Collins's men are trained to shoot people like you and you said yourself you ain't much with a gun, and aside from the fact that you never worked on a safe before, and aside from the fact that even if Collins's men don't kill you there's Jonathan downstairs and a dozen other men with guns in Tres Cruces who wouldn't stand for it, you couldn't go nowhere with the money even if you got away with it, for the same reason the money's sittin' in that safe to begin with, which is that we're all stranded here and the flood's still rising."

"Not entirely true. I know, if I could work with that safe alone, I could figure it out. I'm good with my hands, and there are more ways to open a box than one."

"Don't you think the people who build safes know that? Why do you think they're called 'safe?' Because they're safe from people like you. I may die in Tres Cruces, that much seems certain, but not tomorrow, not strung up or full of holes over some stupid scheme cooked up by a failed blacksmith's apprentice. No thank you."

"Listen to me. My plan is a good one. And now, with Jackson in jail, there's only the one guard and Collins to deal with, which will make the first stage easy."

"Nothing's easy where money's concerned, Moreno. Money and guns. You're either stupid or naive to think a lure as simple as yours would get a hired man with a gun away from a safe full of money. Besides, like I said, even if everyone else in Tres Cruces died this instant, you'd be a million years opening that safe. Have you ever even seen a safe up close, Moreno? It ain't a jewelry box and you ain't got any dynamite and nobody's that smart with his hands."

Moreno drained his whisky, refilled his glass, and then strolled around Diana's room taking soft little baby steps that barely registered against the wooden floor. He muttered wordlessly and noiselessly to himself, just his lips moving in a pantomime of speech. Diana drank off her own glass and refilled it, happy enough for the free whisky and the change of pace from animal sex. The conversation, no matter how pointless, was at least engaging, and Moreno's plan would accomplish one

21

thing for certain if they carried it out: it would put both her and him out of their misery. Which, as Diana thought more about it from the bottom of her whisky glass, might have been worth it, except that she could put a bullet through her head any time she wanted without going to the trouble of making a fool of herself in front of the whole town first. Which, as Diana considered further from the top of another glass of whisky, would still be no loss, since the whole town already thought her lower than a fool as it was. Which was still no good reason to take up with a failed blacksmith who was probably exactly as stupid as Diana originally thought him to be. Diana sighed loudly and looked out at the rain, feeling so sodden by the whisky that the storm outside seemed pleasant for a moment and the man walking strange little mincing circles around her became almost agreeable.

Diana, taking pity on Moreno: "The secret is not to figure out how to open the safe with your own little brains or hands, sweetie. The secret is to make *them* open it. It's called force, Moreno, and guns and fear. You overpower'em, force'em to open the safe, shoot'em, and then get away with the loot. The way things get done in this world is by force, not by being clever or cute, because the odds are stacked against cleverness and even a genius can't beat house odds. Listen. You hear that? It's wind, Moreno, and thunder, it's brute force, it's cold brute force. A slave don't obey his master 'cause the master's smarter than him, he obeys 'cause the master cracks the whip. You see? You think I'm stuck in this godforsaken town 'cause everybody here's smarter than me? It ain't like that. You can't outsmart'em because smart ain't the game they're playin.'"

Moreno, quietly: "There's truth in what you say. But listen to what I say, because there's truth in this as well. Things are not always as they appear and sometimes simple force can be deceived in its simplicity. Because even simple things have meanings that are not always obvious."

"But that won't open a safe. A safe is simple, with no hidden meanings. Anyway, if you're so cocksure, if you're so clever with your hands, what do you need me for? Why don't you just crack the safe yourself and be done with it?"

"Because robbing a bank is not merely a matter of opening a safe. One must get into the bank, one must get out of the bank, one must have an alibi. A woman known in the town can provide a stranger with a good alibi."

Diana: "Good alibis ain't exactly what I'm known for."

"And that's not exactly the reason I want you to help me. That is, it's not the only reason. As I've said—"

A knock at the door.

Diana: "Who is it?"

Gruffly: "David Burns. I came back for my appointment."

Diana, turning sour, with a glance at Moreno: "Just a minute."

"He's here to have sex with you?"

"I put him off this afternoon, and he wasn't too happy about it. You better go. Thanks for the whisky."

"But is our meeting over? Let's finish this bottle and talk about these things. You and I could become very rich if we work together."

"The work I gotta do is outside that door, Moreno. Please go. I don't want to get beat up. I'll think about your little plan, all right?"

Pounding at the door. "Is somebody in there?"

Diana: "I'm almost finished." Lower: "Please go."

Moreno, calmly: "You see, you fear this man because he may hurt you, because the saloon owner may hurt you if you displease him. You are under their control, and that is the power, the brute force, you speak of. I know a thing or two about power, because I've been on the wrong side of it my entire life. But let me show you one way in which power may be diverted, very simply."

Moreno set his whisky glass next to the bottle on the nightstand, cleared his throat, and walked with his soft mincing steps to the door. Diana muttered curses under her breath and foresaw the relatively small Moreno on the short end of a heavy punch from the fat fist of David Burns and then herself on the wrong side of angry brutal sex from Burns and a backhanded slap from Jonathan after that, with probably no money to show for any of it. Moreno unlatched the door and opened it a few inches, allowing Burns to show his scowling unshaven face.

Moreno: "Yes?"

Burns, mildly surprised, but aggressively: "Come out if you're done with her. Let somebody else have a turn."

"What is your name please?"

"What?"

"Your name. How are you known?"

"Burns. What's it to you?"

"Mr. Burns, my name is Arturo Calderon, from San Juan. I apologize for interrupting your evening."

"Apology accepted. Now beat it."

"By chance, Miss Diana and I began talking and discovered that we may have the same father, Señor Wilfredo Calderon, also of San Juan. I believe she is my half-sister. We have been discussing the matter to determine if this is true. I wonder if you might let us have some more time to look into this matter and try to recall certain times and places from our past?"

Burns, dubious: "You fucked this whore and she's your sister?"

"Half-sister, possibly. And no, we have not had carnal relations. Surely, you can understand my concern, but do not worry. I will not try to prevent you from seeing her professionally, and she herself has expressed to me that she will gladly see you later." Moreno turned toward Diana, who nodded reluctant assent and then bowed her head to avoid Burns's gaze.

"And you came up here and started talking with this whore? And now you think she's your sister?"

"Half-sister. It's a strange coincidence, I admit, but all the more reason to pursue it, wouldn't you agree? Mr. Burns, even if we find that Diana is my half-sister, I will not try to prevent her from practicing her trade, as I have said, because that is the life she has chosen. If you will give us a little more time this evening, to pursue what may be an urgent matter for both of us, I would appreciate it. I'm sure you can understand the value of family?"

Burns, scowling: "You say your name's Calderon?"

"Arturo Calderon of San Juan, sir, at your service."

Diana: "Come back in an hour, Mr. Burns, I promise you. Later than an hour, I'll give you one for free."

Withdrawing, with an ominous glance at Moreno: "I'll be back for your sister in exactly one hour."

Moreno closed the door and turned back into the room with a self-satisfied bow. Diana grasped the whisky bottle by the neck, thinking to do some violence with it but certain of the uselessness of such a gesture. She slammed the bottle back onto the nightstand and gasped a great angry sob. Tears of rage streamed down her face. Moreno approached her with his arms outstretched, in part in perplexity and in part to ameliorate Diana's anger, while Diana looked bitterly in his direction without quite looking at him. The tallow candle guttered and shadows advanced and receded up and down the walls, which glowed the color of old butter, and Moreno extended a hand to Diana, which she refused to take. Moreno refilled both of their glasses and sat back down at the vanity while his reflected image appeared and disappeared according to the direction of the bobbing candleflame.

Moreno: "You see, now the man is confused and he'll let you alone for at least another hour. Then you can talk about the ridiculousness of my claim, or you can assert that my claim, though ridiculous, is true, and this sort of ambiguity and doubt will make him more manageable."

Diana's knuckles turned white in her clenched fists and she swallowed the scream that she wanted to direct at Moreno, so that it came out as a sharp screech. She picked up her whisky and hurled it, glass and all, at Moreno's head. He ducked and the glass clacked harmlessly off the vanity. Whisky splashed Moreno's neck and sprayed the mirror and extinguished the candle, and the glass fell to the floor, bounced hard once and then shattered. Diana and Moreno now stared into the darkness between them as the acrid smell of smoke filled their nostrils, and the drops of water dripping into basins around the room suddenly became loud and painfully discordant.

Diana, into the darkness, quavering with rage: "That man is not confused and your little charade won't mean nothin' to him. Now he thinks you're an idiot and a liar, and he'll be the more angry that I went along with the lie, and if he ain't downstairs right now tellin' Jonathan all about it then Jonathan'll hear about it sooner or later and he'll curse me at best or beat me at worst 'cause he'll think I'm gonna leave him and go off to live with my brother Arturo Calderon in San Juan. Your clever game! And what do you think Burns and his friends are sayin' about you right now? They're gonna keep their eyes on you for spoilin' their fun! You better hope you don't come down on the wrong side of a disagreement with one of them boys before the flood breaks, 'cause now they'll cut you or shoot you or just beat all your teeth in for sport. And what was the point anyway, so you could spend an extra hour yappin' about your stupid plan to get yourself killed and me in the bargain? So you could tell me what a great idea it is for a little man like you to rob a bank?" Sobbing: "Well, you done me enough favors for one evening now, Mr. Moreno, and if I don't get beat once tonight I'll get beat twice, and I thank you for your little lesson in how to talk a woman into harm through sheer stupidity. Good luck to you robbing that bank. You can get the hell out of my room now and don't ever come back. And you can leave the bottle."

Moreno did not stir from his chair, but sat pinching his lip at the darkness through which he could feel Diana's anger approach him in waves and snare him in its undertow, drawing him toward her. He extended his hand to her, his hand that became visible in a split-second burst of white lightning before disappearing again into the thundering void between them. Diana was sobbing, and the whisky that had made her feel bemused at this man and his mincing steps and his preposterous plan only minutes before now made her feel scattered and furious, with no easy target for her rage but her own things, because even this little man could overpower her if push came to shove. If she complained to Jonathan, Jonathan would believe Moreno's word over hers, and any action she contemplated led to violence against her, so she stood still and shook with an unpronounceably hopeless hate.

Finally, Moreno stood up and crossed the room and stood at the door, looking back through the darkness in the direction of Diana's low animal sobbing. "Do this, think about this: if they ask you, tell them I am Arturo Calderon, your half-brother, that our father was Wilfredo Calderon, the rancher of San Juan. If they ask for details, make them up, no matter how implausible they are, make them up, but remember them, and tell them to me later."

"Why?"

"I can't say. Only that it may be useful to you in the future, in some unforeseen way. The truth will not help you. Look at yourself, think about your situation, think about the truth of it, and tell me how this truth can help you. There are other ways, other truths, if only we have the courage to imagine them and the faith to follow them wherever they may lead, and the daring to act on them when the opportunity presents itself. Use your intuition."

"I'll think about that tonight while that fat man decides he wants to fuck me for free and Jonathan lets him."

Moreno reached into his waistcoat and withdrew two dollars, walked gingerly around Diana's bed in the dark, found her left hand and squeezed the money into it. "I'm deeply sorry if I've caused problems for you this evening. Please consider what I've said and take my advice in this thing that can do you no real harm: I am your half-brother Arturo Calderon from San Juan. I myself will tell this lie. Make a fool of me if you will."

Moreno squeezed Diana's hand again, walked across her room noiselessly, opened her door and was gone, shutting and latching the door with a practiced grace so gentle that barely a tapping of wood accompanied his departure. Diana threw his two dollars onto the floor and flung herself face down across her bed, but found that she could no longer cry.

* * * * *

By the time David Burns returned to Diana's room, Diana had neither collected Moreno's two dollars from the floor nor re-lit her tallow candle nor even moved a single inch on her bed, where she lay face down in a stupor of anger so inchoate and objectless that it could only be expressed abjectly, as lassitude. Burns knocked on the door and when the knock wasn't answered he let himself in to find Diana lying motionless, without acknowledging his presence, and his first thought was that some harm had come to her. He said her name several times but elicited no response. In the darkened room, barely lit now by the first silver shade of moonlight, Burns kicked over a metal basin filled with rainwater that sloshed across his boots, and the basin clanged and rattled with an eerie hollowness that filled the room.

The rain had relented somewhat, falling now as a whispering susurration against the roof of the inn, streaming softly down Diana's windowpanes in gentle unbroken cascades. Every other sound seemed hard and guttural, especially the gruffness of Burns's voice and the thud of his boots and the protesting creaks of the boards under his weight.

Burns, his hand feeling for the footpost of Diana's bed in the dark: "It's been exactly one hour and I don't want any horseshit about what time it is or whose sister you are. I got money as good as anybody's and I know what I got a right to expect from it."

Diana did not stir. She imagined this fat man's cock in her mouth, a thought that would normally not even register in her mind, much less arouse an emotion; but now, for the first time in a blue moon, she could feel herself beginning to gag, the chalky clay thickness at the back of her throat, followed by the bright metallic feel of too much saliva in the recesses of her jaws. Just lying on her bed, it took Diana every effort of will to keep from throwing up, and when she had finally regained control, Burns sat heavily on the side of the bed and the process of nearly gagging repeated itself. Diana didn't care whether or not she got beaten, whether or not she had to french this man's cock, whether or not she got paid, just so long as whatever happened was over quickly and she could go back to lying this way across her bed. She hoped she wouldn't throw up on the fat man, as that would merely prolong whatever misery ensued and worsen her beating.

Burns shook Diana's shoulder and she lifted her head. Even through all the years of humiliations she had suffered at the hands of men like Burns, Diana had never felt this angry before. That Moreno character, she told herself, there was something about him—the particular way he had embarrassed her, the exaggerated daintiness of his self-assurance, his insane scheme to include her in a hopeless act—he had lacerated her heart, which she had thought too scarred to feel another prick. Diana looked up into Burns's eye sockets, where his eyes receded invisible in the darkness, and watched as he took off his hat, stood, and unbuckled his belt.

Burns: "That little beaner really your brother?"

"Half-brother."

"That little beaner really your half-brother? You make believe all your johns is your brother, like that's supposed to turn you on? Like humping your brother is the only trick that excites a sportin' lady?"

Acidly: "Half-brother."

Pulling off his boots and dropping his trousers: "Maybe you oughta pretend I'm your brother. Maybe you oughta pretend I'm your daddy, come to stick my big hard cock down my little girl's throat. You like that?"

Diana felt even more numbed than usual by the dull cruelty of this man's sexual imagination. She roused herself just enough to lift up on one elbow and pull her torso across the bed toward the man's already erect penis, which she could just see jutting out from below his awful rotund belly. She smelled something fungal and stale like old cheese. Even before she could put out her tongue or open her lips around the soft tip, Burns's large hand had fallen heavily across the back of her head, and he gripped her skull with his fingers. He pushed her face down toward his crotch and then pulled her head back up by the hair. He stepped forward and thrust his penis at her, which Diana opened her mouth to accept.

No art or subtlety was required of her beyond moving her jaw and teeth to avoid cutting Burns's stiffened member, and most of her energy was spent suppressing her newly revived gag reflex. Like many angry men before him, Burns was happy enough with the simple violence of contact and hard movement and subjugation. The back of Diana's neck ached where Burns was pulling and jerking her hair to the rhythm of his movements, and the pain helped distract her from the idea of vomiting down his legs. He spurted into her mouth, and Diana swallowed and swallowed again and let the thick bitter slime coat the back of her throat on its gruesome way into her body.

She coughed and felt a blackness like a steel panel shut behind her eyes. She rubbed her forehead across the rough fabric of the bedspread until the pain in her neck subsided and she could bring herself to look at the semi-naked body of the Virginia miner. Burns had hiked his pants back up and sat down on the bed to adjust himself and breathe a few deep wet breaths after his climax. He reclined onto one elbow so that his face was level with Diana's, and he scrutinized at her. Diana looked back at the round outline where muted gray moonlight found the stubble on his cheeks. The empty blackness of his face in the dark was exactly as Diana thought of him, a shell whose danger lay not in the barbarity of his bulky presence but in his utter emptiness, the excavated mine at his center, which once, maybe, long ago, had held a soul but now contained only an arrogant lack of curiosity. In the presence of this typical man with a typical ambition from a typical place, who had no real idea who he was or who she was or what they had just done, Diana felt as if she were staring at the Angel of Death. Of Death in Life.

Burns: "That guy fuck you? That Arturo Calderon?"

"What business is that of yours?"

"None, just wondering what a swishy little guy like that would do with a woman like you."

"He's not a swishy little guy. He really is my half-brother."

"No foolin'? It's a funny world when a guy pays to get off and finds himself stickin' it in his own sister. Makes you wonder how many other guys you fucked that was related to you."

Diana rolled away from David Burns and retrieved a cigarette from the box on her nightstand and lit it and looked at the three fingers of whisky still in the bottle that Moreno had left. "It ain't like that. My father, Wilfredo Calderon, he was a good man. He wasn't the kind to leave a trail of helpless bastards all over the country. It was just the force of circumstances."

"There's always a reason, ain't there?"

"You should talk."

"I ain't never fucked no whore. I ain't never left my seed in some woman then rode off and not given her a second thought. A real man would take care of his own children, no matter what."

"You sayin' my daddy ain't a real man?"

"What kind of man would let his daughter be a whore?"

"Where do you think whores come from, David?"

"Not from good families. I'd never let my sister be a whore. I'd kill her first."

Diana took a long drag on her cigarette and felt the hardness come back into her chest. She laughed secretly at Burns and thought how many times she would have killed him already if he were her brother, how that probably *was* the mark of a good family. Archly sarcastic: "Maybe I just like being a whore and my daddy's broad-minded. Maybe my half-brother has respect for whores."

Burns, with utter derision: "Nobody respects whores."

"When you say whores, you mean women, don't you?"

"You got a smart mouth, is what I mean. Let me have a swig of that whisky."

"Sure, if you pay for it."

Burns grunted and rummaged in his pocket, fingered a number of coins, and threw one onto Diana's pillow. He lumbered halfway around her bed to grasp the whisky bottle and bring it to his lips. Diana stopped him, got a glass from the dresser, poured him a shot and took the bottle back and raised it to her own lips.

"If you got a daddy down in San Juan, why don't you go down there to him?"

Gesturing toward the window: "Ain't nobody goin' nowhere, honey."

"Rain won't last forever. Go when the storm breaks."

"What do you care what I do?"

Drinking off his shot in one gulp: "I don't. Thought I'd be polite is all, seein' as how you just frenched me."

"Southern gentleman again? You ain't been with too many whores, have you, David?"

"I ain't the kind to go to whores." Pointing out the window at the rain. "It's just a matter of circumstances, is all."

"There's always a reason, ain't there? Let me give you a tip: there's nothin' polite in talking to a whore after you shoot your stuff down her throat. Talk is only polite when you don't pay for it."

"You're sure a uppity bitch, and me just tryin' to be nice and all."

"You're nice enough. You wanna buy another shot, or is my service finished?"

Standing up from the bed, putting on his hat and turning toward the door: "You'd better watch that mouth of yours, 'fore somebody comes along and puts you in your place."

Laughing out loud: "I'm already in my place, sweetie."

Burns stomped out of the room and slammed the door behind, leaving Diana to finish the rest of the whisky in one long convulsive drink and fling the bottle across the room. She fell across the bed, twisting onto her back to keep her cigarette aloft. She thought, so now I'm the half-sister of an impostor and the daughter of Wilfredo Calderon, who probably doesn't exist, and I'll be goddamned if I don't get a beating out of this somehow, and exactly what difference does it make who my father is or where he lives? So much for the truth, she thought, and so much for lies, and so much for all the shades in between; as the whisky splashed through her brains, she took a last long drag on her cigarette and flung it across the room, daring it to catch something on fire. She thought not what Moreno thought—that a non-truth might mysteriously help her in the long run—but rather that the idea of truth simply didn't apply to her, like it didn't apply to animals, and that only people who thought certain things weren't true could be bothered to care which things were. She rolled over, prone on her bed, and waited for the whisky to carry her into oblivion.

RECONNAISSANCE

Moreno walked hunched through the rainy night on Tres Cruces' main street, past El Charro Restaurant, where a few haggard-looking people stared into their lamplit plates of beans and rice, past the barbershop where Doc Drumwright sat crossing and uncrossing his legs to some internal rhythm as he flipped through a magazine, past the telegraph station where Hargis sat whittling, past the post office and the darkened Panaderia Jimenez. When Moreno came to the Hidalgo Trust Bank, he stopped and fumbled in his vest pocket for a cigarillo, then pretended to have trouble lighting a match. He stole glances at the gunman asleep on a cot inside, his belt and holster lying on the floor next to him within easy reach. Behind the gunman was a door made of steel bars whose lock Moreno was confident he could pick in a matter of moments.

Moreno lit his cigarillo and strolled around the bank, stepping off the plank walkway onto the swollen sodden muck that now passed for earth, which made obscene sucking sounds every time he lifted his feet. He looked at the Highland Notions Shop, which sat on a little ridge up above the bank to the south and thought about the possibilities of approaching from that side. The bank's windows were not barred, and the back door appeared to be made of simple wood, which meant, Moreno thought, as he spit a fleck of loose tobacco against the wall, that the door led to an office rather than a secured area with valuables. The main safe, Moreno knew, sat behind a teller counter near the center of the bank; whether or not one could access the safe through this back door as conveniently as through the front he did not know. But this was not critical: the most important element in his scheme was the relatively simple subterfuge he would use to lure the guard and the bank manager away from the bank, so that he would have time to work his magic on whatever he found inside. The details, he thought, would work themselves out in the act.

Moreno finished walking every edge of the bank and found himself back on the main street, bunching his shoulders into his collar against the rain, his face glowing hellish orange in the light of his cigarillo. He leaned against the corner of the bank and imagined himself inside, imagined his hands deftly working his picks into the lock that guarded the clerks' area, darting like a waterbug to the black round-cornered safe and miraculously opening it. He had heard about the clicking of individual tumblers in combination locks, how minute variations in sound revealed the combination, and he felt sure that Doc Drumwright had a stethoscope somewhere in his barbershop, the filching of which would be a matter of mindless patter, misdirection and sleight of hand. Minor details, he thought, and he waved them away with a flick of ash.

Moreno was so absorbed in the grandeur and imminent success of his scheming that he hadn't heard the softly slipping footsteps approaching from his blind side, from behind the bank, and he jumped nearly off the plank sidewalk as a hard clear voice said: "Picked a bad night to stand around the street, Mister."

Moreno turned to find Collins's gunman—the one who, only minutes earlier, had been asleep inside the bank—standing at his elbow with a toothpick in his mouth. He stared matter-of-factly down at Moreno as rainwater flowed in a trickling stream around his belled-out hat. Moreno cleared his throat and laughed with exaggerated ease.

"Haven't had too many good nights of late, have we, sir? Sometimes the inclination to loiter defeats the craving for comfort."

"Is that supposed to mean something?"

Moreno: "May I present myself?" Extending his hand: "My name is Arturo Calderon, from Alto Cedro."

The gunman, looking at Moreno's hand for several seconds before shaking it: "Kerr. Jamie Kerr."

"Mr. Kerr. Scotsman, is it?"

"My granddad was. I don't think about it one way or the other."

"Haven't seen you down at the saloon."

"No, and you won't neither, not after what they did to Jackson. I didn't come to Tres Cruces for trouble. I just got a job to do and I'm doin' it and that's all. That's why I come out here now, to tell you to move along."

"Move along? But I'm not doing any harm, am I, just taking a little constitutional?"

"I've seen you strolling around the bank before, Calderon."

"It's a small town, Mr. Kerr, so one must trace one's steps over and over. But if my presence here troubles you, I'll head back to the inn. I don't want to bother anybody."

"No bother, I just like to keep my eye on things."

"I respect that, Mr. Kerr, I truly do respect that, since I'm a working man myself, and you have to respect the duty of another working man. Well, then, sorry if I disturbed you, and much obliged for the conversation. But I was only out for a breath of air, you know, and you may see me again, if this rain doesn't let up soon. It makes a man nervous, being locked inside every day."

Kerr grunted equivocally and Moreno walked slowly down

the street toward the inn, glancing behind every so often to tip his hat at Kerr until Kerr finally retired into the bank. As soon as he did, Moreno ducked between the telegraph station and the panaderia and raced, slipping and sloshing, behind the buildings until he could clearly see Kerr looking out from the bank's rear door. Moreno put his hand to his chin and considered this back door for a while and considered the demeanor of Kerr, until, unable to draw any useful conclusions, he sauntered at an easy pace back to the saloon.

THE APPEARANCE OF THE HORSES

The bracing aroma of medicinal products, soaps, lotions, and alcohols overwhelmed any attempts at civility in Doc Drumwright's barbershop; even innocuous fat-chewing conversations tended to have an energetic edge to them due to the unconscious effect of the biting pungence of so many distillations, and Drumwright himself was so curt and forceful in proclaiming his opinions that he exacerbated the tension. He had come to relish his own contentiousness: only a complex surgery excited him more than a rousing argument. Doc Drumwright was known to argue one side of an issue one day and then claim the other side the next day and do both with equal conviction and sincerity, because, as he said, the amusing thing was the debate, not which side was right.

When Jonathan Vega blustered into the barbershop the morning after the shooting of Pastor Charles, in a rain driven nearly horizontal by a wicked northern wind, he expected to be contradicted no matter what position he took. Though it was only eight o'clock in the morning, Doc Drumwright was already reclining in his barber chair with a gin in one hand and his other hand soaking in a basin of lilac water. A broken-spined dog-eared tome called *A Medical History of General Zachary Taylor's Army of Occupation in Mexico* lay on his lap, and Drumwright appraised Jonathan as Socrates must have appraised his students: as amusing distractions whose rhetorical maneuvers he had already considered, dissected and dismissed and whose arguments he could destroy with a flourish at any time.

Jonathan respected Drumwright for his book knowledge and rationality, but thought the barber had gotten a bit too full of himself since he had begun "practicing medicine." Drumwright's reputation and influence had grown yearly since he had arrived in Tres Cruces nearly twenty-five years before, even though, in Jonathan's opinion, Drumwright had done little of practical value to earn his stature: he hadn't killed any Indians in the uprisings or helped build any buildings or dug those miners out of the Rodriguez Mine when it collapsed, or any other practical thing that nearly every other man in Tres Cruces had done. And yet, Drumwright had served once as mayor and was entrusted as the acting deputy whenever the marshal was away, and he was the first person anyone approached when questions of civic policy arose.

Jonathan shut the torrid wind out behind him, nodding to Drumwright and taking a moment to right his windblown hair and remove his wind-kinked overcoat. He hung the coat on a rack and set his shotgun down against the doorpost. The wind whistled low and plaintive through cracks between sideboards and rattled the barbershop door back and forth against its loose latch.

"Morning Doc. I'll get right to the point. We decided amongst ourselves down at the inn that we're gonna hang that boy Jackson, and we're wondering if you, as the acting deputy, have any objections."

"Awful sudden, isn't it? Why can't you wait for the marshal, wait to get a judge down from San Luis and do the whole thing proper?"

"Well, Doc, maybe if the case against him wasn't so cut and dried we'd wait, or maybe if he wasn't—you know, half of them down at the inn, they want to string him up just for bein' a nigger in Tres Cruces, never mind what he did to that circuit rider, and I've got half a mind myself, since I been diggin' lead out of my furniture. It's just got everybody riled. But we're all law-abidin' folks, so we wanted to check with you before we strung'im up."

"Reckon on using the scaffold, or just hanging the boy from a tree?"

"Clancy used the wood from the scaffold last winter, Doc. We hadn't had a hanging for so long. We figured we'd take him down to the willow grove and hang'im there and then throw his body in the river."

Doc Drumwright, wiping the lilac water from his hand, taking a ruminative sip of gin: "I have to admit, Jonathan, the case against him is pretty tight, but what about the extenuating circumstances? That preacher was cheating, everybody saw the evidence, and a judge might just chuck him in the hole, put him on a chain gang and get some use out of him, rather than waste good twine on his neck."

"Doc, you know as well as I do that boy's as good as dead, and it'd sure relieve the burden of this rain on the townsfolk if we could string'im up, or at least shoot'im. Give everybody a sense of civic purpose for a couple hours."

"Couldn't you just whip him, Jonathan? All this killing makes me nervous, and if it happened that the marshal decided to investigate the matter and found that you'd taken the law into your own hands and killed a man without a trial, you could wind up in the hole as quick as he could. The marshal doesn't take kindly to vigilantes."

Jonathan opened his mouth to reply but was interrupted by a screeching whinny from just outside the barbershop, and the whinny was followed by the rolling rumbling thomping sucking sloshing clomp of hooves striking the muddy earth on Main Street. Jonathan turned and stared out the window and

Doc Drumwright sloshed gin on his wrist as he twisted out of the barber chair and stood at Jonathan's elbow. The gusting fierceness of swirling rain made the horses appear as ghosts emerging from the watery ether. There were seven: two chestnut mares, a strawberry roan, an appaloosa, a golden palomino stallion, a dirty yellow dun and a cream-colored mustang with ebony points. They galloped by in a froth, their eyes bulging terrified and wild, the mares lagging a few lengths behind, up Main and then to the left around Alberto Torres' Tack Room and Stable across the street from the Coronado Saloon. They disappeared again into the darkness of the storm.

Jonathan, picking up his shotgun: "Were them horses stabled in town, Doc? You think somethin's happened to Torres?"

"No, not Torres. They were Lazaro's, from Rancho Cielito, at least some of them were. That palomino I'm sure was Lazaro's own. I don't think they were stabled in town."

"They couldn'ta come from Rancho Cielito. How would they have crossed the river?"

"I don't know. Maybe somethin's happened out there."

"Marshal's out there. Maybe he found a way across."

Drumwright and Vega stared for several minutes as wind lashed rain against the window and lightning cracked in the distance. Thunder followed, ushering in the horses again. They galloped past with all the real solidity of pounding hooves and flying mud, retraced their steps, and then disappeared in the opposite direction, back into the riled ghostly torrent.

"Ain't no way cross them rivers, Doc, north, east, or west. You wanna get into Tres Cruces, you gotta cross a river somewhere, or you gotta navigate the sand flats away south, which was ten miles of swamp and soup when Saul and me went down even two weeks ago. Either them horses have been lurking around town unseen for the last three weeks or they found a way across, and it don't seem real likely to me that them mares could swim a flooded river or trot all nice and easy through a sand swamp."

"Maybe the boys out at Rancho Cielito found themselves a way through the flood."

"There weren't no boys ridin' them horses, Doc."

Drumwright swallowed the rest of his gin and turned around to look at himself and Jonathan Vega's back in the mirror, framed by the gray wall of rain splattering waves against the window. "Perhaps we should get some men together, follow the tracks out, see if we can't lead'em back to Torres' stable, see if we can't find where they crossed over. Who's got a horse in town?"

Jonathan: "Nobody's gonna go out with the rain like this. We'll have to wait till the wind blows over."

"All right, then. I'll go to El Charro, you see about your customers at the inn—we'll round up volunteers for when the wind dies down. And anyway, that'll give us something to do instead of hanging Jackson."

"You think we oughta wait? That's your final decision?"

"I know y'all are gonna do what you want, Jonathan, but as the acting deputy, I have to say it would reflect better on me if we waited to hang him till the marshal gets back in town."

"All right, then. We won't hang'im yet. But I can't guarantee that boy's safety."

"Nobody's asking you to."

Jonathan put his overcoat back on and took his leave of Drumwright, while the barber drained off another quick shot of gin, outfitted himself against the weather, and made a dash down the street. Drumwright had a bad feeling about those horses and about Jackson, and he had a bad feeling that Jonathan Vega was liable to use that shotgun of his sooner or later, now that he'd gotten the idea in his head. If Drumwright knew

Jonathan at all, the gun was just as likely to go off at the wrong time at the wrong person as it was to do any good, and he feared that the marshal would have more than one crime to adjudicate by the time he got back from Rancho Cielito.

A Diplomatic Visit

Jonathan Vega's nephew, Saul, served as the houseboy, jack-of-all-trades and cook at the Coronado, and Jonathan had made him responsible for Jackson's upkeep: as long as Jackson remained incarcerated in the Tres Cruces jail, Saul was directed to take him two spartan meals a day and, in the company of Doc Drumwright and Jonathan Vega, to escort him once a day to the outhouse behind El Charro Restaurant. On the morning after the shooting, Saul had fried Jackson an egg and refried a mess of beans and heated an old tortilla and a cup of coffee and had placed the breakfast on a metal tray covered with a greasy towel. He was headed out the inn's kitchen door when he was stopped by a hissing whisper. He found Diana skittering across the kitchen toward him in a green mantle whose hood draped so far over Diana's face that Saul had to look twice to make sure it was her. She stepped as quickly and lightly as she could, but her heavy leather boots scuffed and thumped the floor.

"Hey, Di. I ain't used to seein' you up so early."

"Mornin' Saul. You're headin' over to the jail, ain't you?"

"That's right."

"Would it cause you any trouble if I went in your place?"

"Why would you want to do that?"

Flaring up: "Maybe I just wanna save you some trouble. Ah, sorry Saul, it's just early for me. I'm kinda hungover is all. It's just. . . I know they're gonna kill that boy, and I thought I'd say a few kind words to him before they do."

"Kind words from you? I mean, that's mighty generous, Di, I guess. But don't it seem like a waste of time? You think a scoundrel like that, who'd shoot an unarmed man in cold blood, would hold any store in a kind word?"

"Kindness is never wasted, Saul."

Laughing in surprise: "Well, I'll be hanged, what kind of spider bit you this morning, Di? I ain't never heard a word like that from you in all my life."

"Don't you believe in kindness, Saul?"

"As much as the next fella."

"Then let me have that food. I'll take it to him. You don't have to open the cell, do you?"

"I don't even have a key. You're just supposed to hand it through the bars, wait till he eats it, and then take it all back from him. If he gives you any trouble, just holler over to Uncle Jonathan, and he'll come fix'im quick."

"Thanks, Saul."

"Second thought, Diana, if he gives you any guff, why don't you come to me first, and I'll tell Uncle Jonathan? Keep us both out of trouble."

Diana winked conspiratorially at Saul and kissed him on the cheek as she took the now lukewarm plate from him and pulled her cloak a little closer around her neck. She dashed out the door and trotted at an eager clip behind the saloon, past El Charro and the barbershop and across Main Street. She exchanged a greeting with Alberto Torres, who for some reason was on his hands and knees levering up a plank in the walk, and was pointedly snubbed by Mrs. Mathers as she passed the window of the General Store. The towel over the breakfast plate flapped in the wind and Diana jostled coffee into the food and dropped Jackson's fork in the mud—she wiped it off on the towel and then replaced it on his plate.

The door to the marshal's office was ajar when she approached, and she knocked but found the office unattended. Inside the windowless room, Diana was greeted first by the marshal's plain oaken desk, adorned with an oil lamp, a blank writing pad, an empty ink well and a quill pen; behind the desk sat an unvarnished chair, and behind that a green canvas cot covered by a yellow and white checkered blanket. Opposite the desk, against the far wall, was a wooden gun cabinet that normally held rifles, shotguns and pistols, but which now stood empty. Diana wondered who had taken the guns and what they had done with them. The office walls were festooned with WANTED! posters bearing terse but nevertheless florid descriptions of heinous crimes and potential rewards for men pictured as garishly pencil-drawn faces, as if every criminal in the territory had been torn directly from a P.T. Barnum act.

Diana pushed her hood back from her face and deposited the greasy towel on the marshal's desk. She collected her wits and walked the half-dozen steps down the damp fetid-smelling corridor to the two holding cells. Jackson's was the only one occupied, and, besides Jackson himself lying on his cot, the only thing in his cell was a basin half-filled with urine and a tin pitcher half-filled with water. Jackson was fully clothed except that he wore no boots and his boots were nowhere to be seen. Dried blood stained the collar of his white shirt a muddy claret; a scab still oozing clear fluid caked his right temple; and his face was swollen and blue with bruises. He gazed at Diana through half-opened eyes, and she made no further movements until he pushed himself up and sat stiffly on the edge of the cot.

"I brought you breakfast."

Jackson: "The whore feeding the nigger. Almost Biblical, ain't it?"

"You read the Bible?"

"I was on the wrong end of it enough to take an interest. So I guess that makes you Mary Magdalene and me Jesus Christ—that's what I meant, the whore and the nigger. Ain't that funny."

"No, it ain't. I don't recall Jesus carryin' a gun, nor shootin' people down in cold blood."

"He would. If he was alive today, his apostles would be a posse, and he'd need one, the way they'd treat him."

Diana, smirking, but still indulgent: "That's nice and all, but I ain't Mary Magdalene and you sure ain't the Christ. Nothing's anything else but what it is." Diana motioned with the tray and then slipped it between the bars of Jackson's cell and set it on the floor.

Jackson, not budging: "Everything's somethin' else, it's just how you look at it. I ain't no murderer, but they gonna string me up for bein' a murderer. Maybe you ain't no whore, but I bet you been paid for sex, ain't that right?"

"You're a murderer and I'm a whore. Look, I didn't come over here to talk to you about Jesus Christ and whorin'." Pausing to consider: "Ain't you gonna eat your breakfast?"

Jackson stood up and then snapped halfway over again with a cry of pain and clutched his back. He righted himself slowly and shuffled to the breakfast tray. His eggs and beans were swimming in coffee and the tortilla was soggy with rain water. He lifted the cup to his lips and swallowed a sip of the cold burnt coffee and looked at Diana bitterly.

"S'pose I could hardly expect better, right?" Laughing ruefully. "You know, it's my first time in prison. This kind of prison, anyway." He picked up the tray, returned to his cot and set it on his lap. He ate the sodden meal with growing relish.

"I come to ask you a question. You know they're gonna hang you, right? They were talkin' about doin' it today but Doc Drumwright talked'em out of it. So the way I figure it, you got nothin' to lose."

"Nothin' to lose by what?"

"How do you feel about Collins, your boss?"

With a mouthful of beans: "Nothin' against him. Gave me a job."

"What about the guy you work with, what's his name?"

"Kerr. Got nothin' against him neither, except his family was on the Reb side, down in Vicksburg."

"What would you say if I could get you out of this fix you're in, Jackson?"

Running his tongue between his teeth and lips: "Can you walk through walls and make yourself invisible? Can you make me invisible? It don't matter none. Even if you busted me outta jail, they took my guns, and there ain't no way outta town anyway. So I'd say you must be an angel of God almighty if you could get me out of this fix."

"How would you feel about killin' some men? I mean, some more men. Like Kerr and Collins?"

"I'd rather kill that Hargis."

"Kill him, too, for all I care. But Kerr and Collins?"

"Why would I want to kill them?"

"I'm fixin' to rob that bank and all that money you're supposed to be carryin' to San Luis. It'd make things easier if I could count on your help."

Jackson, pausing a beat and then laughing painfully from his gut: "You sure are somethin' else. What's your name?"

"Diana."

"Miss Diana, you must be the damnedest whore I ever talked to. All right, I'll kill Kerr and Collins, and Hargis too, and that Vega fella, and Drumwright and all them that beat me up over at the saloon, and I'll kill the whole damn town, how's that? You just bring 'em over here one by one and let 'em into my cell, and when they're all dead and stacked neat in the marshal's office, you can get away with the loot."

"You're in no position to mock, Jackson. You don't see it now, and I don't blame you, but I'm the only hope you got of savin' your neck."

"With respect, Miss Diana, that makes my hopes very slim. How's a little thing like you plan on bustin' me outta here and robbin' a bank and sailin' off clear as the breeze in the biggest storm this side of Noah? You see my point?"

"I see your point, and here's my point: if you're interested in gettin' free, then you have to trust me to know what I'm doin'. I know this town and I know how to get you out of this jail. But it'll cost you in some killin'."

"I'm interested in not havin' a rope around my neck, but you'll pardon me for not jumpin' with joy. But I'll promise you one thing: all else fails, I'll wave at you from the gallows. Yes I will, Miss Diana."

"Don't be smart, Jackson—I'll put a bullet in you myself and nobody'll care one way or the other. Now, give me your tray. I'll see you again, and you'll see what I got in mind. I ain't crazy, and I know how it can be done."

"But how?"

"Let's just say a fairy gave me the idea."

Handing his tray back to Diana through the bars, with a mirthless grin: "I'm all ears, Miss Diana, all ears for a fairy tale."

"Don't call me Miss. Just Diana."

Diana put the hood back over her face and clomped down the marshal's hallway. In fact, she had only a rough notion how she was going to break Jackson out of prison and only a vague idea how they would then steal the money from the bank and no idea at all how they would cross the river; but Moreno had unexpectedly stirred in her a long-dormant yearning for freedom, for life, and the money stranded in the bank across the street would pay her way out of Tres Cruces, a long way out, far beyond the lurching grasp of Jonathan Vega and the macabre sweaty stiffness of aroused anonymous men. She hadn't thought about running away for years, but she had run away before, only to be dragged back to Tres Cruces by one of Jonathan's hired agents or one of the local ranchers or by her own failures. If she could run away now, if she could somehow manage to cross the river in this storm, no one would dare follow her, and if she could reach the other side with all that money, she would never have to look back again. The freedom of money!

She did not believe the bank could be robbed without bloodshed, and she thought Moreno a fey dreamer: but Moreno had spun the idea like a crude wooden top across the flattened blankness of her mind, and her encounter with David Burns had kept it spinning, the exact painted patterns still indistinct in their swirling motion but the colors gyrating hypnotically nevertheless: freedom. Freedom from pain, freedom from humiliation, freedom from the indignities of sex. How exactly she would escape this flood when no one else could and how she would deal with Moreno and his mincing schemes she didn't know yet. She grabbed up the greasy towel from the marshal's desk and marched out into the rain, calculating, plotting, hoping beyond hope or reason that this rain somehow portended good, after all.

A Puzzling Message

As Hargis followed Doc Drumwright to into the telegraph office, he stooped and picked up a stick and used it to scrape clods of brown clay from the bottom of his boots. He looked bleakly up at the gray clouds bearing low over Tres Cruces and threw the stick disgustedly into the street, where it stuck straight up and down like a survey marker.

Hargis felt on the verge of snapping and falling as surely as the telegraph lines had snapped and fallen in the storm. His lack of occupation made him feel beggarly and worthless and reminded him that in the eyes of the people of Tres Cruces, and therefore in his own eyes, he was a failure. Hargis's mother and father had been killed in an Arivica Indian raid when he was fifteen; unable to sustain their already failing herd of Herefords, he had sold his father's scrawny cows and small patch of stony land and hired his labor out to the neighboring rancheros, all of whom soon discovered what his father had already known—that Hargis tired easily and lacked tenacity. Physically weak, mechanically incompetent, poor with horses and cattle, bad at woodworking, fence-mending and building, Hargis had survived for years mainly on the largesse of Mr. and Mrs. Mathers, who had taken pity on him for the sake of his parents and employed him to run errands to Holguin or Whitney. Only the Russell, Majors, and Waddell Telegraph Company had saved Hargis from lifelong ignominy. When the company ran its San Quentin Line through Tres Cruces and held trials for clerks, Hargis proved extremely clever and fast at learning Morse Code.

Hargis's position as Tres Cruces' telegraph officer had made him an integral part of the town almost overnight and had won him a measure of grudging respect from the townsfolk. Now, however, without a telegraph line, Hargis felt unmanned, unnamed, slipping back into his more familiar lifelong role of failure. In fact, no one in Tres Cruces thought about Hargis at all, but he imagined that everyone singled him out for judgment, and he felt everyone's stares on the back of his neck like worms boring into his flesh. He hated the storm for making him so conspicuously useless.

Doc Drumwright sat down in a lashed rawhide chair, while Hargis rummaged in his desk for the message he had sent on behalf of the marshal. The raindrops pelting the office's pitched wooden roof sounded flat and close and angry, without reverberation, and Drumwright felt in special need of a drink.

At the back of the telegraph building, separated from the main office by a waist-high partition of crateboards, was Hargis's tiny living area. A small cast-iron stove squatted near his tie-hack bed: on the stove sat a tin coffee pot and a flat iron, and across the bed lay a light patchwork quilt. Hargis used a shipping box for a bedside table, and atop the shipping box stood an oil lamp with a blackened hood. The entire telegraph building measured only twelve feet by twelve, and Hargis's living space comprised less than half that area. There was only one window, which could not be opened, and the office smelled flatulent and stale.

Hargis, shuffling papers back and forth across his desk: "Normally I wouldn't do this, Doc. The telegraph company'd have my head if they knew I was showin' around other folks' telegrams, but the more I thought about it, the stranger it seemed. And what with the ferry down and the parson gettin' killed, it might be important that somebody see it, in case the marshal really ain't out to Cielito, as everybody's sayin'. You know, in case there needs to be justice done with that boy in the jail, or what have you."

Drumwright: "Everybody wants justice done with that boy right now, don't they?" Drumwright stared at a blank space in front of Hargis and chewed the word aloud: "Justice." Shaking his head: "When did the marshal actually send this message?"

"Same day the rains started. Matter of fact, now that I think about, this is the last message that went through before the lines went down."

"And what about it makes you think the marshal didn't go out to Cielito?"

"Nothin' exactly. I mean, nothin' I could put my finger on, Doc. It's just strange, is all, and I thought you better have a look at it."

Hargis lifted a box off of his desk and looked underneath it and moved the telegraph key back and forth and looked all around it, and then he opened the desk's middle drawer and repeated similar gestures with the pencils and rubber insulators and spare wire trimmings inside the drawer. He put his hands on his hips and tapped his toe against the puncheon-log floor and thought for a moment and then duplicated the exact same series of motions, again with no success. Finally, as if seeing it for the first time, he lifted a scrap of brown paper that had been sitting on top of his log book all along. "Ah, here it is." He handed it to the doctor. "Maybe it don't mean nothin', but maybe it does."

Drumwright took the paper from Hargis, stepped over to the window and held the message up to the light. Hargis's scraggly printing showed faint against the sepia paper, and the doctor squinted and winced.

Drumwright, reading: "Have seceded from union stop taking stock stop will see to union as arranged stop take Blackwell's Celerity to Union Pacific stop arrangements secured stop end." Drumwright contemplated the message and then reread it to himself and looked a question at Hargis.

"I told the marshal it didn't make no sense, but he said the person gettin' it would know what it meant. Folks do that all the time, you know—chop messages up till they sound all garbled, on account of the cost."

Drumwright: "How much did the marshal pay to send this?"

"Seven dollars."

Letting out a low whistle: "Must have been important."

"What do you think it means, Doc?"

The doctor read the message several more times. "He says the word 'union' three times in three different ways, but I can't figure if that's a code or a coincidence. Blackwell's Celerity is a stagecoach out of San Luis. Where did he send this message to? Who was it addressed to?"

Hargis opened his log book. "To a Mrs. Repilado, in San Luis."

"Repilado? I've never heard of any Repilado family roundabouts."

"Me neither. But it's a big place, San Luis."

Outside, the rain hushed suddenly into a drizzle and the drops against the roof sibilated suggestively but would not quite coalesce into words, as if the rain were murmuring the secret of the marshal's message in a language neither Hargis nor the doctor had troubled themselves to learn. Drumwright continued to stare at Hargis's scribbles, and Hargis shifted uncomfortably from one foot to the other, looking out at the sludge of the street with a defeated bitterness depleted of vigor.

Drumwright: "I don't know what union the marshal might

have seceded from, though that does sound a bit ominous." He thought of his favorite subject, the Mexican-American War, and how Texas's declaration of independence had eventually led to sustained bloodshed; and then he thought of the secession of the Confederate States of America, which had wrought even more bloodshed; but he couldn't devise any sound analogies between those wars and the marshal's mention of secession. In fact, the word didn't seem to make sense in this context. "'Take Blackwell's Celerity to Union Pacific' seems to mean 'catch a stagecoach and then take a train,' but from San Luis, you could just take the Addison Survey Train to the U.P. line, so that doesn't quite add up. 'Will see to union as arranged' and 'arrangement secured' seem like they might be saying the same thing, unless the secured arrangement is something other than the union. Whatever that means."

Hargis: "You think it might be an arranged marriage? That's a kind of union."

Drumwright rubbed his chin. "Could be. But for the marshal? Who's arranging it?"

"Maybe he bought himself a bride."

Drumwright looked at Hargis critically: "Then what about his seceding from the union? What does that union mean?" He read the message again, but remained as baffled as he had been to start. "Well, based just on this message, I can't see any reason to believe there's anything wrong, or that the marshal isn't out to Rancho Cielito. I don't see that this has anything to do with the marshal's whereabouts, or should give any cause for concern."

Hargis, defensively: "He seems to be talkin' about travelin' here, and now he's disappeared. Strikes me as more than a coincidence."

"He hasn't disappeared if he's stuck out to Rancho Cielito on account of this storm, has he? I'm sure there's some small piece of ordinary information we need to make sense of this message, that it's all logical and sensible, if only we had a proper idea what it's about. I don't think we have to assume the marshal's run off somewhere or that he's buying wives."

Hargis, discouraged, taking the message from the doctor's hands: "Well, you know, Doc, it was just a feelin' I had. All these strange goings-on, maybe they put some funny ideas in my head."

Drumwright, patting Hargis's shoulder condescendingly: "I admit that this is a strange message, and it's good that you showed it to me, but I don't want everybody getting riled up over something that might be perfectly normal. You see?"

"Sure."

"On top of everything else, if the rumor got out that something had happened to the marshal, we might be in for some real disquiet. I've already got half of Tres Cruces ready to lynch that boy Jackson just because the marshal isn't in town—imagine what would happen if they thought he'd gone to San Luis or caught a train or some other such far-fetched nonsense. Everybody's nerves are on edge enough. So why don't we just keep this between us and let the marshal tell us about it in his own time, when he gets back from Cielito?"

Hargis walked to his desk and dropped the marshal's message back into the scrap paper bin that comprised his filing system. "I wouldn'ta even showed it to you, Doc, except that everybody's settin' around waitin' for the marshal to come back, and. . . I got a funny feelin' about it, like maybe he ain't comin' back."

"He'll be back."

Drumwright and Hargis looked at one another for a long moment and then Drumwright nodded and stepped into the doorway. "You keep your eyes open, though."

As the doctor tilted his head back and wet his face in the

drizzle, he tried to remember the exact script of the marshal's message, which disturbed him more than he wanted to admit: in Drumwright's experience, the marshal tended to be square and forthright, and the very fact that he had sent a cryptic message was vexing. The doctor nonchalantly took his leave of Hargis and retired to his barbershop, where he could indulge his craving for a shot of homemade applejack that, he felt sure, would help him sort out the grave vagaries of the last twenty-four hours in peace.

In the telegraph office, Hargis sat down at his desk and stared for a long time at the marshal's message, convinced that there was something in it to be concerned about. Like the doctor, however, he wasn't sure what.

THE FIRE

The first person to notice the fire was Jamie Kerr, the bank guard, because the Hidalgo Trust Bank was closest to the building that abruptly began spewing black smoke into the pale afternoon sky: the Highland Notions Shop. A shift in the wind had wafted the sooty, sweet-smelling smoke through the open front door of the bank and Kerr had leapt up from his cot and run outside and seen the building on fire. He had hustled down to the Coronado Saloon to tell Mr. Collins, and soon most of the town had assembled around the perimeter of the burning building.

The Notions Shop sat on a rise at the far south end of town, set apart from the rows of buildings that made up Main Street by a small ridge. A widow named Highland still owned the building, though she had become too old and ill to run the shop. She had tried for years to sell it, but no one was interested in opening a new shop of any kind in Tres Cruces any more, so the widow had finally rented it out at a modest rate to the marshal, who used the space to indulge his woodworking hobbies. Now, the building was little more than a wooden storehouse for wooden work benches, wooden sawhorses and the wooden artifacts of the marshal's boredom, all of which made excellent kindling.

By the time the congregation of people arrived from the Inn and El Charro and the General Store and Alberto Torres' Stable, the Notions Shop was too hot to approach and windows were shattering like popping corn. The low rumbling whooshes of oxygen being consumed and objects being sucked through fiery vacuums inside the building filled everyone's ears. On this afternoon, the rain was little more than a drizzle and so could not be counted on to extinguish the blaze, and Doc Drumwright sent men to the main well at the other end of town to pump buckets full of water and bring them back, and he stationed a man on every rooftop in town, so that, if a fiery brand were blown from the Notions Shop onto another building, there would be no chance of the fire spreading.

Drumwright, announcing in his most judiciously calm voice: "There's little enough reason to fear folks, just an unfortunate accident of nature. You see how this building sits up higher than the ones where we are, and you know how lightning likes these taller buildings. No reason for us to fear down below." Suddenly realizing: "Say, did anybody hear any thunder? I don't recall there being any lightning this afternoon."

Everyone looked at everyone else and saw confirmed in all the faces that there had, indeed, been no thunder that afternoon and no lightning. Everyone wondered aloud how the fire could have started, because the only person who ever used the building any more was the marshal, and no one had any reason to go inside since the marshal had left for Rancho Cielito. Jonathan Vega and Saul and two ranch hands from Rancho Mirabal and David Burns and Jerry the miner from Virginia all made a sweeping circle around the Notions Shop, to inspect the surroundings for clues. As they did so, the building itself heaved and cursed with fiery tongues and shot shards of wood and glass into the air. They slipped and slid across the ridge and stumbled knee-deep into great holes that looked like shallow puddles and scanned the ground for any evidence that someone had approached the building. It was David Burns who first found the footprints south of the shop, leading up to the back door. He called out and everyone came running, giving the crackling coughing structure a wide berth, until a knot of men stood staring down at the suspiciously lonely boot prints crossing the muddy ground to the rear entrance.

Jonathan: "Guess we should follow'em back where they came from, see what this is all about. Who here's carryin' a gun?"

Some men volunteered that they were carrying guns, some said they could get guns and some stared at their feet. There was a pensive lack of movement until Drumwright pointed at the prints the way a man surprised by a wolf will simply point instead of crying out.

Jerry the miner: "Hey, the Doc's right. We can't follow these prints."

"Why not?"

"Look, they start up here in this pool. We'd need an Indian to track where they came from." The prints did indeed emerge from a slough that stretched a quarter of a mile or more behind the shop. "And they lead *to* the building, but there's no tracks leadin' away."

They looked from the prints to each other to the burning building back to the prints, none of them exactly sure what to do. "Look how strange they are. That ain't slippin' from the mud—there's a pattern!" Whoever had made the prints had not been walking normally, as the left and right feet didn't follow one another in regular strides, but slopped and slid a bit from side to side, with the right foot pointing out and the left foot always exactly perpendicular to the Notions Shop.

"Somebody's in the building!"

"We gotta get'em outta there."

"We can't go in there, we'll get ourselves killed."

"If somebody's still in there, they're already dead."

"Who woulda gone in there?"

"Are we gonna go in there?"

"We gonna risk our necks for some arsonist and we don't even know who it is?"

"Somebody's gotta go in there. Maybe it's the marshal back from Rancho Cielito."

"How could it be?"

"Who else would be in the marshal's workshop?"

"I'm goin' in." Jonathan's nephew Saul stepped forward with a grim, frightened look on his face and moved toward the door of the Notions Shop.

Jonathan: "You can't go in there. I won't allow it. You'll get killed."

Drumwright, yelling: "Somebody fetch a bucket. You, run around front and bring back two buckets of water. I'll go in."

Saul: "You can't go in, Doc, everybody needs you."

David Burns: "This is crazy. Somebody's gonna risk his life to go in there and find a dead body? There'll be time enough for that when the fire's burnt itself out."

"We don't know that. We don't know but it might be the marshal and somethin' terrible's happened to him and we gotta save him."

"It can't be the marshal, there ain't no way he coulda got back across the river."

Drumwright: "What about those runaway horses? And now this. They must've repaired the ferry or found some way across."

"Impossible!"

Saul: "While we're standing here jawin' about it, a man might be burnin' up alive. I'm goin' in."

Jerry ran up breathless with two buckets of water and Drumwright grabbed one of them and started to pour it over his own head. Saul stopped him and took off his hat and poured first one and then the other bucket over himself, drenching his clothes through to his skin. He turned and ran toward the shop before anyone could react. He put his hand to the doorknob, which burned as hot as a branding iron, and he cried out and yanked his arm away and shook his blistered fingers. He kicked at the door several times until the frame around the latch gave way and he crashed inside.

Saul was greeted by a heat the likes of which he had never imagined before, so dry that his skin felt like ancient parchment and his eyeballs shrank in on themselves and teared up, and the tears were sucked down his face and dried before they reached his cheekbones. He felt as if he had entered hell itself.

He found that he was standing directly in fire and jumped to one side and tried to catch his breath. He choked and felt his lungs seize, as if they were turning inside out, and his heart pounded wildly. Black smoke filled his eyes. He squinted and then stooped and found a tiny pocket of air and a tiny sliver of light, and he peered at a pile of clothes that looked to be a body, only a few feet away. Again he gasped for breath but choked blankly and felt his hands and feet grow heavy and his head turn light. His body was like a great block of burning wood floating up from the bottom of a fiery lake, and he had almost no control over his limbs as they swelled and bobbed before his eyes. The air around him was filled with low cackling, the gargoyles of hell closing around, laughing, inviting him to join them in the flames. With a tremendous effort of will, he took two steps forward and knelt down to touch the body.

His eyes burned like glowing coals and his hands felt lumpen, but he managed to stoop bent-backed and drag the body backwards across the burning planks, until he felt searing pain in his right leg and looked down to find his pants on fire. As his lungs fairly burst against his ribs, he let go of the body and heaved himself back, striking the door frame with his spine and falling halfway outside.

Saul lost consciousness in a clamor of voices. Buckets of water were thrown over his body as he was dragged out of the building. The other inert body, whose shirt was on fire, was spotted inside the door and three men wrestled it outside coughing and gagging, and more buckets of water were thrown on it, and the knot of men stumbled and lunged backwards away from the building as if they were all one creature. They dragged the bodies through the mud to a safe distance from the inferno and doused them with even more water.

Jonathan, cradling Saul as Saul sputtered and revived: "Can you hear me? Boy, can you hear me?"

Saul gasped for breath and came to with a pained wail. "He's in there, by the door!"

"We got him out. Are you all right?"

"My leg, shit, my leg."

"Doc!"

Drumwright, kneeling over the other body: "He's still breathing. Carry him back to my shop, quick as you can, you and you. You in the brown shirt go with'em and fetch some more water."

"Doc!"

Drumwright, approaching at a trot, then stooping to peer beneath Saul's singed and tattered pantleg: "Do you think you can get up? Here, put your arm around me, and the other around your uncle. Ready? We're just going down to my shop. You think you can make it? If we go too fast, you tell us."

They made their way down the ridge, through the crowd, and away from the Notions Shop, past Moreno, who hovered in the doorway of the bank. After spluttering some more and coughing and trying to catch his breath while hopping along between the two older men, Saul said, "Who was it? The marshal?"

"Otis."

Jonathan, pulling up a little: "The Frogboy? What the hell was he doin' in there?"

Drumwright: "I don't know, but he's lucky he didn't die doin' it. He may die yet."

Jonathan: "Jesus Christ almighty! I nearly sacrificed my own flesh and blood for a freak of nature. I bet he set the fire himself."

"Let's get this boy inside and see to his wounds."

MIDNIGHT RENDEZVOUS

The fire in the Highland Notions Shop lasted the whole afternoon, until the flames had gutted the building. A sudden downpour extinguished the last lingering embers, but Jonathan sent four men to douse the ashes some more just the same. He gave free meals and drinks to the water-bucket men, who had manned their posts all day on top of the other buildings.

The burns on Saul's right shin and calf swelled angry red, but Doc Drumwright said they were minor and would heal in time, and he wrapped them in bandages laced with a buttery smelling ointment. Jonathan presented his nephew as a hero at the saloon, and Saul got drunk on his uncle's best private rum. Otis the Frogboy still had not regained consciousness by the evening, and Doc Drumwright said he didn't know if he would pull through: he had burns over half his body and his breathing was labored and shallow. They laid Otis out on the "surgical table"—a long steel plate that had once been part of a boxcar, suspended across sawhorses in the back of Doc Drumwright's shop—next to the shrouded body of Pastor Charles, which had begun to stink in spite of Drumwright's efforts.

That night, the Coronado was abuzz with speculation about the fire, about what Otis the Frogboy had been doing in the building, about how the Frogboy had managed to set the fire and why he had lingered in it. The general conclusion was that no one could ascertain the motives of such a mentally incapacitated man, and a few people wondered aloud why people such as Otis were allowed to live. They said, Thank God nobody else had been in the building, and Poor Saul, who injured himself to save that cretin! A man from Rancho Cielito was stationed in Drumwright's barbershop with instructions to fetch the doctor the moment Otis revived, though the feeling in the saloon was that, even if Otis did survive and return to his normal self, he would be unable to account for his actions.

As the indignance and self-righteousness over Otis's deed became almost celebratory, Diana lingered quietly at the bar and thought to herself how odd this fire was, especially on the heels of the shooting of Pastor Charles. Tempers were growing shorter and harmless diversions were coming fewer and farther between, and the revelry in the saloon over the fire and Otis's burned and comatose body frightened her.

Moreno, who had remained inconspicuous all evening, approached the bar and ordered a drink, pointedly turning his back on Diana; when he returned to his seat, Diana found a folded slip of paper on the bar, within easy arm's reach, and she nonchalantly scooted her drink to and fro on the bar until she captured the note under her glass and slid it into her hands. She glanced around to determine that no one was paying attention and then opened the note, which read: "Please come to room 13 after midnight tonight to discuss some matters arising from the fire this afternoon." It was signed Arturo Calderon. Diana tore the note into tiny pieces and set them on fire in her ashtray as she lit a cigarette.

The night wore on and the crowd thinned as they exhausted the possibilities of their discussion. They returned to their rooms upstairs or to their makeshift cots in various downstairs nooks of the saloon or to the other businesses that provided sleeping spaces around Tres Cruces. Diana went to her room.

No clients approached her, and not even Jonathan came

in to vent about his problems or to have sex with her; she was thankful that, since the rain had begun, Jonathan had grown less and less interested in her, and she was relieved of the burden of his tedious conversation and sweaty body. She emptied the rain basins around her room through the window and then lay on her bed; and then, as she was thinking about Moreno and Collins and Kerr and the bank, she remembered Jackson, and she recognized that everyone had forgotten him in the commotion and that he had not been fed since breakfast. She decided to take advantage of the opportunity to go down to the jail again, to convince Jackson to throw his lot in with her.

Saul, she knew, was passed out drunk in his room, so whatever food she offered Jackson for dinner would have to be scrounged willy-nilly from the kitchen. Diana dressed to go out and pattered as quietly as she could down the back stairs.

She assembled a plateful of unsavory leftover glop and slipped out the kitchen door, surprised to find the night sky relatively light. She made out a sliver of moon bobbing between clouds, like a silver needle sewing patterns into the sky. As she passed along Main Street, the moonlight caught wet porch beams and reflected white off the faded paint of gently swinging signs, making small patches of wood glow ghostly against the shadows. Diana felt less like a whole human being than an occupied body whose spirit was as fleeting and insubstantial as the glimmers of moon mirrored in the rivulets of rainwater running beneath her feet.

The street was empty as Diana clopped across to the marshal's office. The only lamplight glowed from Doc Drumwright's shop. She tried the marshal's door—this time it was locked. In a futile exercise, she walked around the entire jail, which she knew had neither alternate doors nor windows nor any opening except the front door. She knocked lightly on the door, on the chance that someone might be asleep on the marshal's cot, but she received no answer and, frustrated at this reminder of her helplessness in the face of real walls and real locks, she stamped her boot heel into the plank sidewalk and banged her fist once into the door. She returned to the inn, sneaked back up the rear stairs, and set Jackson's food on her dresser.

As she lay on her bed contemplating Jackson in his cell, she felt overwhelmed once again by her own weakness, by the stupidity of Moreno's plan to rob the bank and even more by her own even stupider idea that she could accomplish what she knew Moreno could not. She put her fingertips against her windowpane and thought that this rain must finally be driving her mad and that she would be better off doing nothing and saying nothing and just lying here in her room until the storm blew over and everything returned to normal; but she was agitated the more by the knowledge that a return to normal would mean being fucked and beaten and sitting here miserable in her room until she died. She checked the ticking clock on her dresser: a few minutes before midnight, and though a visit to Moreno seemed idiotic, it was her only option, and so she fixed her hair and applied perfume to her wrists and neck, as she hadn't bathed in three days. She changed from boots to slippers and trotted down the narrow hall and around the corner to room 13.

She knocked softly twice and entered. Room 13 was tiny, perhaps ten feet by seven feet, with just enough room for a small, shoddy chest of drawers, a three-legged table holding a basin and a pitcher, and a narrow bed that was nothing more than pine boards and blankets. Moreno lay on his side on the bed, fully clothed, with his boots still on, squinting at a thin book by the light of a candle. He waited until Diana had come all the way into the room and closed the door behind her before sitting up and checking the time on his pocket watch.

"Midnight. I'll take your punctuality as a sign of enthusiasm." Motioning with his arm for her to come in: "The only seat I can offer you is my bed, but please sit down."

"I'll stand."

"As you wish. I'm glad to see you've changed your mind. What convinced you to take part in my plan?" Diana shrugged and looked away. "Well, no matter. Did you tell that man Burns that I'm your brother? I ask only so I'll know how to approach him the next time we meet."

"Half-brother. Yes, that's what I told him."

"And he believed you?"

Diana: "It's hard to tell, since he don't care one way or the other, and honestly, right now, I don't care a damn about that either. I need to know some things about this plan of yours."

"Very well, what would you like to know?"

"For starters, why me? Of all the people in Tres Cruces, why choose me for your partner? You think I'm more desperate, or just easier to use? You think you can trust me?"

Moreno put down his book and walked to Diana. He raised his hand to Diana's face and she flinched and backed against the wall. Moreno held his hand palm outward in a gesture of peace and stepped forward again. A loose strand of hair had escaped from behind Diana's ear and he caressed it back into place with his fingertips, then traced a gentle snaking 'S' along Diana's jaw from her earlobe to her chin.

"If you don't already understand why I chose you, then I couldn't explain it. Do you know what I mean?"

Diana took a breath and became deeply angry and felt the anger flow outward from her chest through her arms into the backs of her wrists, and her hands began to shake. "That ain't no answer. That ain't about robbin' no bank."

Moreno, sighing: "There are many reasons for doing anything. Perhaps there is no reason, other than the fact of you."

"That still ain't no answer."

Pausing to clear his throat, looking at the floor: "I'm just a vagabond and you're a scarlet dove. How could I speak to you of love and not appear foolish?"

"Love?!"

"Perhaps you've never known love? Real love." Pausing to search Diana's eyes: "Have you ever felt loved?"

Diana rolled her eyes toward the ceiling and felt her anger become the disorderly and inexpressible rage that Moreno had inspired at their original meeting. With every other man, in every other hopeless situation, she was icily dismissive, but something about Moreno compelled her, perhaps because he was so much more ridiculous than anyone she had ever met, perhaps because he seemed proud of his ridiculousness in a way that couldn't possibly benefit him. He maddened her, and yet she wanted to keep poking around him, the way one pokes the edges of a painful scab to satisfy an itch that only grows deliciously worse with pressure.

Diana, sarcastically: "I feel loved all the time. All right? And that still ain't got nothin' to do with robbin' a bank."

"Let's just say that some choices are simply fortuitous—not necessarily driven by logic, but by feeling."

"Let's just say you got your reasons, and leave it at that." At this, Moreno gave a thin, quixotic smile and rested the palm of his right hand gently against the nape of Diana's neck. "So let me ask you somethin' practical, Moreno, 'cause whatever reasons you got for choosin' me, I'm goin' along for the money. All right?"

"All right."

"How do you plan to open the doors guardin' that safe? Not the safe itself, but the bank doors, the ones leadin' behind the counters? How you even gonna get inside?"

Moreno continued to stare at Diana's face in a simultaneously chaste and libidinous way that Diana hadn't seen since her childhood, a look of lustful ignorance, and he took the liberty of caressing Diana's neck so gently that she barely felt the tickle of his fingertips as they traced her collarbone to her shoulder. Neither of them breathed.

Diana: "If you ain't gonna answer my questions, you can stop pawing me. Or you can pay me for the pleasure and do it right."

Moreno looked away, embarrassed for himself and saddened by Diana's hardness. He stepped back, opened the top drawer of his dresser and retrieved a small black box just larger than the palm of his hand. He held it out it to Diana. The box was hinged, and when Diana opened it, she found it lined in red velvet. It contained several small pockets and cloth eye-hooks that held tiny steel rods, silver dowels and miniature pikes that were curved and bent in unusual ways and whose shapes seemed to twist and change in the light.

Moreno: "A lock-pick set. I worked for a time as a mechanic on a riverboat, where I met a few interesting people. I acquired that from a confidence man, who was caught stealing and thrown overboard: as luck would have it, I was the first person in his cabin after he was ejected, and I found those picks in a hollowed-out Bible. I taught myself how to use them, and I can now pick most locks with ease. What else would you like to know?"

Diana held each little shaft up to the light one by one. She ran the tip of her index finger up and down them, over their little curves and points, and she manipulated them between her fingers, getting a sense of their weight and the quality of their machined hardness.

Diana: "You ain't a blacksmith's apprentice at all, are you? Nor a mechanic, nor a vagabond, nor whatever else you said. You're that confidence man, from the boat."

"Hardly. I just know an opportunity when I see one."

Moreno held his hand out to Diana, who reluctantly took it. He held her fingers in one hand and stroked her forearm with the other. He looked at her with dewy eyes.

Diana, blanching: "Can you show me how to use them?"

"The idea is for me to use them."

"But could you? I've got a use for'em that has nothin' to do with the bank."

Moreno, letting Diana's fingers drop: "I suppose I could, but I don't think I will. What if you get caught trying to break into some room before we have a chance to rob the bank? Suppose they take the picks away from you and lock you up, leaving me with no tools and no accomplice?" He held up his index finger to keep Diana from speaking while he paused for emphasis. "Show me what you want done, and I'll do it for you."

"I don't need you to do my dirty work, Moreno. It's a matter that just don't concern you. And I won't get caught. If you're willing to trust me with your little plan, if you're willing to trust me as a partner, then you oughtta be willing to trust me this far."

Moreno turned his back and stepped lightly to his bed, hovering above the candle and tapping his fingertips together rapidly. "Perhaps you're right, but I don't believe this line of talk will get us anywhere tonight. Perhaps I'll show you how to use them, but later. Right now, I think we should discuss the conditions under which we might act. That's why I asked you to come here."

Diana stared for a few moments longer at the lock pick set before snapping it shut. She clutched it in the palm of her hand. "Show me tonight."

Sighing: "Very well. If that's a condition you're placing on me?"

"All right, then, we're settled on that." Nodding acquiescence: "Your note said something about the fire."

Moreno: "Correct. It has given me certain new ideas. You see, I was responsible for that fire."

"You were? But how?"

"I asked that man, Otis, to do me a favor, but he botched it and burned the building down."

"You asked Otis the Frogboy to do you a favor?"

Grinning ironically and shaking his head: "You all call him Frogboy, like he's some kind of monster, but it isn't so. He merely thinks about the world differently than you and I."

"Moreno, he has a brain problem. He doesn't think about the world the way we do because he can't."

"He's not a monster. He has talents." Moreno paced back and forth with his hands behind his back, taking soft steps. "When I discovered that the marshal used that Notions Shop as a workshop, I figured there might be some tools inside that could help us, so I broke in one night and stole a few things." Moreno opened the bottom drawer of his dresser and moved aside some pants and shirts to reveal a mallet, a handsaw, a hand drill, a wood pick and a plane. "But then it occurred to me that, although the marshal was out of town, it's conceivable that he could make an untimely return and discover the items missing, or that someone else might use the shop. I thought it would be a good idea to create an alibi for the missing tools. So I sent Otis in and instructed him to do some things that might draw attention. That way, someone would discover him inside the building and when the items were missed, they would blame Otis. It wouldn't matter then that they wouldn't be able to find the tools. Everyone would assume that Otis had done something irrational with them and they would pay it no more mind."

Diana, scoffing: "That makes sense like a five-legged sow." She slid a short distance along the wall, farther away from

Moreno. "If you'd bothered to ask anyone, you'd know nobody else is even allowed inside the marshal's workshop, so nobody would have found out about the missing tools, and the marshal's stuck out to Rancho Cielito as sure as we're stuck here. Do you ever do anything that just plain makes sense?" Calming herself: "Anyhow, how does that make you responsible for the fire?"

"I sent him into a tinderbox with a lighted oil lamp. He didn't seem comfortable with the lamp, I admit."

"Why the hell'd you give him a lamp, in the middle of the day?"

"As I said, I wanted him to draw some attention."

"No one would see a lamp flame in the middle of the day!"

"Maybe. Anyway, it was a little joke of mine. A harmless personal joke, I thought, about Diogenes and his lamp. You know?"

"No, I don't know, and I don't want to. Jesus! How am I s'posed to trust you, with your stupid lies and your stupid plans and your stupid jokes, and now you nearly got two people killed and burned down a building over nothing, and how is any of this supposed to make sense?"

"Everything has to make sense to you, doesn't it? The whole idea of robbing a bank, though, simply does not make sense."

Moreno stopped pacing right in front of Diana and squared his body to hers. He leaned into her with his hand against the wall just above her left shoulder, so that she felt the warmth of his body all along hers. She struggled to remain still. Moreno's figure was slight, and though he was taller than Diana by three inches, up close they seemed paradoxically of equal stature. Diana was repulsed by his body the way she was repulsed by all male bodies, and yet she felt unintimidated by him, almost as if he really were her brother. She turned her face away and then turned back and found his gaze oddly unaggressive, almost apologetic, and yet calculating in a way that registered poorly in the pit of her stomach.

Moreno: "There is no design in this world beyond sheer luck, Diana, luck and the thrill of opportunity. The thrill of weaving an insignificant thread through the loom of fate with your own small shuttle. You want me to make plain sense, but there is no plain sense for me to make."

Diana drew herself up against the wall and stiffened her posture to gain as much distance from Moreno as she could. "I don't know if you're as dumb as you sound or dumber. All I'm askin' is for you to lay out the whole plan, all at once. If it don't make sense, then it don't make sense, but you can't tell me that there ain't no plan."

"As with every ambition one can have in life, we have an outline—an idea of what we want to happen. We have a goal, a direction, and a way to move in that direction. The rest will have to be improvised along the way."

"But you're gonna rob that bank, ain't you? You obviously have some sort of plan."

"Perhaps I can illustrate my point this way: consider the bank. The concept of the bank is just an accident of history, not a design that necessarily makes sense. A locked building where people give other people paper and metal to hold for them? It's a convention improvised from somebody's idea, and then it just grew and grew and developed the form it has today, until now, no one can imagine life without banks. And my idea to rob the bank is a result of this accident of history: it's especially accidental, since I'm sure I would not attempt it except for this storm. There wouldn't be enough money to bother robbing in such a farflung outpost as Tres Cruces, without the entirely coincidental intervention of the rain. You see? Such is always the way with accidents, with surprises. With history, and the future. We act on an idea and then see where it takes us, and we look back to see where we've been, because nothing is quite certain. Nothing quite makes sense unless we make the meaning up ourselves."

Moreno breathed in the florid perfume on Diana's neck and closed his eyes to savor the intoxication of it. He wished he were far away with her, alone, somewhere he could enjoy the crane-like grace of her movements and the lines of her high cheekbones and the salt and tang of her kisses, without these complications.

Moreno, whispering confidentially: "The fire. The fire was an accident. But it has given me the idea for another fire, a bigger fire, a better diversion than I had originally conceived. You probably didn't notice, but during that fire at the Notions Shop, I sneaked into the bank and picked the lock of the teller door and walked right up to the safe, and then I locked it again and sneaked back out. You see? The entire town was, so to speak, consumed by the fire. So now my idea is to set another one—that is, for you to set another fire—and while they run to put it out, I'll open the safe and we can get away with the money."

Moreno opened his eyes, stepped back from Diana and surveyed her face, as if finding something new and freshly appealing there. Diana shook her head as if trying to wake up from a particularly ugly dream. "And what building am I gonna burn down?"

Moreno, more and more pleased: "The tack room, the stable across the street. That should burn for quite a while. The hay, the stalls, and they'll be distracted getting the horses out. It's at the opposite end of town from the bank. It's ideal."

Diana, suddenly angry: "God damn it, Moreno. And explain to me again why you can't just burn the building down yourself? What's the point of havin' me run into harm while you dance around by yourself in the bank?"

"You shouldn't come to harm."

"Not like Otis the Frogboy, for instance."

Insinuatingly: "But he's not like you, is he?"

"Why do you even need a partner, you're so clever?"

Moreno squeezed Diana's shoulder reassuringly, almost playfully, as if they were having a harmless lover's spat. "There are always complications. People in places where you didn't expect them. You see? It's good to have four eyes, four ears, to be in two places at once. We'll have more resources at the crucial moment."

Diana, through clenched teeth: "Why not hire a gang, then? You been doin' a lot of thinkin', Moreno, but I don't see that you've thought any of this through. You got a plan, but you don't call it a plan because one thing just sounds less likely than the last."

Moreno, leaning closer to Diana again, his warm breath moist on her forehead and cheeks: "I don't know how much there is to think about. You create a diversion. I steal the money. And as for needing a partner. . . I don't need one. I want one. I want you."

"Christ, Moreno."

"So, you'll do it, then?"

"I'll do it."

"Good. You must not think I'm so crazy then?" Whispering: "I like this tension."

"Moreno, you could just pay to have sex with me. Wouldn't that be easier?"

"I know you're angry, Diana. If I were you, I'd be angry too. But not everyone in the world wants to hurt you."

"No, you'd never hurt me, would you? You'd never get me hurt."

"No, Diana. Honestly, I wouldn't. I have only your best interest in mind."

"You don't even know what my best interest is. Look, Moreno, I'll do it, I'll go along with your non-plan, but only if you show me how to use these picks. Tonight."

Casting his eyes down disappointedly and taking a step backward: "Oh, I see. You won't trust me. You still make demands." Moreno turned away and considered for a long moment. "Very well, if that's your price."

"We already agreed!"

"What door do you wish to open?"

"You don't need to know. I don't think this is asking so much, in exchange for burnin' down a building."

"Burning down that building will benefit you as much as me. Maybe more." Sighing, to himself: "But who doesn't have conditions, eh?"

"That's right. Even you, Moreno."

He took the lock-pick set and told Diana the purpose and use of each tool, the ways to manipulate them for different kinds of locks. After checking the hall several times, he quickly and breathlessly demonstrated how they worked on his own door and then stood guard while Diana picked his lock as well.

Diana felt an elation that resembled pure freedom as she knelt in the hall and twiddled a pair of spiky shafts into Moreno's keyhole. She felt the hard resistance of tumblers and latches pressing against her fingertips and then giving way as the door swung a quarter of an inch into the room.

Moreno, gesturing dismissively: "This door has an easy lock. Very poor quality, and the knob and latch are also cheap. Not every door will give so generously. But now you have the idea."

"Which of these would I need to open an outside door?

Say the door to the saloon?"

Moreno selected two little rods from the set and held them up. "These would probably do."

"Then lend me those. Just those two. If somebody does catch me, you'll still have the rest of the set."

"But without those two, the number of combinations of picks, the number of locks you can breach, goes down drastically. At least tell me why I should take such a risk."

"There's no risk. I won't get caught. And, on second thought, if I get caught, I'll hide 'em. I'll stick 'em up my ass, all right? You'll get your little rods back."

Diana held the picks up like a question mark between her face and Moreno's, and Moreno took her hand in his and lovingly kissed each knuckle of each finger and then turned back into his room without looking at Diana again. Diana slipped the picks into the frilly hem of her camisole, one below each breast, and stepped into the hall. She looked at Moreno lying on his bed facing away from her. She closed his door and tiptoed down the hall to her room.

DRUMWRIGHT CONSIDERS

Alcohol had precisely the opposite effect on Doc Drumwright as it did on everybody else: he had been drinking so much for so long that he could no longer achieve a satisfying state of inebriation, and hard liquor had a stimulating rather than depressing influence on his psyche. Fueled by gin or rum or sourmash whisky, he could spend whole nights awake reenacting Mexican War battles in his mind, playing them out from different vantage points on the field, changing the outcomes, watching the dead die slowly or reviving them with a medical miracle of his own devising, reversing the fortunes of the Mexicans or the Americans or the Texans as he saw fit; or he would ruminate over rare diseases of the human body based on case histories he had read, spinning elaborate theories about the workings of the nerves of the spine or the spleen. He would sit up all night in dipsomaniacal reveries over his favorite apothecary book, *Dr. Chase's Recipes*, musing to himself about the potential effects and dosages of certain drugs, or he would stand in front of his medicine cabinet and regard his miniature vials and vessels: of morphine, extract of ergot, calomel, tincture aconite, bromide of potassium. On especially torpid nights, he would leave off speculating and administer some laudanum to his drink and whet a straight razor and prove his steadiness to himself by shaving his own forearm as if for surgery, and then he would congratulate himself on his poise by draining another shot and trying it with his opposite hand on his opposite arm. Tonight, however, he simply sat in the darkness with a flask of rum at his elbow to aid his concentration, dwelling not on his own magnificence but on the events of the day. He tried to ignore the piteous moaning of Otis in the back of the barbershop.

There was something about the fire in the Notions Shop that struck the doctor as cock-eyed. The idea that Otis had wandered out of town in all this muck and rain and had somehow found himself on the south side of the Notions Shop perturbed Drumwright no end. Why had Otis ventured out in the first place? From what point in town? Where had he circled back? Drumwright had known Otis to behave irrationally, even to hurt himself deliberately, so he wasn't surprised at the fire itself; nor was he surprised that Otis had gone into the Notions Shop, since the marshal occasionally fashioned wooden toys there, and some of those toys had found their way into Otis's hands. What perplexed the doctor was the fact that Otis had entered the Notions Shop from the rear, leaving no tracks at all around the building, but only a simple trail in a straight line from out of town. How had he gotten in? Wasn't the back door always locked? It was impossible to tell what went on inside Otis's diminished mind, but the doctor could not help wondering by what strange initiative Otis had traipsed that far out of town, all alone, then back through a swampy pool to the shop.

Drumwright took a thoughtless swig of rum and considered the claustrophobia of the rain, the likelihood that Otis had become confused and had wandered without deliberation or purpose in one direction and then another, until he had recognized a familiar building and headed for it. The doctor cleared his throat and spit into the porcelain basin at his feet, then wiped his mouth and his mustache with the back of his sleeve. Otis was an imbecile, Drumwright thought: there was the explanation. And yet the doctor did not feel satisfied and vague premonitions nettled his conscience. His bones ached, more with augury than rheumatism, but neither his bones nor his conscience could read the omens. Otis and the fire, the marshal's telegram, the seven horses. He took another drink of rum.

He was keenly aware that the rest of Tres Cruces remained ignorant of the marshal's odd behavior before the storm and were not as concerned as he was by the appearance of the horses. He suggested to himself that he was merely inventing mysteries to ward off the monotony of the rain. But there was something urgent in Drumwright's anxiety, an acute fillip that these signs portended violence.

He stood and ambled over to his desk and lit a candle. He held the guttering light up to the medicine cabinet and stared hard through his reflection in the glass. Mix some Dover's Powder in his rum? The blend of sugar, ipecac and opium would comfort him against these infertile contemplations.

He listened to Otis moaning wretchedly. What design could that retarded man possibly have had in setting that fire? None. Rum cascaded through the empty arroyos of his mind. And the marshal's telegram: though Drumwright feared that Hargis's ill feeling about that message might prove true, he could see no connection between it and anything else. The horses? Perhaps they had escaped from some corral destroyed in the storm, and maybe they were just as confused as he was; yet, how could they have crossed the Fuerte from Rancho Cielito?

Drumwright mulled and mulled and drank and drank, and the night wore on, but if there was any tie between Otis's pyrotechnics and the marshal's telegram, he could not find it; and if there was a solution to the conundrum of the horses, he could not discover it standing in his barbershop. He opened the medicine cabinet and gauged his supply of Dover's Powder, then tapped some into his flask. He shook the flask vigorously and drank its contents and waited for the opium to float him away.

THE CONSEQUENCE OF AN ARTLESS LIE

Diana had closed her door behind her, had rolled her eyes to the ceiling and heaved a huge sigh of relief, was already planning her next gambit before she realized that the air in her room was wrong. She turned from the door in the darkness and recognized the smell of Jonathan's specially blended tobacco mingling with her own stale cigarette smoke. A little red point of burning paper lit up next to her vanity and the floorboards creaked as Jonathan took a drag on his cigarette and stood up. He lit the oil lamp he had brought from downstairs, revealing his face haggard from sleeplessness, the skin puffy around his eyes and taut around his mouth.

"Where you been?"

Diana stepped out of the lamp's direct light and kicked her slippers off. She took a moment to remove some pins from her hair, as nonchalantly as possible. "I was down in the saloon. Tryin' to drum up some business."

"There ain't nobody in the saloon."

She bent to turn down her sheets. Outside, the beat of raindrops slackened for a moment, then suddenly crashed down like a wave breaking over the Coronado, and slackened again. A raven, scared out of its nightly hiding place and attracted by the lamplight, banged against Diana's window, fluttered and staggered on the sill, then dropped out of sight.

Jonathan: "You know what I say?"

"What?"

"I say you're a liar."

Jonathan took a long drag on his cigarette and moved toward Diana slowly, hesitating at the foot of her bed, watching her. She turned her back to him and removed her white cotton blouse and camisole. She palmed the little lock picks and dropped them to the floor with her clothes. She selected a threadbare blue nightgown from her tiny wardrobe, removed her bodice, then casually pulled the nightgown over her head, unfastened her skirt's eyehooks and let the skirt fall into the pile of clothes on the floor. She was shaking inside, but continued preparing for bed as if it were any other night.

Jonathan: "What do you know about a drifter named Calderon?"

"What do you want to know?"

Jonathan threw his lit cigarette at Diana's head. She yelped in surprise and put her hands up too late to prevent the cigarette from striking her neck. She yelped again at the sting.

Jonathan, stepping closer: "You worthless bitch. This dude Calderon's gonna take you down to San Juan, ain't that right? They say he's your brother. That's who you went to see just now, idn't it?"

Completely acquiescent, with downcast eyes: "No. Like I said—"

"You weren't in the saloon. Where were you? You're thinkin' about runnin' off with this Calderon, ain't that right?"

"Jonathan. I couldn't run off nowhere if I wanted to, which I don't. You think I'm stupid?"

"You're worse than stupid: you think you're smart."

Motioning toward the rainy night: "Well, I ain't smart enough to think I could run away in this storm."

"That's just how stupid you are, which is why I come to put a stop to this right now. You ain't goin' nowhere. This here is your home that I provide for you, and there ain't no call to ever think about leavin', you understand? You got a roof and you got three square a day that I provide for you, understand? You ain't never had another home and you ain't never gonna. Anyway, there ain't nowhere to run, 'cause nobody'll ever want an ugly bitch like you. Now who's this Calderon?"

Jonathan reached into his belt and unsheathed a five-inch buck knife. He held it up to the lamplight. The blade shone in the wavering, bulbous, rusty yellow glow, and Diana caught her breath. She took an instinctive step back toward the wall and brought her hand up to her chest.

"He's nobody. Just some asshole from San Juan."

"Not your brother?"

"I swear. He said that 'cause he wanted to fuck his sister, that's all. Burns came in before he finished, and they both got sore. It was all just a story."

"That's a funny kind of story."

Shaking her head no: "Everybody's got their little things they like. I've heard a thousand times worse than that, ten thousand times, and so have you."

Jonathan grabbed Diana's wrist. "And what about Burns?" Moving the blade of his knife slowly up to Diana's face and pressing the flat of it against her cheek: "He wasn't too happy, the way you treated him."

Diana closed her eyes. Her heart beat so wildly that it was all she could do not to leap away and throw herself out the window. She felt the knife cold and hard against her cheek, and she had to speak through gritted teeth, barely opening her mouth, to avoid being sliced by the pressure of the blade. "Ah, you know how it is sometimes." Between shallow breaths: "It was a bad day, Jonathan. That's all. It wasn't the right time. It was just wrong. Just wrong, you know how some days are just wrong? I didn't mean no harm by it." On the verge of sobbing: "I'm sorry, Jonathan, I'm so sorry. It won't ever happen again,

I swear to God. Don't cut me."

Jonathan lowered the knife, letting his knuckles graze Diana's jawbone and sternum and left breast, until his fist rested against Diana's side and the point of his knife pricked upward into her exposed armpit. With his free hand, Jonathan grabbed at Diana's face and kneaded her cheeks angrily into her teeth. Diana's neck muscles stiffened and she made an involuntary grunt as Jonathan pushed her head back and forth, from one side to the other. After what seemed an eternity of kneading and crushing his fingers and knuckles into her face, he squeezed the back of her jaw with his thumb on one side and his ring finger on the other, forcing her mouth open, and he pulled her mouth into his, a hard, angry, grinding open kiss, teeth against teeth and teeth against lips. He bit into Diana's bottom lip so hard that she cried out, and blood seeped against her gums.

Jonathan let go her jaw and grabbed at the neck of her nightgown. With a reckless motion, he jerked the gown away from her skin and brought the knife up, almost into her chest. The nightgown tore away with a loud rip. Diana hurled herself back in surprise. Her foot struck a basin on the floor. She lost her balance and fell heavily against the wall. The basin splashed rainwater over her stockinged feet and clattered across the floor, where it spun slowly and loudly into angry silence. Her nightgown was slit wide from the belly, exposing her breasts and stomach.

"Get up and come over here." Trembling, Diana stood up, using the wall behind her as a prop. Motioning with the knife: "Come here." She walked the few feet to Jonathan with frightened baby steps, wringing her hands, her shoulders stooped and her chest concave, her eyes cast down.

"I didn't do nothin', Jonathan. I swear to God, I didn't do nothin.'"

"You're not gonna do nothin' neither, you hear?"

"No, I swear."

"Turn around."

She turned around and Jonathan grabbed a handful of her nightgown. With a few deft cuts, he shredded it and ripped it off of her shoulders, so that she stood before him naked except for her cheap cotton underwear and stockings. He turned the dull side of the blade toward her and slid it in between her buttocks. He ran it up one side and down the other, bunching her underwear into the crack.

Diana shook with a tremendous sob of fear. Her entire body quivered. She steeled herself: this wasn't the first time Jonathan had raped her, but it was the first time he had used a knife, and Diana felt that this time, with the smothering dread of the rain and Jonathan's bloodlust with Jackson and Saul burned in the fire, he might do more than just beat her. The knife blade, which had felt cold at first, grew warmer and more terrifying as he continued rubbing it up and down the inside of her buttocks, between her legs and thighs. Up and down, now faster, now slower, and with each change in the knife's speed and direction, Diana held her breath, waiting for the blade to slice her.

Jonathan pulled out the waistband of her underwear. He sawed through it and then sliced down, tearing away the cheap fabric and exposing her skin. Then he made the same motions again, over and over, running the blade up and down her buttocks, up and down, pressed now against Diana's naked skin. Occasionally, the point of the knife began to prick her ever so slowly, until Jonathan pulled it back and slid the broad face of the blade to another part of her ass. She felt the sharp edge shave against flesh, until the suspense of the moving blade made her weep and cry out from the back of her throat.

"Don't cut me, Jonathan, don't cut me. Please don't cut

me."

"Spread your legs."

Crying harder now: "Please don't cut me, Jonathan, please!"

Jonathan punched Diana's left thigh and forced her legs apart. He shoved her forward, against the bed, and then he struck the middle of her back between her shoulder blades with his closed fist, so that snot from Diana's nose streamed out into her mouth and she lost her breath and lunged forward against the bed. The knot of Jonathan's fist remained imprinted in her back as she curled defensively into herself on the edge of the bed. Jonathan grabbed her between her legs, hiking her ass up toward him. He opened his trousers and then laid the knife blade across the small of her back, which was convulsing with spasms of fear.

He lined himself up and thrust the hard thick knot of his cock roughly into Diana's ass. They both cried out, and Jonathan's hand holding the knife slipped, and the knife blade clipped her right shoulder and cut her. She felt the cut at first as an emptiness in the pit of her stomach, and then as a sharp wire strung taut across her skin, and then as a weltering pain growing by the second as blood ran out in a stream down her side. She screamed and tried to heave herself away onto the bed, but Jonathan caught her around the waist and thrust harder and deeper into her, half a dozen times, both of them growling like animals in rage and pain, until he came inside her and let her squirm away across her bed. She huddled, facing him, in a defensive ball against her headboard.

Jonathan let out a long breath and grabbed at Diana's footboard for support. He wiped the knife blade on Diana's bedspread, leaving a trail of her blood across the rough fabric, and then tucked and cantilevered himself back into his trousers and zipped them up. He wiped the sweat away from his upper lip and stared at the heap of Diana's naked body. His hands shook. Pointing with his knife: "You cut bad?"

Diana neither answered nor looked at Jonathan, but remained curled into herself on her bed, arms wrapped around her knees, rocking herself gently as blood trickled down her side and onto her pillow. She could feel Jonathan's semen seeping out of her, oozing across her right buttock.

"Have the Doc look at that cut if you want. Tell him to bill me." Walking to Diana's vanity and picking up the oil lamp he had brought from downstairs: "I don't want to hear nothin' more about this Calderon character. Nor about San Juan, nor about anybody's brother. And if David Burns comes back to see you, you treat him special. That boy's got some money laid up, him and his partner both, and I don't mind if they spend it in my saloon."

He stared at Diana a while longer. Though the night was warm and the air in her room close, she shivered uncontrollably. Jonathan rummaged in her wardrobe, found a heavy cloak, and threw it at her. "Mind you don't make yourself sick."

He exited the room, leaving Diana gnarled up, shivering in the dark, listening to the drops of her own blood against her pillowcase mingle with the raindrops splashing into basins around her room.

No Plan, No Choice

Diana lay curled on her bed for a long time before she was able to think a thought of her own, and then what she thought was that she hated herself and hated Jonathan and hated Moreno even more. The cut on her shoulder had stopped bleeding but had not stopped hurting. Time accordioned around her. It seemed as if hours passed without a single blink of her eyes, as if her whole life up to now hadn't been half as long as this single night. Still, when the force of her hatred finally overcame her benumbed terror and she dragged herself out of bed, it was only three in the morning. She opened her window and threw the clothes that Jonathan had cut off of her into the street. She washed herself, put on fresh underwear and a clean skirt, and pulled on her boots. She carefully slipped a blouse over her cut shoulder and, though the night was still warm, she wrapped herself in her mantle.

She took Jackson's plate of encrusted gruel from her dresser and tiptoed rather too heavily for her own liking down the back stairs and outside. The clouds now obscured every trace of light from the sky. Diana moved by memory and intuition in the darkness around El Charro, across the street to the eaves of the Mathers' General Store, down along the sidewalk to the marshal's office. She stopped now and again, listening for movements; and though she noticed the faint burnt-ochre glow of candlelight wavering in Doc Drumwright's window, she heard nothing besides her own breath and the pattering drizzle draining off the lips of the overhanging roofs. When she was certain she was alone on the street, Diana set the plate down on the walkway, scooped Moreno's picks out of her pocket and set to work on the marshal's lock.

For a long time, she found no tumblers or ratchets to manipulate, just blank metal seemingly without teeth; but as she calmed herself and breathed deeply and evenly, as Moreno had showed her, her fingers became accustomed to the subtleties of the mechanism and she discerned grooves and niches. She found a combination of nooks that resisted her pressure in a promising way, and she fumbled and failed and dropped one of the picks and re-found her grip. She used her mouth to alter the angle of the picks just slightly as she applied tension against the tumblers and rotated the rods. Her shoulder stung where it was cut. The joints of her fingers began to ache and her head hurt, until suddenly all the tension in the muggy air dissipated at once, as the tumblers gave beneath her fingertips. She heard the click of the latch, and the door swung in on its hinges.

She pushed the door wide and put the picks back in her pocket, then picked up Jackson's food and went in. She stood just inside the doorway for a long moment in the pitch dark, listening, feeling the whole blackened room around her pressing stale against her skin. At last, she closed the door again, felt her way across the room and down the hall to Jackson's cell.

Jackson, recognizing Diana, breathed a sigh of relief. "I thought you'd be one of them men, come to kill me."

Jackson had gotten nothing to eat since breakfast and had been forced to defecate in his urine basin, and he had sat in his cell outwardly riled and bitter but inwardly terrified in the manner of all condemned men whose punishment remains in doubt. He thought more and more about being killed in some unexpectedly gruesome way, perhaps by starvation. Diana handed the plate through the bars.

"If it wasn't for you, I expect they'd just let me starve."

"Maybe. There was a big commotion today, a fire down at the Notions Shop, and you know how people are—one thing pushes out another."

Between greedy mouthfuls of stale food: "And it's better not to be a thing."

"I'll make sure somebody comes at breakfast. But probably not me. Now, listen, 'cause I don't have long. There's a little Mexican man named Moreno, you know him? About five six, maybe, soft features, walks kinda funny, talks real mannered."

"I met a guy like that at the saloon, only his name wasn't Moreno, it was Calderon. Real polite but kinda strange."

"Same guy. Anyway, this Moreno is plannin' to rob the bank."

"I thought you was plannin' to rob the bank."

"Just listen. This guy's kind of a dreamer, and he thinks he's gonna rob the bank. He's gonna try to jimmy the safe or somethin'."

"No way, no how. For one thing, it's a combination lock, can't be jimmied. For another thing, that safe's a solid steel pig, and nobody gonna crack that thing but Collins. He's the only one knows the combination."

"That's what I said, but Moreno's got his own way of thinkin'. I'm tellin' you this 'cause Moreno's prob'ly gonna be in the bank when we go to rob it, and I don't know how it'll all play out. So you should be aware. Anyway, what's gonna happen is, I'm gonna set the stables on fire for a diversion, then I'm comin' down here to spring you, then we're robbin' the safe and gettin' free. So that's the plan."

Jackson, scraping his plate clean: "That don't sound like much of a plan. And I don't see how you can get that safe open without Collins. You're gonna need to collar him and make him tell the combination, and you can't do that without causin' some kind of a ruckus and havin' a score of guns trained down on you."

"We don't need the combination. The real plan is, we're gonna blow the safe. I think I can get some dynamite."

"Dynamite? Well, that's more ruckus still. You'll never make it out alive, and even if you blow the safe, you got nowhere to go once you got the money."

Diana, impatiently: "Look, here's the crux of it. I figured a way across the river, and if you don't wanna end up hangin' from a tree, you're gonna go along with me. Got it? Like I said, we're prob'ly gonna have to shoot our way out of town, but we can help each other in this thing, and then I'll get us across the river. I guarantee it."

Jackson handed his empty dinner plate through the bars of his cell. "So now, let me see if I understand. You gonna burn down the stables and then break me outta here while this Moreno character does somethin' to the safe, but that don't matter none 'cause we're really gonna blow the safe, and I'm gonna shoot the hell outta everybody with some guns you're gonna get me, and then we're gonna ride blazin' out of town and somehow hocus-pocus make it across the river and get away. Is that your plan?"

"That or rot in here till you hang."

"And why won't they just follow us across the river and round us up, supposin' we get that far? I mean, if you got a way across, why can't they come right after us."

"I know it don't sound good, Jackson. It don't sound that good to me. But that's what we're gonna do."

Shaking his head: "I'm gonna be earnest with you, Miss Diana—"

"Just Diana."

"It looks like I'm gonna die here pretty soon one way or

another, and much as I'd like to get free, I don't think you got a chance in hell of making any of this work. So why don't you save your own little neck and just let mine hang? 'Cause this so-called plan of yours sure ain't gonna save me, nor you neither." He rattled his cell door and fixed Diana with a look that was as hopeless as it was compassionate. "There's what's possible, and there's what's not possible, and I ain't fully convinced you know the difference."

"You ever been a slave, Jackson?"

"What if I was?"

"Why don't you think about that when you're askin' yourself what's possible?"

"I'm not sure I take your meaning."

"Well, you ain't a slave now, Jackson. There's a time for everything, and there's a time for gettin' free. I'm gettin' free now, that's all. And you can help yourself by helpin' me. All right? You wanna get free?"

Jackson made no response.

Diana: "Now sleep tight and heal yourself up a little. I don't know when this thing's gonna happen, but it might be soon and you're gonna have to move fast."

"This is the craziest thing I ever heard of. It's suicide."

"You committed suicide when you shot that preacher, and you know it. Just be ready when I come for you." She strode down the hall, opened the marshal's front door, peered quickly up and down the street and left Jackson behind to stew.

A QUESTION OF MOTIVES

Jackson dozed and woke and dozed again and nothing changed inside the darkness of his cell, so that sometimes he didn't know if he was asleep or awake or merely dreaming that he was awake. When he felt paws against his cheeks and the tips of claws digging into his flesh and his arms jerked up to ward off the faceless animal that tore at him, he was sorry to recognize that that was the dream. He ached from so many places that his body seemed alien and hostile to his mind. His tongue felt swollen and dry and his head felt shrunken and hot. Colorful lines undulated before his eyes, and the profuse sweat trickling down his brow was cold. He could not lie in any one position for any length of time without panicking. When he dozed, he felt hunted and when he woke he felt caught.

It was near dawn when he heard the latch of the marshal's door open. Footsteps approached and his heartbeat skipped, for these were not Diana's soft quick careful footsteps but the clumsy slow boots of a man. There was no reason for any man to come to Jackson's cell before dawn, except to do him harm. Jackson continued to lie still, his hands trembling where they gripped the cot.

The footsteps stopped outside his cell. The person they belonged to remained silent for a long time, and Jackson cringed from the anticipation of he knew not what. A shot? A pronouncement of judgment? The cuff of a blade against a strop? Thunder knelled ominously in the distance, and as the last echoes rippled away, Jackson swallowed hard and turned his head toward the man's figure, which was a deeper blackness in the pitch dark of the corridor. A board creaked beneath the man's boot as he shifted. Jackson heard the cold caress of the man's hands against metal, the faint ring of it as the stranger wrapped his palms around the bars.

"It's a bad way to die, ain't it?"

Jackson did not recognize the voice. He seethed inside. He swung his legs around and sat up on his cot, but there was nothing else for him to do, so he just sat there churning.

"It's funny, the things a man'll do to himself. The fixes he'll get himself into. How, if you give a man enough rope, he'll hang himself with it, as the saying goes. How some men are born to cages, and even if you let'em out they'll find their way right back in." The stranger let go of the bars and took a step back. He leaned against the bars of the cell opposite. "It's funny." Jackson heard the man's bated breathing as an arrhythmic counterpoint to the steady drone of water splashing off the roof, and he found his own breathing following the stranger's. "No one to blame but yourself."

Jackson: "What would you know about it?"

"I know I'm free to walk out that door yonder. I know you ain't. I know you put yourself in this cage of your own free will by your own actions."

Jackson shivered feverishly and gazed at the outline of the stranger's body.

"You're like a dog that goes back to its own vomit. What are you doin' in here, Jackson? Do you even know? I bet you do."

"What do you want?"

"What do *you* want, Jackson?" The stranger's voice was flinty and unbroachably superior. "You want a chance to defend yourself? You want your motives pronounced sound and your actions allowed as fitting? You want to be free? I don't think so. I think you like bein' locked up, you and all your kind. I think you like it. You wasn't made to walk free like a man."

Jackson: "You don't know nothin' about bein' a man."

"I know that a man don't kill another man over a dollar in nickels."

"It wasn't the money."

"No? What was it, then? The principle?" The stranger guffawed, a dusky sneering that echoed around the cell. "You killed a man for the principle that you shouldn't-a been cheated out of a dollar's worth of nickels? That's a powerful principle, Jackson. You musta been ready to shoot every last man in that saloon for a principle that powerful, 'cause you surely knew them folks wouldn't set idly by while you gunned down one of their own."

The stranger scuffed his boot back and forth against the floor, and Jackson felt the abrasions of leather against wood as sandpaper scouring the inside of his forehead.

"See, I got myself a theory. Either you was willin' to shoot all of them people for your nickels—I mean, your principles— or you was just hankerin' to find a nice safe cage to rest your bones in. Nice and safe, bein' in a cage, bein' somebody else's animal, ain't it? Bein' a slave?" The stranger began pacing the corridor in the darkness, letting his hand travel with a slow metallic thump from one bar to the next, thumps that clanged with finality in Jackson's ears. The stranger, as if suddenly bethinking himself, musing aloud: "Principles of—what was it again? What principle was it you killed that man for? Of fairness! Was that it? You, a good negro with a job and all, killin' folks over fairness! So, let me ask you, Jackson: was it fair that a man died over a nine-high flush? Even one he got out of his sleeves?"

"Out of his Bible."

"Oh! Now, now I see it then. He was a hypocrite! You could stand a certain amount of cheating, but you've had just about enough hypocrisy, of folks lookin' at you and sayin' one thing to your face and thinkin' and doin' another. White folks, I mean. Now I understand. You went and shot the hell out of that parson to make an example of the principle that you ain't gonna tolerate double-dealin' from no Bible-thumpin' white folks no more. Now I see it more plain."

Jackson felt swollen with hate. He squinted and gaped and followed the footsteps of the stranger as he paced, but he could not guess where this mockery would lead. Jackson racked his memory for all the voices he had heard in Tres Cruces, but he remembered only the shapes of faces disconnected from their voices, and then he heard the voices disconnected from individuals, until it seemed that all of Tres Cruces spoke with one face and one voice, and the cadence of the voice was exotic and outlandish and the words garbled, until Tres Cruces seemed to speak a language not only foreign but repulsive, like the chattering of monkeys. Jackson found himself hugging his waist and rocking back and forth on the edge of his cot. He realized that the stranger was speaking again, and had been speaking all along, and it took every effort of will for Jackson to translate his chattering squawks into words.

". . .that you are destined for servility and death, by your own design!"

Jackson, ardently: "No! This was not my design."

"Then exactly what were you thinkin' when you pulled that revolver and emptied a slug into that preacher's heart? That a room full a white folks would line up to shake your hand and thank you for pointing out that the principle of fairness must be upheld at any cost?"

"No, I—"

Jackson's head rolled forward and he felt light and empty. All at once he realized that the stranger was inside his cell with him. The stranger spat.

"Your principles of justice and right and a dollar's worth of nickels! Admit that at the very bottom of your heart is no principle at all beyond how you hate bein' free and you'll do everything you can to avoid bein' free, like gettin' yourself killed in the nastiest way you can think up. Anything is better *in principle* than the perversity of freedom, even torture and death—especially a martyr's death. You don't wanna be free."

The stranger strode back and forth in front of him, with increasing pace and energy and stomping of boot-heels, outlining in a deliriously contemptuous voice all of Jackson's yellow-bellied chicken-livered principles. Jackson looked past him and saw that the cell door was still closed, had never been opened, and his body jellied with horror.

The stranger stomped closer and closer to Jackson, each pivot another inch closer, and Jackson knew that when the stranger reached him and touched him something terrible beyond his imagination would happen. The stranger's voice grew shrill, until it seemed to come from inside Jackson's own head. With a flash and a sickening clap of thunder, everything in the cell turned bright ghost white and Jackson saw the stranger's face clearly and looked deep into his eyes, eyes filled with wrath and misery and madness and was aghast to see that the stranger's face was his own.

Jackson convulsed with sobs. He fell back into his cot, rolled toward the wall and hid his hot face in his clammy hands. His mind emptied into a liquid blackness of fever and blame and self-recrimination. He heard the cries of a distant croaking voice that could only be his own.

The Second Appearance of the Horses

At ten in the morning, Doc Drumwright sat at the bar of the Coronado Saloon sipping straight gin, waiting for Jonathan to return from the kitchen. With Saul lying for the moment incapacitated in his room, Jonathan was left to perform his nephew's tasks himself, including cooking, which he hated and did poorly. Drumwright was sweating large circles under his arms, listening to the chatter as the temporary citizens of Tres Cruces rhapsodized over a splash of sunshine out on the street, the first sunshine anyone could remember since the storm had swept in. Though heavy raindrops still fell languidly through the hazy rays of sun, people spoke of the clouds breaking, and spirits waxed in anticipation of the first dry afternoon in weeks. Even Collins, usually indefatigable at the piano, had given up his stolid plunking and sat gazing out at the yellow-white sunshine. A dozen people were out walking in the rain, basking in the heat on their ghoulishly pale faces.

Drumwright sipped his gin and felt the sweet lightness of the sunshine in his chest, but figured he'd wait to celebrate until the rain had actually stopped. He feared that, if another wall of clouds muscled through, this brief bright interlude would ultimately lower everyone's spirits even more than perpetual rain and darkness.

Jonathan tramped out from the kitchen and set a steaming pile of eggs and potatoes in front of the doctor, then leaned into the bar in front of him and looked out at the sunshine. "At last, a bit of relief."

"Maybe." Drumwright took up his fork and shoveled potatoes into his mouth. "We'll wait and see."

"Always the long view, huh?"

"There are no straight lines in nature, Jonathan."

Drumwright sat for a while mushing his breakfast between his teeth with gin, Jonathan standing over him enjoying the view of smiling people promenading in front of the inn. After he had finished his breakfast, Drumwright cleared his throat and motioned for his gin to be refilled.

Drumwright: "You know, Jonathan, you oughtta take it a bit easy."

"How so, Doc?"

"I had a visit this morning from Diana."

"That a fact?"

"Yep. She didn't say anything about you, so don't take it out on her." He swirled his gin and looked past Jonathan at the rows of bottles on the wall behind the bar. "I'm not telling you how to live your life, but no woman deserves to be treated that way, cut and battered. Even if she is a whore."

"Ah, Doc, you know how it is with these cowhands—sometimes the boys get a little rough with her. If anybody ever really hurt her, I'd have somethin' to say about it."

"I've been around this town quite a while, Jonathan. There's no need to lie to me."

"And there's no call for you to pry into other people's affairs. I don't tell you how to run your shop, or cut people's hair, or how much gin you should drink at ten in the morning. I mind my own business and I expect other people to do the same."

"I take your point. It just hurts me to see a woman suffer like that."

"No more than it hurts me, Doc."

Thunder rolled in the distance. As it faded away at one end of town, it started up again at the other, and as that rumble died down, suddenly another started, closer and lower, and the people gathered in the street exclaimed and pointed. They ran toward the saloon and stood on the walkway out front, gaping toward the south, until those inside realized that this last booming wasn't thunder at all but the pounding of hooves. Jonathan ran from behind the bar and Doc Drumwright jumped up and Collins strode to the window to see horses on the dead run tearing up Main Street, the same seven horses they'd seen before, lathered and frothing at the mouth, mud flying, the sun catching the sorrel and burnished gold and slate-gray of their coats, their terrified eyes bulging as they clomped past. They rounded the tack shop, where Alberto Torres appeared in the doorway and stared, the chestnut mares a couple of lengths behind, until they disappeared around Torres' barn and over a ridge to the northwest.

Drumwright: "The goddamnedest thing."

"Somethin's wrong, to get them horses so spooked. They ain't runnin' just for the sake of it."

Drumwright, pointing at one of the men in the corner of the saloon: "You're from Rancho Cielito, aren't you? You recognize those horses? They yours?"

"I'd say so, though we never brung'em across the river."

Jonathan: "All right, let's go get'em. Whoever wants to come, meet over at the stable and saddle up your horses. I got some rope, and we can get more from Torres." Half a dozen men headed for the door, including Hargis and Collins. "Since when have you ever corralled anything but ten dollar bills, Collins?"

"I haven't always been a banker, Jonathan. Anyway, you might need an extra man, when the time comes."

As Collins finished speaking, the horses reappeared

around Torres' tack shop. They whinnied and snorted and galloped madly toward the south, as if drawn by some alarm outside the range of human hearing. They ran up the ridge past the burned-out shell of the Highland Notions Shop, across the muddied clay plains, till they dwindled to a mass of flying hair and haunches. As they galloped away, a rapidly rolling bank of clouds obscured the sun, and the rain began falling in earnest once again. An audible sigh of disappointment gusted up from those standing in front of the saloon.

Jonathan: "All right, let's go!"

The inn was suddenly alive with rushing men, and in the midst of this new bustle of activity, Diana descended the stairs in her green rain mantle, with the hood already drawn around her face. She crossed the saloon, past Drumwright and Jonathan, who were exchanging clipped hurried ideas about the horses.

Diana, pointedly ignoring Jonathan: "Doc."

"Diana."

Jonathan: "No greeting for me, though, huh? Where you off to?"

Diana continued past, weaving through the knot of people now gathered at the door to watch horsemen run across the street, to watch the storm gather momentum once again and the wind whip rain out of the air and into their faces. Diana pulled her hood closer and stepped into the silver-gray bluster.

When she had gone, Drumwright looked meaningfully at Jonathan, and Jonathan shook his head in anger. "That whore ain't your business, Doc. You ridin' with us?"

"I'm too old to go chasing horses, Jonathan. I might add you are, too. Besides, I've gotta change the Frogboy's dressings."

"You keep alert for when we come back. There might be a

few more knocks to attend, the way things are goin.'"

A Matter of Business

Robert McKinley sat on a stack of fifty-pound bags of rice, beans and millet in the Mathers' General Store, dangling his skinny legs, chewing on a stick of black licorice, watching the rain and commotion outside with a droll circumspection that belied his twenty-one years. When the horses had run through town for the second time and the men had come running out of the Coronado Saloon, he had stepped out into the rain and inquired what was happening. Having no interest in riding down frothing mad horses, he had returned to his previous inactivity in the General Store.

As a young man working in his family's beanery in the nearby town of Whitney, Robert McKinley had spent untold hours seated at his father's desk, poring over the books, dreaming of the day when he would go into business for himself—not as his father's successor, but as a businessman in his own right, in a business of his own invention. When his grandmother had died and left him a hundred dollars in cash, he had wound his mind tight and schemed and plotted until he had hit upon a plan, and now, on the verge of setting his plan in motion, he had no interest in risking his neck over some fool horses and the helter-skelter of crazy men with guns.

Robert McKinley was set to become a trader. He'd had dealings with a Menodoc Indian woman named Galecia Guzman, who lived in a mud hovel on the plateau, among a tiny collection of hovels that made up a nameless village. Galecia

Guzman had gained some renown for her woven ceremonial rugs, which the local ranchers bought as part of their daughters' dowries, and Robert McKinley had decided to spend his grandmother's entire hundred dollars on these rugs and then take them east and sell them as Wild West artifacts. He figured the society bluebloods would have no gauge for judging the worth of Indian rugs and he could gouge them for enough money to start a shop, a Western novelty business.

Robert had ridden out to Galecia Guzman's hovel, purchased the few rugs she had on hand, paid some money up front for more rugs and then waited. He had drudged through the tedium of day-to-day tasks working for his father, saving money and biding time, as Galecia painstakingly wove his fortune. At the appointed time, Robert had bid farewell to his only home and his family, loaded his few belongings onto a mule, and had journeyed to the nameless Indian village to collect the rugs. But the last rug wasn't finished and Galecia told him he would have to wait three more weeks; and since the Indian village was closer to Tres Cruces than to Whitney, Robert had decided to lay over at the Coronado Inn and act like the businessman he now was, taking the best room, paying Drumwright to shave the peach fuzz from his face, dreaming euphorically of his imminent arrival in the unreal-sounding city of Philadelphia.

When the rains had started, Robert had bethought himself to abandon Tres Cruces and cross the Fuerte and bide his time somewhere farther east on the plains, perhaps in the Menodoc village itself, where he could keep an eye on Galecia; but even as the Fuerte rose and the rains continued, Robert lingered in Tres Cruces, because he couldn't imagine asking those Indians to give him space in their hovels, couldn't imagine sleeping near them and trusting them not to slit his throat and steal his money. He didn't want to return to Whitney so soon and empty-handed, so every day he walked down to the Fuerte in the rain, watching it swell, until one day he saw the wall of water from the levy-break crash over the ferry and he had to scramble pell-mell to escape the flood.

Now, Robert ruefully spent his days walking back and forth between his room at the Inn and the Mathers' General Store, where he had struck up a friendship with Donald Mathers based on their mutual interest in trading. The days turned into weeks, and Robert wondered how they were faring out at that Indian village, and whether the Indian village would still be there when the storm finally broke.

Robert, sitting on the Mathers' sacks of grain: "Seems to be quite a ruckus over them horses."

Donald Mathers stood across from Robert, rearranging jars full of jerked meat for the second time that morning, to keep his hands busy. He was bald but for a gray band of coarse, dandruffy hair above his ears. His brown canvas pants and brown shirt, which Mrs. Mathers had made for him, fit his lean body awkwardly.

Mathers: "Full of sound and fury, signifying nothing."

"Don't it bother you at all, Mr. Mathers?"

"Does it bother you at all, Robert?"

"But I don't live here."

Mathers grimaced dismissively. "Even if you did. . ." He pulled a feather duster from his back pocket to clean the freshly-rearranged jars, which were spotless from the wiping Mrs. Mathers had given them an hour before. "I've seen horses run through Tres Cruces before. I expect I'll see it again, and I don't reckon it'll mean much in the future, either."

The bell above the front door rattled and Mr. Mathers turned to see Diana bobbing in out of the rain. Mrs. Mathers, wearing a dowdy hand-sewn yellow dress, peeked her head out of the storeroom; when she saw that the new customer was the whore from across the way, she leaned against the door frame and watched. Robert McKinley hopped off of the grain sacks and peered around an aisle of dry goods to take in the view of Diana pulling back her hood and shaking mud from her boots. Mr. Mathers continued dusting the jars of jerked meat, then moved on to jars of licorice and hard candy, without greeting Diana.

Diana: "Morning Mr. and Mrs. Mathers."

Mrs. Mathers: "Just get what you need."

"I apologize for bein' polite, Mrs. Mathers. Any event, I didn't come to spend my hard-earned money on your pretty things. I come to talk to your guest here."

"How dare you speak of earning money!"

Diana, letting her hand fall heavily against her thigh, sighing: "How long have we known each other, Mrs. Mathers?"

"Too long."

"Long enough that we don't have to do this every time I come in here. Really."

"If you'd stop coming in, we wouldn't have to."

Mr. Mathers, setting his duster on the counter: "Sophie. That's enough. State your business, Miss Clayborn."

"As I said, I come to talk to Mr. McKinley here, if he wouldn't mind a word."

Robert McKinley stepped around a vat of molasses and considered Diana, trying to figure out why a Tres Cruces prostitute knew his name. He ran his fingers along the underside of the hat he held in his hands, to keep himself from stammering.

"Yes, ma'am?"

Mrs. Mathers, guffawing: "Ma'am!"

Diana: "Perhaps I could interest you in comin' back to the saloon with me. We could talk a little more private. I could buy you a drink."

"I don't drink, ma'am."

"Coffee, then."

"It's awful hot out."

Impatiently: "The point I'm makin', Mr. McKinley, is that I'd be obliged if I could talk with you privately."

Robert McKinley looked at Mr. Mathers, whose face was carefully blank, and then at Mrs. Mathers, whose features were pulled into a mask so witheringly grim as to turn comic. Mrs. Mathers shook her head emphatically no.

"What's this about, Miss. . . uh. . . Di. . . uh. . . ma'am?"

"You can call me Diana. It's a business matter." A long pause. "Talk down at the saloon says you're a businessman. That right?"

Robert, perking up: "That's right. I'm a businessman."

"Well, I have a business proposition for you."

Mrs. Mathers: "Think of what business she's in, Robert. Think of the kind of propositions a scarlet dove can make."

Talking past Robert to Mrs. Mathers: "It's a legitimate proposition."

Robert: "What kind of proposition is it, ma'am?"

"Could we please talk about this at the saloon? I'll make it worth your while."

Robert McKinley put on his hat and stepped to the corner of the store to retrieve his rain coat from the rack. Looking to Mr. Mathers for approval: "I suppose it can't hurt to listen to a business proposition?" Mr. Mathers maintained his blank mien.

Diana, escorting Robert out the door and into the pouring rain: "Thank you for your hospitality, Mrs. Mathers, I'll come again."

They jogged across the street to the saloon, Robert slipping twice on the freshly churned mud where the horses had swept through. They stomped their boots on the walkway outside, and went in to find Jonathan rushing from his office to the kitchen and back again. As they sat down at a table in an unoccupied corner of the saloon, Jonathan pulled on his poncho and dashed out the front door.

They sat for a while, Robert in embarrassed silence, Diana contemplating the steady rush of raindrops and the shouts from one man to another outside. A few other patrons sat in the dining area, looking out the windows toward the tack shop, where men hidden beneath black ponchos swarmed like drone bees around a hive.

Diana: "I guess I'll just say this plain, 'cause it's gotta come out sooner or later, and better that you know exactly what I want up front."

"Yes, ma'am."

"I need to buy three sticks of dynamite."

"Ma'am?"

"Now, I know you don't have three sticks of dynamite. What's more, I know there ain't nobody in Tres Cruces who sells dynamite, not since they closed the Rodriguez Mine. You have to get it from San Luis. But I believe there's some dynamite to be had in Tres Cruces, and I'm willing to pay for it."

"I'm not sure I understand, ma'am."

"There's a couple miners here in town, maybe you know 'em. David Burns is one and his partner's name's Jerry, last name DeYoung I think. They're on their way to the mines above Menodoc Plateau, in the Dientes de Vacas. The only place to get dynamite in these parts is San Luis, so it stands to reason that if they aim to do any blastin' at them mines, they brought their dynamite along with 'em. You follow me?"

"Not so far, ma'am." Gripping the edge of the table: "If I may offer you a business tip, ma'am? If you want something, and you know who's got it, why not ask them for it direct? I'm afraid I don't have anything like that to sell."

"I know that already." Diana got up and moved toward the bar. "Sure I can't offer you a drink?"

"I'll have a sarsaparilla, if you got any back there."

Diana went behind the bar and returned with a bottle of sarsaparilla and a shot of tequila. "The problem, Mr. McKinley, is that those who own the dynamite won't sell me any. That's why I need you."

Robert, taking a long pull from the warm sarsaparilla: "Just out of curiosity, ma'am, what would you need three sticks of dynamite for?"

"What would anyone need three sticks of dynamite for?"

"Ma'am?"

"To get rich."

"I'm afraid I'm not following you at all, ma'am."

"Where are you from, Mr. McKinley?"

"Whitney."

"Whitney. You ever heard of a man named Barbarito Magana?"

Taking another swig of sarsaparilla: "Used to be a prospector?"

"Not just any prospector. He struck it rich. Really rich. They say he wiped his mouth with hundred dollar bills. He practically built the town of Alto Cedro single-handed, and they wanted to make him governor, but he wouldn't have it. Anyway, he disappeared—"

"Yeah, I remember now. Him and a whole wagonload of loot, somewhere up above Alto Cedro. He just left one day forever and went up to build a mansion, up in the foothills above the town, supposedly to live up there like a king in a castle, but nobody ever heard of him again."

"That's right. He bought himself that mountain, a whole mountain, and he went up there to build his own private paradise and then he disappeared, vanished from the face of the earth. Never cleared an acre of land, never laid a single stone. Just vanished."

McKinley, excited: "And they found those bodies. I remember now. His wife and his mistress and one of his children—"

"A boy about twelve." Diana drank off her tequila.

"That's right, a twelve year old boy, but they never found Magana nor any of his things, and they never knew how those women died." Robert chugged his sarsaparilla with the growing relish of a boy telling ghost stories around a campfire. "They say maybe he's still up there somewhere, gone mad, or maybe he died up there with all his gold and diamonds and things around him like an Aztec king."

Diana, leaning toward Robert and whispering conspiratorially: "Mr. McKinley, I know where Barbarito Magana is." Robert's eyes grew wide. "And I know where his gold is."

Blurting out, nearly shouting: "And that's why you need the dynamite!"

Diana shushed him, although no one in the bar was paying them any mind. "That's right. He's dead, up in a cave above Alto Cedro, and I'm willing to bet there's somethin' worth findin' up there with him."

Robert McKinley sat back in his chair and let this information sink in. He hadn't heard the legend of Barbarito Magana since he was a boy, and now it had come back to life.

"How'd you find this out?"

"You know that fire, at the Notions Shop?"

"Sure."

"When they pulled Otis the Frogboy out, Doc Drumwright found some papers folded up in his pocket. I went over to help, to change Otis's dressings, and Doc had these papers, but they were all in Spanish, and Doc can't read Spanish. So I said they were nothin' and I pretended to throw'em away. Only

I kept'em—"

"And they told you where to find Barbarito Magana!" Taking a moment to consider: "But how can that be? Wasn't that building the marshal's private workshop?"

"That's right."

"Well, what would the marshal be doing with such papers? And if he had'em, why wouldn't he go up there himself to investigate?"

"Maybe the marshal don't want whatever's up there to be discovered. Maybe he's been protecting the family of Barbarito Magana. That's my suspicion anyway." Hurriedly: "Because you knew that Barbarito's wife was the marshal's great-aunt, didn't you?"

"No, I guess I didn't know that."

"So he may have had reason to keep those papers to himself."

Robert, looking from Diana to his sarsaparilla uneasily: "But you really think that retarded boy went in there lookin' for those papers? I'm afraid that don't make much sense."

"I believe somebody put him up to it. I believe somebody sent him in to avoid gettin' blamed if he got caught."

"Well that don't make any sense at all, if you'll pardon me for sayin' so, ma'am. Nobody'd pin their hopes for Barbarito Magana's fortune on an idiot."

Diana laughed. "Idiot? You been payin' too close a mind to Mrs. Mathers, I think. You know, the folks in this town think Otis is some kind of monster, but that's not so. He just thinks different than we do."

Robert considered this while horses whinnied and nickered outside. Close to a dozen men were mounting up in front of the stables, and in their midst Jonathan shouted words that were lost to those inside. Jonathan's voice rose and fell and then dropped in conclusion, and the company rode south out of sight.

Robert: "Well, this little surprise is certainly something else, ma'am, I must say. Makes me glad to be in Tres Cruces for a change." Finishing off his drink: "So what do you aim to do?"

"Go up into those mountains and see what there is to see. There's a cave walled up in the Dientes de Vacas that holds the lost fortune of Barbarito Magana." Leaning over to touch Robert's thigh with her opened palm: "Mr. McKinley, I hope you understand, I mean this conversation to be just between you and me."

McKinley swallowed hard at Diana's touch and breathed her perfume. "Oh, absolutely, ma'am, that's understood. But. . . I still don't see exactly what you want from me."

Diana left her hand on Robert's thigh. "I know, Mr. Mck—. May I call you Robert?"

"I reckon."

"Call me Diana."

"All right." A long pause. "Diana."

"The difference between you and me, Robert, is that you can get some."

"Get some?"

She inched her chair closer to Robert's and whispered. "Dynamite. I know where some is." Diana spread her fingers wide and let the palm of her hand stray for a moment far up Robert's thigh before she sat back in her chair. Her fingertips slid down to his knee and away. "Can I get you another drink?"

Without waiting for Robert to respond, Diana got up and went to the bar. When she returned, she carried a bottle of sarsaparilla, a shot of tequila, and a shot of whisky. Motioning toward the whisky: "In case you change your mind." As she sat down, she pulled her chair even closer to Robert's.

McKinley, queasily: "If you know these miners have this dynamite, I just don't see how I figure into this deal of yours."

"Robert, listen to me. It's in the basement under the Mathers' General Store. They used to trade in such things, mining supplies and gunpowder and such, during the boom, and they built a special storeroom for it. A dry room, with sealed walls. I guarantee if those boys brought dynamite in, they got it stored at the Mathers'. Now, I couldn't get within fifty feet of that storeroom door, but you can come and go as you please over there. Everybody sees you spend all day in that shop."

"Whoa now, wait a minute, what exactly are you asking of me?"

"Frankly, Robert, I'm asking you to get me three sticks of that dynamite."

"You're askin' me to buy this dynamite and sell it to you, or you're asking me to steal it? Either way, I don't think that's exactly a legitimate business proposition like you said."

"Before you go rushin' to judgment, Robert, just listen. It's true, I'm asking you to steal somethin', but I guarantee there ain't no other way of gettin' that dynamite without tippin' off the whole town what I plan to do with it. Anyway, nobody'd sell dynamite to a woman no matter what the reason. Now, some people might call this improper, but those boys won't miss three little sticks of dynamite, and I'm willing to make it worth your while."

"It's not just the stealing. I'd have to betray Mr. Mathers' trust. He's a friend of mine."

"A friend! What did he ever give you that he didn't charge you for, including his advice, I'll warrant. Anyway, that dynamite don't belong to him." Pausing to drink off her second shot of tequila. "I'll put my cards on the table, Robert. I'm willing to pay you fifty dollars for every stick of dynamite you get me. If you bring me three sticks, that's one hundred and fifty dollars. That's all the money I got in the world. And you ain't riskin' nothin', Robert, nothin'. You could talk a little and get into that storeroom and put three sticks of dynamite under your coat and walk out, and nobody'd bat an eye."

Robert sat stooped over his sarsaparilla, affronted, but thinking through this offer. "That's a lot of money, ma'am. Diana." He drank from the bottle and then fingered the shot of whisky before pushing it gently away. "If you've got a hundred fifty dollars, why don't you just go to San Luis yourself, buy the dynamite yourself, legitimate? Seems like you're takin' a mighty craggy path when you could just as easily take a straight road."

"I can't go to San Luis, Robert, I'm not allowed."

"Not allowed?"

"You see Jonathan Vega as just another saloon owner, but he has a lot of power in this town, and in the others round-about. He says whether I come or go. He says whether or not they sell me a coach ticket. He says whether I can buy a dress or a make-up box or a stick of dynamite. He says. And he's not real interested in me goin' to San Luis."

Pinching his lip between his thumbs and furrowing his brow: "Then how do you expect to get to Alto Cedro?"

Diana, leaning over, putting her hand back on Robert's thigh: "I expect to collect all the things I need, and then slip away, like a thief in the night. Surely you agree that it ain't right for one person to own another person? Well, Jonathan may as well own me, and this is how I'm gettin' my freedom."

"You must really think you're onto something with these papers you found, to take all this trouble and put yourself at such risk. I mean, let me ask you: why would you think I'd steal for you? Why wouldn't I just tell Jonathan or the Mathers about your little scheme?"

"Maybe you would. Or maybe you'd be willing to do a harmless little favor for someone for a hundred and fifty dollars."

Robert, taking long pulls at his sarsaparilla: "Is there a map with these papers you found? Is there a map to Barbarito Magana's cave?"

"There are directions. And other things."

She let her other arm fall across the table toward his, so that she could feel the warmth of his hand gripping the bottle of sarsaparilla. They sat with their heads inclined close to one another, and the smell of Diana's perfume and the look in her eye began to preoccupy Robert's mind. He felt the pressure of her fingers on his thigh.

"What if I wanted to go along with you to this cave? To see about this prospect for myself?"

Alarmed: "You mean, to share part of it?"

"Just between the two of us. Seems to me if you need my help so bad. . . well, maybe you could use some help actually gettin' out of town and lookin' for this fortune. You weren't planning to go up there alone, were you?"

"I suppose I was."

"What would you think about that? About having a partner?"

"That wasn't really what I had in mind, Robert."

"As if I had stealin' and lyin' to my friends in mind when I come over here!"

Diana thought about this for a long time. "Maybe. But there's somethin' about you that bothers me."

Taken aback: "How's that?"

"I don't trust a man who don't drink. It's suspicious."

"I'm sorry?"

"You want to be partners with me, I haveta be able to trust you."

Robert: "Yet you're asking me to steal, and to betray the trust of my friend!"

"It's a lot of money. Not the hundred-fifty—I'm talking about a fortune."

Robert, continuing his former thought: "And some folks would say I'd be a fool to trust a painted lady, nevermind you trusting me."

Diana laughed. "You're more shrewd than you let on, Mr. McKinley."

"I'm a businessman, ma'am."

"Diana." She pulled his fingers away from the bottle and took his hand in hers.

"Diana."

"I'll make you a deal, Robert. You bring me three sticks of dynamite, and I'll show you the papers I got off of Otis. If you still want to join me after lookin'em over, we'll talk about that then. If not, I'll give you a hundred and fifty dollars and we'll forget we ever laid eyes on each other."

McKinley took a deep breath. "You know, I'm not the kind of person who steals."

"You're not a thief, you mean. Everybody's the kind of person who steals."

"You think so?"

"I know so. Them miners won't ever miss three sticks of dynamite, Robert. It's a drop in the bucket. And then you'll take a little walk over here and walk back with a hundred and fifty dollars."

"Or maybe half of Barbarito Magana's fortune."

"Maybe."

"All right. I'll see what I can do."

"Good. But first—drink to it."

"What?"

"Like I said, I don't trust a man who don't drink." Robert

looked at Diana as if she were joking, but she only nodded toward the whisky and scooted the glass closer to him. "Do you good." Robert hesitated. "For a hundred and fifty dollars, you can take one shot of whisky."

"For half a fortune, you mean."

"All right."

Robert picked up the shot glass, looked around the room, held the glass up to his nose to smell the alcohol, then took a deep breath and drank it all down at once. His throat burned through and his eyes teared. Diana stood up and leaned over him, caught him by the back of the neck and confused his distress with an open-mouthed kiss. By the time Robert's throat stopped hurting, Diana's tongue was in his mouth and her hand squeezed the inside of his thigh and the alcohol was going to his head. He tried, not altogether convincingly, to pull back, and when Diana finally let him go, she whispered: "Some types of business give a man more than others, Robert. Just ask your friend Mr. Mathers if he don't think so. Ask him when Mrs. Mathers ain't around. Ask him about me."

She stood up, walked behind Robert's chair and breathed in his ear. "You bring that dynamite as soon as you can, and we'll seal this business with more than a handshake. All right? Room number six, down the hall from yours on the left." She punctuated this last sentence by brushing her lips against his earlobe and running her middle finger down the soft of his neck below his ear. "You won't regret makin' this deal, Robert."

She strode away quickly, climbed the stairs and rounded the corner, leaving McKinley staring ahead of him at the silent emptiness across the table, the whisky rushing warm through his chest.

THE POSSE

The posse included Jonathan Vega, Hargis, Collins, Alberto Torres, a few men from Rancho Cielito and several hands from Rancho Mirabal. They rode south out of Tres Cruces at a lope, figuring to overtake the runaways soon enough: the terrified horses had been heavily lathered and bolting at full gallop on both passes through Tres Cruces, and the company figured they wouldn't have much run left in them.

They rode with a warm, driving rain at their backs, following the wide swath of muddy clay paddled and clopped into clods by the fearful horses. An hour and a half outside of Tres Cruces, the trail turned east toward Rio Fuerte, but still there was no sign of the horses themselves. Lightning began to strike in the distance, chasing peals of thunder across the sky toward the riders. Hargis trotted up alongside Jonathan.

Hargis: "Don't make much sense, does it?"

"What?"

"We been out a long time, and we ain't seen hide nor hair of them horses."

"We ain't been out too long."

Collins, riding up to join them: "They aren't headed for the marshes, at least. If they keep on this direction, they'll come right up to the river."

"Maybe there *is* a way across."

"Must be."

The landscape below Tres Cruces looked as if it had hosted

a fierce battle, with small trees snapped in half lying twisted on the ground, bramble bushes denuded and the earth a dark muddy red the color of old blood. It was as if entire generations had drained their lives into the ground and then gathered their skin and bones up out of the earth and marched into whatever grim spirit land had been promised them. Nothing moved across the terrain except the treetops whipped by gusts: the leaves and branches of low-lying bushes bobbed under heavy drops of rain. Though it was only just after noon, the sky was soaked in twilight and the riders could see little more than a hundred yards ahead, to a gray wall that was partly clouds, partly liquid shards of sky already plummeting toward the earth, and partly the dark edges of the their own imaginations. No one could distinguish their own sweat from the water falling down their necks.

Just over two hours out of Tres Cruces, a drover from Rancho Cielito gave a shout and spurred his mustang on. The rest of the company followed, until they approached the seven mysterious horses at the very edge of the roiling brown flood that was Rio Fortuna. The water crashed and roared around a boulder near the far bank, and every so often a grotesquely large branch swept by with remarkable swiftness. Led by the golden palomino, the horses had formed a loose circle and were stamping awkwardly and energetically around a central point, their eyes rolling, baring their teeth and rearing halfway back on their hind legs. One or two at a time would rear sideways, on the verge of trampling one another, moving in leaps and bounds in an ellipse. When the company approached, the horses clustered into a knot, as if huddling in the corner of a corral. They stamped and snorted. They bared the whites of their eyes aggressively, yet their ears stood straight up, caught between conflicting impulses, none of which could be fully expressed.

Hargis, shouting above the roar of the river: "They're actin' like there's a tornado or somethin'." A few of the ranch hands looked up at the sky, as if an *actual* tornado had been invoked right above them.

Collins: "Look how they give that spot in the middle such a berth."

Hargis, trying again: "Like that's the eye and the horses are the hurricane."

Jonathan rode ahead, right up toward the palomino, which at first reared up as if it would fight, but then became confused and, amid much stamping and snorting from the other horses, fell back, one step at a time. He suddenly leapt to one side, causing a chain reaction of leaping horses, dashing at first in their tight knot and then separately toward the river, and then circling back. The company approached the spot the horses had been hovering around and now saw a man's body lying face down in the mud.

Jonathan pointed to some of the ranch hands and ordered them to ride the runaway horses down and get them on leads. Alberto Torres took command, and the men drove the horses toward the river, hemmed them in and began separating them and allaying their fears.

Jonathan, Collins and Hargis dismounted and approached the body. Jonathan was the one to bend down, take it by the shoulder and turn it over.

The muscles of the face had contorted into an ugly mask, the upper lip pulled back on one side to bare teeth, and the skin had bloated with blood and turned dull mocha brown like unglazed pottery. The man's flesh had begun to decompose, and it crawled with gnats and maggots, but there was still no mistaking his identity.

Jonathan: "The marshal! Now how in hell?"

He let the body fall back into the mud with a gasp of disgust. The entire company looked from the dead man to the flooded river to the horses half-wild with fear. There was no evidence of a struggle that they could see, and no clue if the marshal had crossed the river here and then expired from the effort, or if he had washed ashore from somewhere upriver, or if he had never crossed the river at all. Lightning played across the clouds.

Collins: "You think he ever made it out to Rancho Cielito?"

Jonathan: "If he didn't, how'd he wind up with these horses?"

Hargis: "But the marshal's own horse ain't with'em, and none of them other horses has so much as a rope lead. He wasn't ridin' any one of'em, 'less he was doin' it bareback."

Jonathan dug the toe of his boot partway under the marshal's hip and lifted the body. "He ain't armed. I've never known the marshal to go anywhere without a revolver."

"Maybe he left his things out to Rancho Cielito."

"But for what reason? And what about his horse? He surely didn't walk these horses down here, and what would he be doin' with seven horses all untethered and unsaddled?"

"Maybe there were others with him. Maybe they tried to cross the river and this is how they ended up."

The three stood over the marshal's body while the rest of the posse wrangled the runaways. Once separated, the horses became more tractable, until even the appaloosa, the most skittish, let himself be stroked about the neck and bridled.

Collins: "It still doesn't make any sense. The river didn't wash saddles off of these horses, and why would a whole troop of men from Rancho Cielito be trying to cross the river, especially this far down? They could have crossed right outside of town."

Hargis: "Unless they were washed down here. Maybe

there's more bodies along the banks upriver or down."

"Still."

The men tethered the horses on rope leads and led them away from the marshal's body, whose very presence spooked them and caused them to prance like circus jumpers. Jonathan bent down again and rolled the marshal's body onto its side and this time visibly recoiled at the sight. He forced himself to pat the marshal's pockets. He found a sheaf of folded papers in the marshal's vest, and he stood up with the papers and flinched again as he looked at the marshal's deformed face. He rolled the marshal back over with the toe of his boot. The papers were soft with water and soiled with mud.

Collins, Hargis and Torres crowded around Jonathan as he opened the papers. The first page was an expensive-looking, pulpy piece of stationery scrawled with a handwritten message in bold flowery script. The ink had mostly run in the rain, so that only snatches of phrases and fragments of words remained legible. The first sentence read, "Que te importe que te ame. . ." and then trailed into streaky lines. They scanned the letter and scrutinized other disjointed phrases, making puzzled grunts and exhalations: ". . .me voy al trans. . .y ahora si quieres. . .con candor el alma entera yo le. . .a caballo vamos. . .con que tristeza. . ." Finally, though the ink of the signature had fluttered and run, they determined that the name inscribed there was "Alexia."

Jonathan: "Alexia Bauza?" She was the youngest daughter of Jesús Bauza, owner and patriarch of Rancho Cielito.

Jonathan unfolded the other papers, which were set with type, and saw that they were land deeds. Collins read off the markers and measurements specified in the documents and guessed that the deeds belonged to lands adjacent to or within the possessions of Rancho Cielito: the marshal was designated their owner. Hargis, Torres and Collins exchanged looks.

Jonathan: "I never knew the marshal to own any land."

Collins: "And that's quite a stretch of land, if I read those designations right. Quite a tract." A long pause. "And that's a love letter, if I know anything about love letters."

Jonathan, circumspectly: "Maybe. There's not enough there still readable to know anything one way or the other."

Hargis: "Even if it is a love letter, that don't explain nothin'."

Collins: "A love letter and some land deeds and the marshal face down in the mud."

"With seven horses from Rancho Cielito."

"Seven horses. And no saddles."

They stood there looking at the marshal's body, and the roiling muddy river. Lightning snapped so near to their left that their hearts skipped, and they bunched their shoulders around their ears when the thundercrack followed. The horses whinnied and frisked and threatened to bolt, and Alberto Torres spent several panicked moments shepherding them back into order.

Collins: "Let's get back to town. No sense risking our necks out here. What do you think we should do with the body?"

Jonathan: "Well. We can't leave it out here, and this ain't no time for a funeral. It's a wonder the vultures or the coyotes haven't already cleaned his bones, but I ain't seen a thing move since we set out from town."

Jonathan gazed upriver and downriver and at the wide circle of hoof prints surrounding the marshal's body. He took a walk around the circumference of the circle and then went up and down the river for several tens of yards, surveying the ground. "The marshal's body ain't fit to sling across a horse, so let's cut a few branches and lash together a sled and pull him behind us. It'll be crude enough, but the marshal ain't in any position to complain, and we'll at least get him back and bury him proper. I'm glad Nell's already dead. I'd hate for her to see him like this."

Collins and Torres found a hatchet and a machete packed among the ranch hands' supplies. They went themselves to join the work of cutting branches for the marshal's funeral sled, while Jonathan paced his horse downriver to inspect the banks for more bodies or clues about what had happened. The earth at the very edges of the flooded river was too saturated to ride and even several yards back was soupy and sucked at the horse's hooves and pooled in his prints. Half a mile down, without finding so much as a loose thread of clothing, Jonathan turned back.

Even the hardened vaqueros from Rancho Mirabal nearly gagged when they turned the marshal's bloated corpse face up and lashed it to the makeshift dray, which was pulled by Collins's muscular grullo. Unlike the horses from Rancho Cielito, the grullo did not even flinch at the marshal's dead body. The company headed back toward Tres Cruces, this time following the path of the river as nearly as they could around thickets of creosote and mesquite trees. Eight of the eleven riders trailed a horse or a body and their nerves jangled. They felt the weight of the heat, the rain and the landscape, empty of all other creatures, as a mass in their chests which made them breathe shallow breaths. The slow clopping and oozing and sucking of the hoofbeats all around them, the slap of rain across the brims of their own hats and saddles, and the sweet-hot smell of their mounts made the ride seem too real, beyond reality; and the roar of the river was not enough to convince them that what was happening was actually happening, because it simply should not have been. The farther up the river they rode, the more they looked from one to the other, passing the feeling of prickly sensitivity among them, a sixth sense that found danger everywhere in the air and on the land, where there was, at the moment, nothing but themselves.

Jonathan: "If I was the marshal, what reason would I have to try to cross the Fortuna from Cielito?"

Hargis: "Supplies?"

"No. If you're desperate for supplies and the river's flooded, you head for La Union, or Sommerville."

Alberto Torres: "Maybe he saw the smoke from the fire and tried to come in to help."

"On a clear day, maybe, but you can't see beyond half a mile at the outside through this soup. And anyway, why would he bring the horses?"

Collins: "Maybe the horses didn't have anything to do with the marshal. I mean, maybe they came upon his body after he'd already died."

"But then what's the marshal doin' out here all alone, carryin' deeds to miles' worth of land? And that letter? And then how'd those horses get across the river?"

Hargis cleared his throat: "I know I ain't s'posed to tell the contents of other folks' telegrams and all. . ." and he proceeded to tell the story of the marshal's mysterious telegram, sent just before the ferry washed away. He recited the message word for word from memory. Jonathan whistled.

Collins: "You think the marshal was fixing to run away with Alexia Bauza?"

"And what? And he stole a bunch a horses and walked'em down here to the river. That still don't explain it."

"It explains some things."

Angrily: "Not enough. The marshal ain't never been anything but upright."

"He ain't upright now."

"Anyway, why run away when you suddenly find yourself with deeds to half the county?"

They rode in silence, each drifting into his own dark fantasy, each constructing scenarios that became implausible if any detail were questioned. They came across no other bodies, no other clues. After half an hour of struggling slowly through the mucking scrub along the newly-wide river, they abandoned the riverbank and headed back onto the more open plain directly south of town.

The Relative Value of Human Life

Half an hour after the posse had ridden out of town, Moreno had knocked at Diana's door, and when she answered he slid deftly past her and into her room. His face was placid but his dark eyes darted and his hands danced against each other in silent applause.

"The time is at hand. I told you there would be an opportunity, and now we have to seize it. The next few hours may decide our future."

Diana turned her back on Moreno and poured herself a glass of water from the chipped white pitcher on her dressing table. She stepped around the rain basins on the floor and seated herself on the edge of her bed.

Diana: "It hardly seems as if the next few hours could really decide our future."

"Half the able-bodied men in Tres Cruces have just ridden away, including the owner of the stable we intend to burn down and Collins the bank manager. Fate could not have handed us a more ideal opportunity. Any time you're ready, you can slip away to the stable, set it on fire, and then I'll steal into the bank and get our money." Taking an anxious step toward Diana: "Now is the time. Please. Let us have the courage to do this thing."

Diana's brow furrowed. She stared at Moreno's slight figure, standing perfectly still but hopping up and down on the inside. It occurred to her that, though the idea to rob the bank had been Moreno's, she hardly needed him any more, not even as an extra pair of hands or a decoy, and that for once in her entire life she had a secret power over a man, a knowledge that he had no way of knowing, an advantage that mattered. But then it occurred to her that Moreno didn't really need her either, that he could just as easily set the stables on fire himself, or create some other diversion, and then slip down to the bank to try his hand at opening the safe. Of course, she didn't believe that Moreno actually could open the safe. Moreover, she thought, even if they had the nerve to start this caper, that neither of them would finish it alive; but these thoughts flashed through her mind in a moment, and she could not muster the necessary anxiety for them. Instead, she sat puzzled by the fact that her partnership with Moreno was based on absolutely nothing but his wanting her as a partner, and she would betray him for that reason alone. She vowed silently to herself that, no matter how she died, she would stay alive long enough to see Moreno die first.

Moreno: "Why do you just sit there? You must prepare to act."

"I need to know something, Moreno." Pausing for effect. "Once everyone's distracted by the fire, and you get the safe open, and you have the money, what happens then?"

Moreno, surprised: "Nothing. Nothing happens then."

"Something must happen. You're not gonna stuff the money into your pockets and walk down the street whistling."

"Oh, you mean what happens to the *money*? We hide it. We will hide the money, and we will stay here in this saloon just as we have been, like everybody else. We'll walk down the street whistling, if you like. When the storm breaks, we will collect the money and ride away with it."

Diana: "If that money disappears from that bank and then we just sit here and give Collins time to find it, time to find us, nobody'll leave this town with so much as a nickel. If you get the money, you gotta get away with it quick. It's all gotta be a surprise. Otherwise, between Jonathan and Collins, they'll personally search every man, woman and dog in Tres Cruces till they find it."

Moreno ran his fingers through his hair and looked at Diana as if she were speaking a language invented by children for the purpose of communicating with imaginary friends. "How do you propose to get away quick? Eh? There is no way. And why do you talk like this—Collins will do this, we must do that, the men of the town will behave this way, as if you can see the future? Like there might be a solution at hand, this moment, for every problem that will happen in the future? What is the point of thinking this way? First, you will set fire to the stable while I go to the bank to watch. Then, when the bank guard goes to help put out the fire, I will steal the money from the bank. I will close the safe again as if nothing has happened. We will hide the money and then come back to our rooms. If events unfold as we intend them to, or even if they don't, then there will be other circumstances to deal with later, circumstances we are not able to predict now, so how could we make a plan for them? How can we make a plan for what Collins might do in the future? Why do you insist on drawing maps for trails that have not yet been made?"

Diana: "You keep talkin' like this whole stunt'll just work itself out, like magic. Like you'll actually have the exact right idea whenever you need it, and nobody's gonna give you any problems. But let me tell you, if you can't get outta Tres Cruces right away with that money, I guarantee that Collins and Jonathan and half the men of this town will go huntin' for whoever stole it, and it don't take no crystal ball to see that future. You think you're just floatin' along in some big calm river and all you gotta do is paddle around the rocks. But you're makin' waves in the river, Moreno. See how I mean? I *can* predict the future. And I'm only sayin' it'd be reassuring to know you had some idea what you might do if certain things happen one way or another."

"I do, we do have some idea. But not in the way you want, not in a way we can articulate now. What we have is belief that we can do this thing and faith in our ability to navigate obstacles as they arise. I like this analogy you make with floating in a river, because that is just what we're doing, swimming with the flow of the current. We are not building a town or planting an orchard or establishing a company. There is no blueprint, no tried and true model for stealing, Diana. We are testing our own luck against the luck of others."

"Well, you must at least have some idea where you're gonna hide the money."

Moreno, turning on his heels and pacing back and forth in front of Diana: "If I'm not able to open the safe, then there will be no money to hide, and we'll be relieved of that burden. If I open the safe, I'll hide the money where no one will ever look for it, and where it will be easy to move when the time comes."

"But where?"

"In the outhouse behind El Charro."

"That's no hiding place. Everybody in Tres Cruces goes into that outhouse some time or another."

"Yes, exactly. But they don't go there to look for money. In the third stall, below the seat, at the front edge of the hole, I have dug out a niche and tacked a leather band. If you lean far enough into the hole, you can reach underneath the planks themselves. Now all I have to do is tie a satchel containing the money to this band and fill in the niche with dirt. You see? The money will be in the latrine, secured in its own earthen pocket, where no one can see it and no one will look for it."

"God, Moreno, I'm gonna be sick just thinkin' about stick-in' my head in that shithole."

"Yes. Yes. It's perfect, isn't it? And you can go into and out of the outhouse with bags—empty bags, full bags, no one will search the bags of a woman going into an outhouse—and you can go any time you please, as many times as you please, no questions asked. The money will be there for us whenever we want it, however we wish to move it out of Tres Cruces, or if we wish to spend it right here at this saloon. We simply walk into the outhouse to relieve ourselves and walk out with thousands of dollars under our clothes."

Diana started to take another drink of water but could only think of her own body draped across the third stall of the outhouse behind El Charro, her head halfway down into the waste. She had heard stories of the Arivica raids, when set-tlers had thrown valuable into their outhouses so the Indians wouldn't get them, but she didn't remember those stories end-ing well. She consoled herself with the fact that this particu-lar aspect of Moreno's plan would not actually be carried out; that, in fact, very little of Moreno's plan would be carried out. She wondered how he would react when she showed up at the bank with Jackson, some six-guns and her hands full of dyna-mite.

Moreno: "But before we are able to hide the money, you must first slip out of here secretly and sneak around the far side of the stables and set them on fire."

Diana walked around her bed to her dressing table and looked coyly over her shoulder at Moreno. "There's nothin' for you to get all worked up about. Those boys ain't been outta town too long, and the last thing we want is a whole posse of men ridin' back unexpected while you're twiddlin' the dials of that safe."

Moreno put his fingers to his mouth and rested his chin on

his thumbs and considered. "Yes, but we can't wait long. The fire will take a little time to blaze up in earnest, and it will take a little more time for everyone to organize themselves around this new calamity, and I will need an undetermined amount of time with the safe. We cannot squander this opportunity. So I suggest you dress for your mission and put some oil and matches in a bag and be ready to go, if not now, then at the moment we deem appropriate. I'll wait here with you, so we can coordinate our efforts when the time is right."

A knock at the door. Moreno closed his eyes and took a deep breath.

Diana: "Who is it?"

"It's Robert. McKinley."

Moreno, hissing: "What does he want?"

Whispering: "He's a client."

"There's no time for that now. Get rid of him."

"No, there is time. Go back to your room, and I'll get you when I'm done."

Moreno, beside himself: "No, Diana, this would be the height of stupidity. Don't tempt fate: if we work this scheme right, by tonight you'll never have to do that for a man again."

McKinley, from outside the door: "Diana? Can I come in? I think I have something you might be interested in."

Diana: "Just a minute." Whispering to Moreno: "He won't be long, I promise."

"Have you taken leave of your senses?"

"And anyway, he'll give me an alibi."

Moreno: "No. Remember, you're *my* alibi."

Diana: "You take risks your way, I'll take 'em mine. Just wait for me in your room, and I'll be at your door in twenty minutes. Twenty minutes, no more. We'd wait that long anyway."

"Why are you behaving so foolishly?"

Diana, shouting at the door: "Come in, Robert."

McKinley slipped through the door, a half-formed vowel stuck in his opened mouth, which dropped a little slack when he saw Moreno. McKinley let his right hand, which had been poised to sweep open his dripping wet poncho, fall slowly to his side.

Robert: "Pardon me, ma'am, I didn't realize you had company."

Diana: "Not at all. We were just finished."

An awkward pause. No one moved. Moreno glared at Diana, and Robert stared at Moreno. Finally, Robert stepped forward smiling a pinched, formal smile and greeted Moreno.

"Good afternoon, Señor Calderon."

Moreno, bowing slightly and stretching out his hand: "Mr. McKinley."

Diana: "You know each other?"

"Señor Calderon has been giving me advice about what to do when I arrive in Philadelphia."

Diana: "Oh? I didn't know you had been to Philadelphia, Señor Calderon."

Moreno, looking at Diana darkly: "Twice. But it has been many years." Moreno stepped toward the door. "Now, if you'll excuse me, I have some business to attend to." Looking at Diana with an arched eyebrow: "As we all know, certain kinds of business require the utmost timeliness." Moreno walked with his mincing little steps around Robert McKinley. As he closed the door, he shot Diana a look, his eyes filled with disappointment and anxiety.

McKinley stood at the end of Diana's bed, grasping one of the poorly carved asparagus-tip footposts, unsure what to do. Diana picked up a bone comb from her vanity and began running it through her hair, combing it forward and playing with the ends of it to draw Robert's attention to her breasts.

"I must say, Robert, that was mighty quick. Did you get

the. . .?"

"I did. It was even easier than you said." He opened his poncho and withdrew two sticks of dynamite from a game pocket inside. "I didn't even have to ask, and Mr. Mathers didn't bat an eye. I just walked right out with'em. But I could only get two. The way they were bundled, any more'n that would have been missed." Robert wore a gloating smile, as if he had figured out how to print his own money.

"Robert, have you been drinking?"

McKinley, laughing out loud: "I did maybe have another whisky." Suddenly self-conscious, removing his hat: "I got to thinkin' about what you said, and. . . you know. . . I think you're doin' me a world of good, just like you said. Diana. I think maybe you're doin' me a world of good." He handed the sticks of dynamite to Diana as if they were long-stemmed roses, and she set her comb down and held his hand in hers a moment before taking the dynamite and placing it in the top drawer of her dressing table.

"Why don't you take off your rain gear and make yourself comfortable? Would you like something more to drink? I like to see a man drink."

"I feel a bit giddy already."

"It gets better the more you have, Robert. Up to a point of course. And it makes sex better, too." Robert chortled nervously. "If you don't mind my askin', Robert, have you? Well, that is, if you don't mind a personal question?" She stepped over to him and put her hand on his chest.

"No, I don't mind. Fire away."

"Have you ever been with a woman, Robert?"

McKinley turned red and his laughter changed to skittish tittering. "Ma'am, I, I, I don't s'pose I have." Looking down into his chest, ashamed. "I hope that don't make no difference to you, 'cause if it does. . . well, really, I just came up here to look at them papers about Barbarito Magana. That was the deal we had."

Diana laughed, saccharine and false, and let her voice trail off to a mellifluous ululation at the back of her throat. "You don't have to be embarrassed with me, Robert, not now that we're partners." She rubbed her knuckles in little circles against Robert's chest. "And you're not mistook about my intentions: if we're gonna be partners, we're gonna be partners all the way, 'cause that's the only way I know how." Slowly, with studied drama, Diana flattened her palm against Robert's shoulder and let her fingers slither up his neck to his cheek, where she tiddled his earlobe with her index finger, all the while holding his gaze in her half-closed eyes. She allowed him to swallow nervously once and shift his weight from one foot to the other before pulling his mouth down to hers and kissing him, letting the fullness of her lips envelop his mouth, forcing his lips open with her tongue. Theatrically, she broke the kiss and turned away.

"I'm afraid I don't have any whisky, but I can offer you a glass of rum."

"Whatever you have is fine by me. Diana."

She reached under her bed and brought up half a bottle of white rum, poured two glasses, then sat on the bed and patted it. Robert sat down like an eager choirboy in the front pew, wide-eyed, and took his sacramental drink.

"Relax." She put her hand on his thigh.

Robert, again chortling nervously: "I never imagined myself a thief before. Nor an adventurer. Till today, it was always my dream just to be a businessman, not a highwayman or nothin'."

"You are a businessman, Robert. You can pay them boys back for that dynamite, if thievin' makes you so nervous. Anyway, when we find Barbarito Magana's fortune, you can start any kind of business you can dream up. Legitimate."

"Oh, I paid for the dynamite already. I stashed a little money there in their bundles."

She slapped his shoulder playfully. "Why, that was mighty considerate. So you aren't really a thief, after all. More like a gentleman."

McKinley: "I believe takin' what don't belong to you without permission makes you a thief. But at least they won't suffer any loss for it, if you see what I mean. I mean, I don't think it right that my gain should be their loss, because that would be truly dishonorable. But I ain't proud of it, and it ain't proper."

"Maybe most business transactions ain't exactly proper, Robert. Cheers."

They drank their rum and Diana moved her hand up Robert's leg to his crotch and rubbed slow circles over the hardening lump there. Robert swallowed the rest of his rum in a gulp, and Diana took his glass away and continued rubbing him.

McKinley: "Do you think maybe I should see those papers you found?"

"Don't be nervous, honey."

"No. Okay. But." Swallowing hard. "Just to see'em?"

"You don't trust me?"

"I trust you, Diana. I'm just curious, is all. I mean, that's what we're partners for, isn't it?"

Diana stopped and surveyed Robert's face. "Do you read Spanish?"

"Yeah. A little."

She got up, opened her wardrobe and rummaged in the bottom of it, fumbling with scarves and underwear and some small, hard objects that clacked against the wood. She finally pulled out a yellowed sheet of parchment. "Come here." Robert jumped up and went to her side. As Diana stood upright, she hooked Robert's arm and pulled him toward the window, waving the parchment in front of his face with her free hand. "Come over here where the light's better."

She let go his arm and placed the heel of her right hand, the hand holding the derringer she had palmed from the wardrobe, between Robert's shoulder blades. As she handed him the paper, she made gentle, loving circles in his back with her gun hand.

Robert took hold of the paper and bent closer to make out the fine scribblings in a woman's hand, and only just registered a sound like a hammer falling against hardwood before the bullet tunneled through his brain and he fell forward onto the floor. Diana knelt down and put the gun's only remaining bullet into Robert's left temple for insurance, splattering her arm and legs and face with blood. She dragged his body into the corner and stuffed a towel around his head to soak up the blood that flowed out, alarmingly freely.

The room smelled of firecrackers. Diana pulled the sheets and bedspread from her bed and flung them over Robert's body, as if she had merely left a pile of bedding there to wash. She was sweating like she had never sweat before, and her hands shook and her heart pounded like an endlessly reporting canon in her ears. As she reloaded the derringer, she noticed that she had stopped breathing, and she reminded herself consciously to breathe in and out. A fluttering began in her chest and moved up to her throat, then spread to her cheeks and eyes. She blinked back tears.

A knock at the door. Diana jumped and nearly cried out. She ran across the room and turned the lock shut.

Her voice came out froggy and desperate. "Who is it?"

"Moreno. I heard shots. Are you all right?"

"Yes. Yes. It must have been the storm."

"No. I heard shots. They came from this direction."

"I don't know, I don't know. It wasn't here. Go away. I'll

come down in a minute."

She waited, leaning her ear against the door, until she heard the sound of Moreno's light footfalls recede down the hallway. Still she waited, but no other steps approached, and after several moments, she scraped herself away from the door and put on her rain mantle. She slipped her derringer and some extra bullets into an outer pocket and retrieved the two sticks of dynamite from her vanity and put them into an inside pocket. In the vanity mirror, she noticed the blood on her face and right hand and she took a minute to clean herself with a towel already so begrimed with old make-up that a little blood would not be noticed. Then she saw the blood on her legs and skirt, and she was forced to change into an entirely new dress.

As she turned to go, she saw that a stream of blood was leaking out from under the towel and sheets at Robert McKinley's head. She stepped over to contain it with another bedsheet and to hide the bloodspot with a pillowcase. She doused the area with water from a rain basin, and then, satisfied that the heap on the floor didn't appear obviously at first glance to be a body, she unlocked her door and stepped out into the hall, closed the door behind her and leaned against it.

Diana, to herself: "Well. That's it, then." She felt a slow motion sinking from her chest to her stomach, like mercury falling in a thermometer, and her sweat turned cold. She hurried to Moreno's room.

A Horse of a Different Color

Moreno, hissing furiously: "Are you quite through playing games? I give you the opportunity to leave this miserable life behind forever, to make something clean and new of your life, and you jeopardize everything to satisfy another customer?"

"Clean and new?" Diana stood with her back to the rickety dresser in Moreno's room, her skin crawling and her hands shaking. She saw Robert McKinley in her mind's eye splayed across the floor of her room.

Moreno, softening: "You look sick." Putting his hand to Diana's forehead: "You're damp and cold. Are you all right?"

Diana, flaring up at Moreno's touch: "I'm fine, goddamn it, I'm just—"

"Frightened? Don't be. You're not doing anything wrong. If anybody sees you, you're going out to coo at the horses. To relieve your boredom. You can't be caught doing anything wrong because you're not doing anything wrong."

"Till I set that fire, you mean."

"You're in no danger. If you're spotted in the stable, if there's someone there—if there's any problem at all—do nothing. Simply come back. You have nothing to fear." Moreno took both of Diana's trembling hands in his, steadied them, and kissed her forehead, which had the effect of strengthening Diana's resolve, but not in the way Moreno intended.

Diana, using Moreno as a cipher for all of her hatred: "Good luck."

"Yes, good luck to us both." Moreno squeezed her hands and ushered her toward the door of his room. "I'll give you ten minutes. Then I'll slip out toward the bank. After you've set the fire, get away quickly, and circle back into town from the northeast. Return to your room by the back way. I'll meet you there as soon as I've hidden the money."

Diana slipped into the dark, dank hallway, and Moreno silently latched the door behind her. As she approached her own door, the smell of fresh blood became so strong that she could feel it in the back of her throat, and she stood outside her room for a moment, fearful that the entire saloon might be drawn like carrion to the stench. She forced herself to breathe deeply, and as she did so, the smell subsided into the normal corruption and decay of the moldering hallway. She found herself on the verge of tears, and she became angry with herself, both for killing McKinley and for not being icier about killing him. She reminded herself of her disgust with Jonathan and David Burns and for the man McKinley would have become, and for all of Tres Cruces, and she walked on past her room and down the back stairs.

Aside from the marshal, Jonathan Vega was the most heavily armed man in Tres Cruces, a holdover from the rowdier days when a gunfight could break out at any time over anything, and Jonathan had found it judicious to hide weapons all over his saloon. Diana had found it judicious to know where the weapons were hidden. Now, she found Jonathan's Winchester rifle hidden in the broom closet below the stairs, and his Colt pistol in the kitchen larder behind the sacks of dried black beans, just where it always was; she stole his .32 pistol from behind the mirror in his bedroom and a couple of boxes of ammunition from his nightstand, but she couldn't find any other guns in his dresser or under his bed, so she assumed that he had taken them out with the posse. Most of them hadn't been touched in years, and Diana hoped they were still in good working order.

After she had placed the pistols in a leather satchel, along with some tortillas and dried meat and rice, and after she had wrapped the rifle as inconspicuously as possible in a blanket, she set off, out the back of the saloon. She walked first toward Rio Fuerte, then circled back at a run through a stand of scrubby mesquites and palo verdes north of town. The trees were as green as the Garden of Eden after all the rain, with mistletoe choking the branches and strange growths of moss that Diana didn't recognize creeping along the trunks. Bright pliable thistle grew all along the ground. She came upon Alberto Torres' stable from the west, peeked inside and went in. She found it empty but for four horses and a couple of pack mules.

She saddled a matched pair of auburn quarterhorses and slung the satchel filled with Jonathan's guns across the saddlehorn of the nearest one. She put the second horse on a lead, and then set the rest of the animals trotting away, toward the west, out of town. She doused the straw and the baled hay and some of the stalls with oil, set it on fire and galloped off with the quarterhorses, back toward the north.

The horse she had chosen for her own proved to be unruly at first, but she leaned forward and whispered in its ear the first thing that came into her mind, which was the legend of Barbarito Magana. She told this story with the utmost conviction, as if she were recounting the horse's own history, and after a while he was convinced enough to stop fighting her every step and see where she would take him. The horses seemed brighter and more spry for some reason the wetter they became and the muddier their path: they seemed to enjoy the rain and muck, and after a while, Diana's own mount even nickered cheerfully.

She traveled at a trot back the way she had come, through

the living vibrant pale green of a landscape overwhelmed with growth, all the way to the clearing overlooking the Fuerte, and she rode a short distance along the swollen river. The dirty brown water churned and roared. Little white caps appeared above breaks and around swells over unseen objects below the surface. The river had long since overflowed its banks and was now wider by many yards than she ever remembered it, and it was impossible to judge the lay of the new boundaries, to determine the depth of the water at any given spot. Diana spied a placid, seemingly shallow stretch that reached halfway out into the river and imagined that a crossing could be attempted at just that point, when suddenly a massive tree branch reared out of the water and flopped rolling back into the current right where she was looking. The river seemed to be dragging half of the countryside down in its undertow, chewing and breaking and bloating it and then spitting it up toward the ocean. It was impossible even to find familiar landmarks, such as the short jut of earth where the ferry's dock had stood: the land itself had been transformed, and again the Garden of Eden came to Diana's mind, and Noah with his ark. Diana considered the possibility that, unlike Noah and his floating zoo, no one in Tres Cruces would live to make a new covenant.

She stared at the uncertain banks on the Fuerte's opposite side. If she could somehow gain that ground, she would be free.

Diana, doubtfully, to her new horse: "We're gonna do it, ain't we, boy? We're gonna get free."

* * * * *

David Burns and his partner Jerry DeYoung sat in the tiny, dark, cave-like dining room of El Charro Restaurant, smoking hand-rolled cigarettes. The windowpanes at El Charro were nothing more than tacked-up sheets of writing paper rubbed with cooking grease, which gave the paper a nearly transparent opacity, allowing the diners to see the world outside as a wispy shadowscape where distant shades darted and weaved. The yellow-gray light filtering through these mocked-up windows accentuated the dreariness inside, where the tables were all roughhewn and craggy. Instead of chairs, splintery benches wobbled precariously with any shift in a diner's weight.

El Charro was a favorite stop for drovers and ropers from the surrounding haciendas because the food was cheap and you could sit all day if you wanted, just smoking and trading stories with other ranch hands and drifters. The Alvarados, who owned the restaurant, would sometimes give you a meal if you were short of cash. Now, the dining room was empty but for David Burns and Jerry and Hector Alvarado, who was noodling a melody on his guitar across the room.

David Burns, blowing a smoke ring: "Ain't exactly get-rich-quick any more, is it?"

Jerry: "Never was. No part of life is quick. That's just a story people tell 'cause they got nothin' else to occupy their minds. Everything's gotta be 'now' with people."

"Ain't that the story you told me? Get rich quick?"

"We'll get rich quicker prospectin' than balin' cotton or shippin' tobacco from Norfolk—it's all relative. But we got some work ahead of us, some time to spend, even after this storm breaks. Get rich quick is one thing, get rich now is another."

"I never said get-rich-now. I said get-rich-quick. Why you gotta be so contradictory all the time?"

"I just voiced my opinion is all."

Burns sighed heavily. "I'm so sick of this town I could eat my own mule."

Jerry stared past Burns into the smoky dimness. "We're all

147

right. We come this far, and we're just a couple-a days out of them mines. That's where the fun begins. Gotta expect a little bit a everything, else it wouldn't be an adventure."

"I reckon. Makes me mad though, just sittin' around here every damn day with nothin' to do."

"Everybody's gotta be somewhere."

"What's that s'posed to mean?"

"Nothin'. Just, if we wasn't holed up here, we'd be out in them mountains somewhere doin' somethin' else. Know what I mean?"

Burns stubbed out his cigarette, withdrew his tobacco pouch from his shirt pocket and rolled another one. He coughed and asked Alvarado to bring him a shot, and Alvarado told him he could help himself. Burns snarled under his breath and went behind the counter and poured himself a whisky. He returned to his seat and drank and smoked.

Burns: "I think this rain's addled your mind a bit, partner. If we was up in them mountains right now, we'd be gettin' rich—maybe slow and sure, but rich. Here, we're just a couple-a sweaty bodies for flies to land on. Makes me madder'n piss."

"There ain't nothin' to be done, so it don't help to get riled."

"Makes me feel like stranglin' somebody."

"Yep. Well. Can't really do that. Just gotta figure out how to live with it, how to work around it. This storm—it's like when you're a kid and your ma wouldn't let you out to play, that's all."

"I feel like goin' down and doin' that nigger in that jail cell."

Jerry stubbed out his cigarette and rolled another. He lit it, inhaled and held smoke in his lungs so long that David Burns thought it might come out through his skin. He blew the smoke in Burns's face.

Jerry: "Don't go makin' trouble for yourself. There's still gold in them mines, if you want it. You wanna start somethin', start it where it don't matter none."

"Where's that?"

"I don't know, but it ain't with no boy in no jail that they're gonna hang anyway. You always gotta be against somethin', don't ya? But I'm tellin' you there ain't nothin' to be against this time, so just let it be."

Burns grunted. "You're the one always against somethin'." He pushed his rickety bench back from the table and walked out the back door. He smelled the smoke of a fire. His mouth watered and he imagined the taste of a fresh-cut steak, which he hadn't had and hadn't stopped thinking about in weeks. He felt himself sopping and drowning and angry at the sound of rain day and night, felt the drops hitting his neck and shoulders like pins sticking a voodoo doll. He felt ragged and palsied, and he wanted to do something, anything at all to prove that he wasn't as helpless as he felt.

He stepped into the outhouse and was braced by the bright stinging odor of lime at the roof of his mouth and then by the rank heavy blanketing of human waste at the back of his throat. He left the outhouse door open as he urinated into the hole. He kicked the wall in anger and sent a spray of urine over the wooden seat and onto the pair of corncobs resting on the floor beside it. He returned to the dining room seething with exasperation, to find Jerry calmly eating a potato taco.

Burns: "Think I'll go out and shoot somethin'. You wanna come?"

"Whatcha gonna shoot?"

"I don't know. Shoot up a tree or something. See if there's a dog left in this town."

"I'm content to sit. Don't you get into any trouble."

Burns put on his hat and poncho and stepped out the front

door, only to rush back in a moment later. "The mules!"

Jerry peered through the paper-windows but saw only ghostly shadows outside, so he picked up his potato cake and continued munching it as he walked to the door. He followed Burns's finger to the stable across the way and saw smoke curling out between the cracks of the main doors, filtering up through the roof.

"The mules!"

At that moment, Burns's mule appeared around the far corner of the barn, trotting at a steady clip. It let out a guttural "eeee-yeh" and headed north past the saloon. They heard footsteps on the walk behind them and turned to find Doc Drumwright running up, trying to pull the wire rims of his spectacles over his ears. Smoke began to roll out of the stable in billows.

Burns: "I'm goin' after my mule." He rushed off with a rolling fat-legged gimp.

Drumwright, throwing up his hands: "Let's get the horses out of there!" He started to run off, then thought a moment and poked his head into El Charro: "Hector, the stable's on fire! Find some men to run buckets down here." Drumwright and Jerry ran toward the stable. "At least we're next to the well this time. Let's see if we can save her."

They rushed up to the tall front doors and wedged them open, but the straw inside was guttering fire and smoke too dense to see through. They ran around to the rear and found two horses and a mule standing a hundred yards behind the stable, looking at them as if awaiting instructions. Drumwright motioned for Jerry to collect the animals, then he pushed open the rear doors and looked inside. The smoke was wispier and whiter on this end and he fancied he could see nearly all the stalls. They appeared empty. Some of the stalls were black and burning, but the fire hadn't yet taken hold of the building's frame or outer walls.

He ran back to the front, where he met a cluster of men sprinting from the Coronado Inn. Mr. and Mrs. Mathers rushed up from the General Store, and Saul came limping behind. Drumwright directed them all to fetch buckets from wherever they had laid them after the last fire. He told Saul to get to the well and fill the buckets everyone brought with water, and the rest to form a line from the well to the stable. "This time we save the building!"

Doc Drumwright stared into the distance south of town and willed the posse to finish their business and ride back into sight just that minute, but nothing moved on the horizon. He unleashed a stream of silent curses at the storm and the fire. "Worst rain in a hundred years and the whole town's on fire!" He turned back to the stable and ran half way around it, staring intently at the roof and walls. Rain spattered and beaded against his spectacles and a gust of wind drove a plume of smoke into his face. He coughed and his eyes teared, and still he stared and ran around the building. No sign of lightning! He realized with a violent bewilderment, an indignance that affronted him personally, that this fire, like the last one, had been started from inside the building. He swore so loud and so long that Mr. Mathers finally shouted at him to consider the ladies, and Drumwright ran to fetch a bucket from his own barbershop. Someone in Tres Cruces was trying to burn the town down.

* * * * *

Moreno waited behind the marshal's office, across the street from the Hidalgo Trust Bank, observing alternately the first curls of black and gray smoke trailing into the air above Torres' Tack Shop and the front door of the bank. He was armed with the tools he had stolen from the marshal's workshop, his lock pick set, a highball glass from the saloon (for amplifying the clicks of the safe's tumblers), and a small pocket knife whetted to razor sharpness. It wasn't long before he heard shouts from the other end of town, and Hector Alvarado appeared at the door of the bank and summoned Kerr. Kerr rushed with Alvarado toward the fire.

Moreno gave them a little time to run and took out his lock pick set. When he stole around the corner of the jail toward the bank, Alvarado and Kerr were three-quarters of the way to the stable, their backs to him. He scampered across the street, beneath a dense gushing monochrome of milky gray sky, to the bank door. He had picked this lock once before and it presented no difficulties now.

Inside, he shed his coat and wiped his boots with it, so as not to track mud around the interior: his intent was to leave the bank exactly intact, whether he got away with the money or not. He rushed to the locked teller door, behind which sat a pair of desks holding neatly stacked account books and transaction records. He could see, at the very back center of the bank, peeking through green partitions, the heavy black safe.

Moreno had previously conquered the teller door as well, and it proved little match for his dexterity now. He inserted a pair of rods from his pick set, wedged them nimbly into the lock, and the door gave after half a minute of tinkering. He put the picks away and walked behind the partitions.

The safe sat flush against an inner wall. It was coal black, about three and a half feet across, four feet tall, and four feet deep, with a shiny silver lever in the door just below a silver dial. The dial was inset with copper numbers from 1 to 39. Moreno put both hands flat on the safe and laid his ear down on top of it. Despite the afternoon's sultriness, the safe was cool to the touch, and as the chill of the steel spread down his cheek and across his neck, Moreno imagined the bounty that awaited him inside, so close he could almost feel it: stacks of bundled paper bills, probably not an outrageous sum, but enough to start a new life of anonymous prosperity. The ranches round-about were still wealthy enough, and the people of Tres Cruces may have placed their life savings in this very safe, and there might even be jewels or valuable documents, deeds, mining claims, wealth from the whole county on its way to be recorded in San Luis. It was all so easy, Moreno thought, standing here alone with this safe full of money, and he wondered at himself for never robbing a bank before; but then, the circumstances had never been this peculiar, and such a crime would probably never be this easy again.

Easy! He stepped back and was abruptly reminded of the reality of the situation, of its utter lack of ease or simplicity. Though he did indeed stand in the Hidalgo Trust Bank alone, the money was not yet his. He tried to peer underneath the safe's curved edges, ran his fingers along the hair-thin crack where the door met the steel casing. He took a sheet of paper from one of the teller desks and tried to slip it into this crack, and found that the paper penetrated only a quarter of an inch and then stopped.

He slid his fingertips along the base of the safe and came across some raised black lettering at the bottom. The light be-hind the partitions was quite bad, and he had to squint hard and guess at the letters, feeling them like Braille with his fin-gertips, until he deciphered that the lettering was French: "Bil-lecard," possibly the name of the safe company, he surmised, and then "Ghent, Belgique." Moreno marveled that a safe such as this, which must have weighed a thousand pounds empty, had found its way across the Atlantic Ocean from Belgium and then across most of North America, all the way to Tres Cru-ces. He stepped back and surveyed the safe again, expecting an idea to materialize with the discovery of the safe's origin. But none did.

The gears of his mind raced without biting the cogs of other gears, spinning faster and faster but failing to turn the works. He pressed his ear against the door and turned the combination knob, listening for variations in clicks, but found that he heard no clicks at all. He retrieved his highball glass and the rest of his tools from his coat, then put the glass against the safe door and pressed his ear against its bottom and twirled the knob. Still he heard nothing. He took out first his pocket knife, then the pick he had stolen from the marshal's shop, in an attempt to wedge a small opening in the door near the lever. Not only did this not succeed, but Moreno's efforts left two noticeable scratches in the surface of the door.

Moreno knew he had only a little time before Kerr returned or the posse rode back into town or both. With the rain as heavy as it was and the town's main well so close to the stable, the fire Diana had set would not last all afternoon, and Moreno's heart pounded. He stared at the two teller stations, their thin stacks of standardized forms and quills and ink wells; and at the two desks behind the teller stations, with their neatly ordered writing pads and green-boxed kits of sealing wax. He opened all of the drawers of the desks but found only pencils and more forms and a few personal notes from unnamed hands to unnamed eyes. Moreno chewed his lip.

Except for the rain falling heavy as stones against the roof and walls, all was quiet, and the air was stiflingly close and eerily still. Not knowing exactly what he was looking for, he stepped outside the teller area and followed a little corridor that led to a waiting area in the corner of the bank. As he passed a side window, he stared out in dreadful anticipation and saw the bleak, burned-out remains of the Notions Shop, but nothing stirred. He moved along the corridor toward the back of the building and was surprised to find the back door unlocked, and this made him extremely nervous.

The hall turned a corner and ran a short way along the back wall of the bank. Moreno followed the hall feverishly until it dead-ended at another door, which was locked. He took out his picks, fiddled with the lock for several minutes while the sound of his own breath grew louder in his ears, and finally felt the latch click open.

He stepped through the door and found himself in utter darkness. He felt for the box of matches in his waistcoat, struck one, and saw that he was in a low, windowless cube—an office, empty except for a gray steel filing cabinet on his right and a long low desk in front of him. Badly realized paintings of idealized young men and women in eastern finery hung on the walls.

The match burned out and Moreno struck another and used it to find and light a lamp on the desk. He rifled through the contents of the desk's drawers but found nothing of interest, and he felt the fire in the stable burning down to embers and the posse returning, and he felt in the bones of his chest that it was time to give up and flee the bank. Jittery and tense, Moreno turned his attention to the filing cabinet, to take one last long shot at finding something of use.

The top two drawers of the cabinet were unlocked and contained scores of creamy brown file folders, slick to the touch, each of which bore a name and records of transactions for many months, with interest calculations, debtor's notes and the like. The third drawer was locked, and the lock was set into the side of the cabinet, between the second and third drawers. It looked something like the end of a rifle clip and was inset with a tiny keyhole.

Moreno tried his smallest rod on the lock, but found the keyhole too tiny to manipulate and so returned to the bank's main room to retrieve his mallet and wood pick. He listened at the bank's front door for a moment and still heard nothing but the rain, and then he peered out the front window and saw nothing but a wall of sky dappling the earth with water. He forced his feet to move with precision, back to the manager's office, forced his mind not to heed his body's foolish trembling.

When he came back to the filing cabinet, he ran his thumb over the tiny keyhole several times to get a feel for its construction and tested it for movement side to side. The lock was not sturdy, probably a simple spring mechanism. Moreno had seen such locks before, though he had never worked on one. He took his best guess about the location and depth of the tumblers and the spring, about the direction the latch would turn, and he wedged his smallest rod a little way into the opening, just at the bottom. Then he took his wood pick and pressed the tip of it into the top of the keyhole and pointed it down at a forty-five degree angle to the rod. He tapped the pick's wooden handle several times as tests, and then he brought the mallet back and swung it down in earnest, striking the pick handle a sharp blow. It gave and he heard a sound like the metallic thump of a cash register opening. The lock shuddered inward, the little rod fell to the floor and the drawer slid open.

Moreno felt a triumphal lightness in his chest and a thin involuntary smile played across his lips. He listened: still nothing but the rain. He brought the lamp closer and peered into the drawer.

The bottom drawer was not notably different from the top two: more folders containing more ledgers, this time with larger numbers; a few envelopes with old, official-looking letters from the railroad company and a mining concern; the last will and testament of Julio Rodriguez. Finally, at the very back of the drawer, wrapped in soft calfskin leather, Moreno found a little black notebook closed with a latch. He opened it, and there on the pages in-between he read a long series of oddly arranged numbers that could only be code—which, he thought, might contain the combination of the safe out front. Maybe. Something.

He tried a simple alphanumeric translation, but it made no sense. Perhaps, he thought, the combination was simply hidden there in plain sight, if only he could select the right sequence of numbers. He would have to figure out the notebook's significance in his room at the inn and leave the main assault on the safe for another day. It was unfortunate, he thought, and he would probably never have such a lovely opportunity again, but at least this development represented progress. He was one step closer to the money.

He closed the filing cabinet and noticed that the teeth of the keyhole were hopelessly bent and misshapen and that the silver shuttle of the lock casing was no longer flush with the side. This could not be helped. Moreno gathered up his tools, set the lamp back on the desk extinguished it, and left the room.

He relocked the office door and returned to the front of the bank. Just as he became sure that his getaway was complete, that this part of the caper had been a success—a mitigated success, a half-success, but a success nonetheless—he heard a sound outside the door.

His insides seemed to empty, as if his guts had been scooped out with metal spoon. Footsteps on the wooden walkway! He leapt away from the door as sleek as a frightened lizard and slithered as quietly and quickly as he could toward the rear exit.

* * * * *

After surveying a quarter-mile stretch of Rio Fuerte without finding a likely crossing point, Diana headed back to Tres Cruces, and when she came within sight of the town, she saw the stable burning and the line of men and women between the well and the barn doors. She hunkered low in her saddle and used the horse's body to shield her own and clopped slowly further away south, behind the buildings, toward Doc Drumwright's barbershop. As far as Diana could tell, everyone in town was occupied with the stable fire, and she expressed to herself a rueful amazement that Moreno had been right about that one thing, at least. For just a moment and not for the first time, she wondered who this Moreno character really was, this liar and thief, this blacksmith's apprentice who had worked on a steamboat, who was traveling west, who carried a set of lock picks and used a false name for no obvious reason. A confidence man. He would be in the Hidalgo Trust Bank right at that moment, staring down a dumb steel box, and Diana wondered at herself, that she was sitting astride this stolen horse, that a young boy lay dead in her room, that by entertaining this character Moreno she had set in motion a series of improbable events whose outcome was uncertain but could only involve more death, most probably her own.

She dismounted behind the barbershop and tied her own horse and the second horse she was leading to bent irons that the doctor used to pitch horseshoes against. Unexpectedly, she felt a lump in her throat and tears came into her eyes, and she was forced to kneel down for a moment and catch her breath. Suddenly she was sobbing. She felt panic so strong she thought she would leave her body, and it was all she could do to stay there and not leap back onto her horse and clutch at its neck and whip it and let it take her wherever it took her, to fly away from that place and forget everything she had ever been or ever wanted. She thought of taking Jonathan's guns to the stable and opening fire at random and continuing to fire until she had run through her bullets or was gunned down herself. As it grew, the lump in her throat seemed to embody a deep, angry regret that her life was no other life than her own, that these deeds were her own, that her presence behind Doc Drumwright's barbershop with two stolen horses and stolen guns and the blood of a young man on her hands was as despicable as her whoring and her inescapable servitude to the coarse, gross, vicious-minded tyrant Jonathan Vega. She loathed herself, and she loathed everyone in Tres Cruces, and she felt as hopeless as she had ever felt.

When her sobbing fit passed, she removed her derringer from her coat pocket and held it in front of her face and imagined its little barrel in her mouth, imagined squeezing the trigger, and then everything would be over, and god damn them all to hell forever. She knelt in the rain, for how long she didn't know, feeling the lightness of the gun in her hand, hearing in her mind the crack of the little hammer drop, and then nothing but darkness. But just as suddenly, she came to herself again and felt embarrassed, on her knees in front of the horses. She stood up, put the derringer away and grabbed her satchel off of the saddle. Holding the Winchester rifle in one hand and the satchel in the other, she sneaked around Doc Drumwright's barbershop.

She opened the front door and went behind the doctor's wash basins and shaving supplies to his writing desk. She set the rifle on the desk and opened the top right drawer and found the doctor's key ring, right where she knew it would be, alongside his flask of gin and a plain cylindrical glass bottle with a red cross painted on it, that was filled with the doctor's homemade sourmash.

A moaning came from the back, and then a loud crash and a scream: a miserable, hopeless animal cry, like the howl of a wolf caught in a trap. Diana reached into her satchel and brought out Jonathan's .32, and then tiptoed toward the crying.

She saw Pastor Charles's body, the putrefying smell of which was overwhelming, and then she saw that the noise had come from Otis the Frogboy. He had rolled off of his "surgical table" and now lay coiled into himself on the floor, like a burned spider. When she appeared in the doorway, Otis looked up at her, and she saw a look in his eyes that she had never seen before in anyone's eyes, part pain and part fear and part pure stupid bewilderment, and he stared without blinking or moving the rest of his spindled body, as if he were looking out from some place other than himself, somewhere far away. She brought the .32 up and thought for a moment to shoot Otis, and she was surprised at herself that, having shot one boy dead, the idea of shooting other boys and even herself came as a relief. It was as if she might absolve herself completely, if only she could shoot enough people.

She left Otis lying there on the floor, his body a twisted, fetal grotesque, his eyes still following her from some other place. She put the gun back into her satchel, put the doctor's key ring into her coat pocket, picked up the rifle and slipped out the front door.

She flattened herself against the barbershop wall and sneaked back around it, to her newly acquired horses, which she patted and reassured. Then she ran haltingly and with fervent looks in all directions behind the buildings on the east side of Tres Cruces, past the bank, past the exhausted remains of the Notions Shop. When she could no longer see the stable, she crossed the open plain beyond Main Street and ran back up toward the jail.

On the off-chance that someone had had the foresight to leave a guard posted in the marshal's office, Diana clutched

Jonathan's .32 inside her satchel and knocked on the door. No answer came. She reached for Drumwright's key ring, but, to her surprise, when she turned the knob, the door swung in, unlocked. She rushed inside and set the satchel and the rifle down on the marshal's desk.

"Jackson!" No answer. "Jackson!"

She ran to the jail cell and found Jackson sitting on his bunk with his head in his hands. He looked up, and the whites of his eyes were yellow. The swelling around his eyes had gotten worse. The smell of urine pervaded the hall.

Diana used Drumwright's key to unlock Jackson's cell. She opened the door and motioned for Jackson to come out. He remained seated.

"You comin' or not?"

Jackson did not answer, but simply looked through Diana listlessly, like a dog looking at an old tired hunk of rawhide that had long since lost its flavor. With no sense of urgency whatsoever, he stood up, and winced as he did so.

"They been beatin' you again?" Jackson shuffled toward Diana, through the open cell door, and walked past her toward the marshal's office. "Who done it this time?"

Jackson: "Did you bring my boots?"

"I don't know where they are."

She followed him and when they both stood over the marshal's desk, she unwrapped the rifle and laid the Colt revolver out for him to see. When he didn't look at these weapons, she followed his gaze to the marshal's empty gun cabinet.

Jackson: "That usually full of guns?"

"Usually. I don't know where they put'em."

Jackson, slowly, as if considering for the first time: "So the marshal and the rest of'em are walkin' around out there with a cabinet full of guns? And we got these here?"

Diana, impatiently: "Don't worry that we're outgunned.

What counts ain't the number of guns, but where the bullets land. Now you feel like makin' it across to the bank, or you feel like waitin' here for them boys to beat you to death?"

Jackson puffed out his cheeks and blew air and stared at his feet. He picked up the Colt and felt the weight if it in his hand and then opened the chamber to see that it was loaded. He searched the satchel for bullets, then he picked up the rifle and checked that it was loaded as well.

"These all the bullets we got?"

"The faster we get movin', the fewer bullets we'll need." She withdrew one of the sticks of dynamite from her coat and showed it to Jackson, and his eyes brightened. "I got a pair a horses waitin' for us behind Doc Drumwright's, and we're about two minutes from blowin' that safe, and then we just ride outta here and get ourselves free. So pull yourself together."

"And the river? How we gonna cross the river?"

"You leave that to me. I got you outta this jail, didn't I? I'll get you across that river."

"All right, then, Miss Diana, I guess you the boss."

"Don't call me Miss, you hear me! Just Diana." She pulled a stick of dried venison out of the satchel. "You eat lately?" Jackson took the meat and tore off a hunk of it with his teeth while Diana slung the satchel over her shoulder and held the .32 in her hand. "All right. You finish that and I'll have a look."

She opened the door and looked down the street toward Alberto Torres' tack shop. To her surprise, the billow of smoke that had been rising steadily over the stable had disappeared, and the crowd around it seemed to be moving more leisurely. A knot of people had formed right in front of the stable doors, but there was no other activity for the moment and she judged that they could cross unobserved. She turned to Jackson.

"You ready to go? I know you're feelin' bad, but you pull yourself together and we'll get through this, and then you can nurse them wounds proper."

The venison had a salutary effect on Jackson's outlook, and he readied himself to follow Diana into the rain. She gave the signal and ran out, and Jackson hobbled along as fast as he could behind her, feeling rocks ooze away under his feet as mud sludged in-between his toes. The muck felt good, and so did the rain on his bare head, and he looked up and down the street and felt naked and open for anyone to see.

They reached the front door of the Hidalgo Trust Bank and Diana once again withdrew Doc Drumwright's keys, but after trying half a dozen, she realized that he didn't have a key for this door. Jackson turned the knob and banged against it with his shoulder, but the door did not budge, and he winced in pain.

Diana wished she had held onto Moreno's lock picks; in their place, she reached under her hood and took a couple of pins from her hair and tried her luck with these, but she was anxious and scattered and so was Jackson, and she couldn't locate a latch or tumbler to work on.

Jackson, brandishing the Colt: "Get back. I'm gonna blast it."

"No, here, use this." Diana held up her derringer. "It's quieter. Maybe they won't pay it no mind."

"A shot's a shot."

"This ain't no time for arguin'." Diana waved Jackson aside and put the derringer up to the door herself, between the knob and the frame. She fired a round and then lunged hard against the door, which popped open. She felt a stinging in her hand and looked down to find a large wooden splinter lodged between her thumb and forefinger. Blood streamed into her palm.

They rushed inside, Jackson waving the Colt and leveling the Winchester at the emptiness that greeted him. Diana threw herself back against the door and slammed it shut. She winced as she yanked the splinter out.

"Moreno!" She stanched the bleeding in her hand with the sleeve of her coat. "Moreno!"

Moreno emerged from the hallway with such astonishment on his face that, in any other circumstance, Diana would have cracked a malicious joke. Moreno's relief that he hadn't just been discovered by Kerr or Collins was more than offset by the fact that Jackson was pointing two guns at him. Diana, whom he had thought to meet back at the Coronado Saloon, was staring at his confusion peevishly, as if he were an unruly child who was misbehaving.

One Fire Out

Doc Drumwright stood inside Alberto Torres' stable, surrounded by chattering men and women with buckets, looking up at the damage. For once, he was thankful for the hard rain. They had fought off the fire and at least saved the stable's structure. Still, he was unsure how much good they had really done. Half of a burned stable wasn't worth much, and he thought that, for all their effort, Torres might have to start over again from scratch. Flames had licked most of the inside walls black and the stalls were charred nearly to cinders.

Drumwright walked out the back door and stood staring into the distance, until Saul limped up and patted him on the shoulder. He yelled over the clattering of rain against the building. "Looks like you're the hero today, Doc. I s'pose you and I'll have to trade off bein' heroes from one day to the next."

Drumwright: "I didn't do anything, Saul. We all did this together. Anyway, I think our effort was in vain."

"Saved the building."

"Maybe. I'd give my last drop of bourbon to know how these fires started. This wasn't lightning, and the more I think about the Notions Shop, the stranger it gets."

"Ain't nothin' stranger than the Frogboy, Doc, you gotta admit."

"Otis is no arsonist, and he didn't do this."

"You think somebody set it on purpose?"

"I do. Maybe somebody lost their mind on account of the

rain. Maybe something worse than that. Whatever the reason, we're all stuck in this together, and we can't let mischief go unpunished."

"Whatta ya aim to do?"

"I guess for the time being there's nothing to do. Except get these good people some food."

The doctor gathered everyone around him and announced that, as an appreciation for everyone's hard work, they could adjourn to the Coronado Saloon for a free meal and drinks, and he'd take it upon himself to pay out of the town's emergency fund. Then Drumwright announced that he would personally pay a reward of ten dollars for any information about the cause of the recent fires; and that he suspected there was an arsonist in their midst, perhaps someone standing among them at that very moment. The doctor apologized for any offense he might have caused by saying this, but then went on to say that if the perpetrator were indeed in their midst, that he would be brought to justice, and that they might look more forgivingly upon this crime if the guilty party surrendered himself and gave some explanation, these being extraordinary circumstances.

The doctor finished his speech and waited. No one came forward. But as they stood staring at him, the doctor had a moment to reflect, to survey the faces looking back at his, and he suddenly remarked to himself not who was there, among the crowd, but who wasn't. Diana, for one, was missing, and Drumwright now racked his brains trying to remember exactly when and where he had last seen her; and he couldn't recall precisely which of the drovers from Rancho Cielito had gone with Jonathan and which had stayed behind; or if that fellow Calderon, from Holguin, had ridden out with the posse or not. Lightning sizzled audibly overhead, followed by a crack of thunder that made even David Burns flinch. With a yell and a wave of his arm, the doctor adjourned the people to the saloon.

Everyone but Kerr headed for the shelter of the inn. The bank guard pulled Saul aside and made him promise to save him some free grub, then he trudged through the rain toward the bank, to make sure everything was still secure.

No Honor Among Thieves

Inside the Hidalgo Trust Bank, Moreno was too flabbergasted to speak. He had been halfway out the back door when he'd heard Diana's voice calling him; he had already spun an elaborate tale in his mind to tell Collins or Jonathan Vega, was already concocting an alibi that would protect both Diana and himself. When he appeared in the bank's main room and found himself staring at the wrong end of Jackson's guns and saw the look of urgency and contempt on Diana's face, his mind simply froze. All of his contingency plans fell and splattered like ordinary raindrops piddling into the muck of the street outside.

"What the hell are you doing?"

"We're blowin' the safe."

Moreno's confusion turned to anger. "You're ruining everything."

"Oh? Did *you* get the safe open yet?"

"And this!" Moreno gestured toward Jackson, suddenly unafraid of his guns. "You bring a killer and you shoot through the door! You might as well put a gun to your own head. And mine."

Diana brought out a stick of dynamite. "This is how you open a safe, Moreno. We're blowin' it, and then we're ridin' outta here."

Moreno was beside himself. He took the stolen notebook out of his pants and waved it in Diana's face. "No, this is how you open a safe."

"What's that?"

"It's the combination. I'm sure of it. I found it in back."

"Then why haven't you opened it?"

"It's in code! I need time to decipher it! You see? I could have figured out the combination and come back again later. But it doesn't matter now, there won't be any later with you shooting through locks and setting murderers loose." He looked at Jackson with disgust and then back at Diana with a rage born of disappointment and betrayal. "I thought you were smarter than this."

"What made you think so?"

Jackson, insistently: "If we gonna blow that safe, I suggest we do it and leave the fightin' for after."

Diana made a move, as if to step around Moreno toward the safe, but Moreno grabbed her by the shoulders and forced her to meet his gaze. "If you do this, you kill us all. We can't get away with the money like this. Let's get out of here while we still can and put Jackson back in his cell and see if we can't at least come out whole."

Jackson: "I ain't goin' back in no cell."

"There ain't no goin' back, Moreno, not for me, not for him. You wanna get out, then get out, but we're blowin' that safe and takin' that money."

Moreno looked from Diana to Jackson, then hurled the notebook across the room. It smacked against a partition near the safe and fell to the ground, and Moreno turned and grabbed Diana's shoulders again and looked into her eyes with such hurt that Diana almost felt moved. "You didn't understand what I was offering you, Diana. I thought you did, but now I see that you didn't."

"What were you offerin' me? A safe full of money you didn't have? A chance to get killed?"

"I thought you were smarter than this."

"Sayin' so over and over ain't gonna make me smarter. Anyway, I got no illusions how smart *you* are."

Moreno put his hand to Diana's neck, so that Jackson stepped over to defend her, but Moreno merely caressed the skin below her left ear, then wistfully twirled a lock of Diana's hair around his index finger, before stepping aside and muttering into his chest. "I'm leaving. I'll be sorry to watch you die." He pushed past her and opened the front door, only to slam it shut again instantly.

Jackson: "What is it?"

"It's Kerr. I think he saw me."

"Move away."

Jackson handed Diana the rifle and then braced himself against the front door frame. He cocked his revolver and grabbed the doorknob with his left hand and eased the door open a couple of inches. There was a guttural cry from outside. Jackson flung the door wide, leveled the Colt and fired once and then leapt back inside and slammed the door shut.

Diana: "Did you get him?"

"I believe so. Why don't you get to blowin' that safe?"

Moreno actually jumped up and down, and for once his steps didn't seem mincing and effete. "You've killed us! They'll all be coming now. If they weren't before, they'll be coming now."

Jackson: "Diana, why don't you blow that safe?"

Moreno ran down the hall toward the rear door. He unlocked it and stepped out behind the bank, but as he did so he caught some movement out of the corner of his eye, and he turned just fast enough to see the ghost of a man disappear behind the telegraph office. He stared for a moment longer to see if this was an illusion, a trick of his fear, or if a man would reappear around the corner. Nothing stirred. The sky turned a little blacker and the rain fell harder. He stepped back into the bank, locked the door and ran down the hall into the main room. "There's somebody else out there. Drag that body inside, quick."

"Why?"

"We could use his gun, for one thing, and there's no sense showing off. If that posse rides back in, that body will be the first thing they see."

Jackson and Moreno stepped into the street, Jackson with his pistol leveled and eyes darting all around. To Moreno's amazement, no one shot at them, and, in fact, they still seemed to be alone on the street, though he fancied he saw a pair of figures duck inside El Charro. It was hard to tell through the rain, which was falling in sheets. Moreno grabbed Kerr's legs while Jackson covered him with his pistol cocked; he dragged Kerr into the bank, leaving a wide swath of blood on the boards outside, and Jackson closed the door behind them.

Kerr's face was ruined. The bullet had passed through his nose, just below the bridge, and his forehead had collapsed into his eyes and sagged into the hole in his face. Moreno thought he would vomit.

Jackson: "You know how to shoot?" He unfastened Kerr's belt and holster and handed them to Moreno, who put them on ashen-faced.

Meanwhile, Diana had gone to the safe and realized that she had no way of fixing the dynamite to the door. She had searched frantically for some sort of fastener or strap big enough to fit around the body of the safe; but, finding nothing, she'd dragged a chair over and set it flush up against the safe door. She stood the dynamite on its end on the chair, right next to the combination dial. Then she took out a box of matches and looked back at Moreno and Jackson.

"Hey! Ready?"

Moreno came hurrying over, Kerr's gunbelt flopping around his waist. "That's it? You're just going to set the dynamite up against the safe and light it?"

"What do you suggest?"

"How do you know there will be enough force directed at the proper location to open the lock? How do you know where to send the explosion so it won't destroy what's inside?"

"I don't know. You told me yourself—we're testin' our luck against the luck of others. I'm hopin' to get lucky."

"That's not what I meant."

Jackson, watching the door: "Shut the hell up and get on with it. Somebody's gonna be comin' presently, and I'd just as soon walk outta this building alive."

Diana struck a match and held it to the fuse, which lit with an angry hissing. She and Moreno rushed out from behind the partitions, through the teller area, toward the hallway in back.

"Jackson, get some cover."

Jackson hesitated only a second before rushing to join them. They crouched down with their backs to the wall and plugged their ears. For a long time, nothing happened. They looked at one another.

"Something's wrong."

"No."

"How long was the fuse?"

"I don't know."

"You didn't time the fuses?"

"How could I have?"

"Should we go check?"

"No."

They waited. Moreno's face turned ashen and his eyes milky.

Jackson shifted. "I'm goin' to check."

"Don't be a fool."

"Foolish is settin' in this hallway waitin' to get caught."

Diana: "No. Give it a minute. You gotta wait. I've seen dynamite used before."

Again they waited, each of them staring straight ahead at a void just a few inches in front of their faces, every muscle tensed. Thunder boomed overhead and they all jumped. Jackson stood into a crouch and peeked around the corner. Nothing stirred, and as the thunder reverberated away into the distance, the tiny creakings and rustlings of their own bodies seemed amplified.

"It's too long."

"Just wait."

"It's too long."

Jackson ran down the hall. Diana stood up. Moreno remained seated on his heels, glassy self-pity in his eyes.

Moreno: "There is no way out. You know this, don't you? There is simply no way out."

Diana: "If we all die like this, it'll be better than livin' like that."

"You should have listened to me. You should have waited."

"Waited for what? How many more diversions you think you could get away with?"

"You can't shoot your way across the river."

Diana, yelling: "Jackson! Hey, what's wrong?" To Moreno: "You're too clever to help yourself, Moreno. That's your problem. You're sooo clever." Again yelling toward the front of the bank: "Jackson!"

Moreno: "We are already dead."

THE POSSE RETURNS

After the fire in the stables had been put out, David Burns followed the rest of the crowd into the saloon, got a free glass of whisky, and then stepped outside to the porch. Burns was in a pent-up, angry mood and wanted no part of the celebration. Jerry followed him outside, smoking a cigarette, thinking to placate Burns with conversation. Though Jerry was the nominal leader of their mining expedition, Burns was bigger and stronger and Jerry needed him to do most of the heavy work when they actually got to the mines. The last thing Jerry needed was for Burns to get into some kind of trouble and get jailed or strung up and leave Jerry stranded alone in Tres Cruces.

Burns: "I'd like to get my hands on that sumbitch settin' them fires."

Jerry, taking a long drag at his cigarette: "What do you care? You should thank him for givin' you somethin' to do, to pass the time. That's what you wanted."

"That guy didn't do us no favors burnin' that stable down. Where we gonna put our mules now?" Burns finished off his whisky in two quick gulps, then breathed through the burning at the back of his throat.

Jerry: "We didn't lose nothin'. Anyway, there's nothin' we can do about it."

Confrontationally: "You ever just get riled? About anything?"

"What if I did?" He took a heavy drag on his cigarette and

flicked it into the muddy street. "Ain't you tired out from that fire? What are you in a lather about? Have another whisky. It's on the house."

Burns sniffed at Jerry and looked out at the gunmetal gray clouds firing hard pellets of cold sky to the street. The rain's renewed ferocity seemed almost welcome after the scorching dry gasps of flame in the stable, and the wind swept water across their grimy necks and faces. They listened to a baleful version of "Cotton-Eyed Joe" being wrenched from the piano inside.

From down the street, a single gunshot muscled through the noisy afternoon rain, and Jerry jumped and Burns stood up straight and peered down the street. All they could see was the row of buildings on Main Street disappearing into a murk of gray. Burns threw his shot glass down in the mud and waited, but nothing moved on the street.

Burns: "That was a shot. No question."

"Let's get the others."

From inside the saloon, the raucous piano playing and clambering of voices continued without a pause. Burns strode off of the porch toward the bank.

"Where you goin'?" He watched Burns duck into El Charro, and he debated for a moment whether to follow him or run inside to get Drumwright; finally, he leapt off of the porch and ran into El Charro, just in time to see Burns disappear behind the counter. "Burns!"

Burns hurried past the shelves in back and opened up the larder. He picked up a double-barrel shotgun leaning against the wall on the floor. "I seen this in here earlier. Tell Hector I'm borrowin' it."

"Whatta you gonna to do?"

"I'm gonna catch that sumbitch myself."

"Burns, we don't know who fired that shot or why, and

there ain't no sense gettin' killed over it. Come with me and fetch the others."

Burns hefted Alvarado's shotgun and pushed past Jerry, back out into the rain, toward the bank. Something about the moment, about the audacity of Burns's foolhardiness, mesmerized Jerry, and he slunk alongside Burns as if drawn magnetically. They crouched and lurched forward clumsily, skulking along the front of the buildings.

As they passed the barbershop, they saw a heap on the planks in front of the bank, and Burns clutched the shotgun a little tighter. They passed the telegraph office and made the heap out to be a body.

Burns: "I'll be damned." He remembered the bank guard taking his leave of the saloon earlier. "It's Kerr. Somebody shot that bastard dead, right in front of the bank." This broke the enchantment that had momentarily captivated Jerry, and he pulled himself away and ran in the opposite direction, toward the saloon.

Burns held Alvarado's shotgun at his hip, slipped behind the telegraph office and crept toward the bank. As he flatfooted forward, he felt a sudden change in the air and stopped in his tracks. The tension grew inside him. All at once and for no reason he could name, he ran back and darted around the building, holding himself as flat against it as his fat body would allow. He waited a moment, then peered around the corner and saw standing at the back door of the bank, looking almost directly at him, none other than Arturo Calderon of San Juan, half-brother to the whore at the Coronado Inn. Calderon looked as if he were about to step out of the bank, but then his eyes seemed to find Burns, and Burns pulled his head back. When Burns summoned the nerve to look again, Calderon had disappeared, and lightning snapped and thunder roared in Burns's ears.

Burns peeked around the corner again, waited to see if Calderon would reappear; when he was convinced that he wouldn't, he ran forward and flattened himself up against the side of the bank, holding his shotgun close to his chest. Burns felt personally insulted, as if his confrontation with Calderon in Diana's room had humiliated him in light of these present circumstances. He decided to kill Calderon.

* * * * *

Jerry rushed into the Coronado Saloon and found Doc Drumwright at the bar, midway through his third shot of rum, the doctor's cheeks puffy and his eyes narrow and watery. Hector Alvarado was playing "Hills of Mexico" on the piano, and what he lacked in talent he made up for in enthusiasm: his clumsy off-kilter pounding filled the air. People were still in a state of dishevelment from fighting the fire, toweling themselves off and congratulating one another more heartily than they actually felt necessary, to ward off the imminent return of their discontentment.

Jerry yelled his news over the noise, and Drumwright just looked at him. "It's the honest truth, Doc. Kerr's laid out down there front of the bank."

"Who shot him?"

"I don't know. We heard the shot, and then we run out and seen the body."

"Who did?"

"Me and Burns."

"Where's Burns?"

"He went down to the bank with a shotgun."

The doctor motioned for Jerry to follow him, and together they went into the kitchen, where Saul was hobbling around in circles, wielding an oversized iron skillet, trying to prepare a meal for the entire town of Tres Cruces. "Saul, you got any guns?"

"Why? What's wrong?"

"Somebody shot Kerr."

"No kiddin'?" Considering: "Ah. . . well. . . I seen my uncle took a fair number of guns with him when they went out after the horses. He mighta left his shotgun under the bar, though. You ain't gonna go out there, Doc?"

"I'm afraid there isn't much choice. Most anyone who could handle a gun already rode out of town, and I'm the acting deputy."

"But who shot him?"

"We don't know."

Saul set the skillet on the stove and limped back into the tavern, behind the bar, where he knelt down and found the shotgun. He broke the barrel, saw that there was a shell already loaded, and reached below and handed the doctor four more. Drumwright put them into his vest pockets.

Saul: "You think it's the same fella set the fire?"

"Maybe."

"Hey, Doc, why don't you wait till Uncle Jonathan and the rest of 'em ride back in? Ain't no call to risk your neck like this."

"It's my business as much as anyone's whether or not people get killed in Tres Cruces. I've already got a dead body in my shop, and another nearly roasted alive, and now Kerr. I won't stand for this kind of disregard for human life."

"But you don't stand a chance against a real gunfighter."

"There aren't any real gunfighters in Tres Cruces, Saul."

Jerry: "Burns is down there, too. So you got another gun on your side."

"Against how many, you think?"

"I don't know. There was only one shot."

Saul: "Just wait, Doc. Hole up here and wait for the others. There's a dozen guns out there, prob'ly ridin' back in right now."

Drumwright finished his third shot of rum and wiped his lips. He looked into the future to see himself—a slow old man with no taste for fighting, out in the rain confronting an unknown gunslinger. His first mission would be to find Burns and join with him, and hopefully they could corner the killer and pen him down somewhere until reinforcements arrived. The killer could be anyone anywhere out there on the street, even Diana, he thought, with a quick glance toward the upstairs landing. Though his mind was lubricated with adrenaline and cheap rum, no inferences he could make added up to the truth, since the truth was too desperate to be plausible.

Drumwright: "Is this the only gun you've got?"

"Uncle Jonathan's got firearms stashed all over the inn, if I can just remember where."

"Well, collect some weapons and keep your eyes peeled. You and Hector are going to keep watch over the inn. DeYoung, you cover me as I leave and follow a ways behind me on the street. Nobody else leaves the inn, got it? And nobody gets in. Whatever you do, don't let the killer mingle back in with the rest of 'em unaccounted for."

By this time, the crowd gathered in the saloon had noticed Doc Drumwright at the bar with a shotgun, and the urgent manner in which he and Saul and Jerry DeYoung were talking. Many eyes now fixed on them. Hector Alvarado, with his back to the room, was still pounding away at the piano, and Drumwright had to shout repeatedly to quiet the saloon.

Drumwright announced the situation. He told everyone either to sit tight or go to their rooms but under no circumstances to leave the inn, and that he would get to the bottom of this appalling crime and bring the perpetrator to justice. With this new calamity, and with the absence of the most able men, a premonition of doom cloaked the tavern.

Drumwright slung his poncho around his shoulders and headed out into the rain. He hadn't seen this much gunplay in decades, since he had first arrived in Tres Cruces. As a medical doctor, he was now better equipped to deal with bullet wounds than ever before, but as a resident of Tres Cruces he was deeply appalled. He wondered if the rain had driven everyone mad.

The doctor's first worry, as he trod heavily past El Charro, was that Burns would surprise him and shoot him by mistake. He had spoken to Burns only once, but that had been enough to warn the doctor away from him, and he trusted Burns with a gun about as much as he trusted Jonathan. His second worry was that the killer would simply pick him off from some hidden vantage point, that by walking so openly out on the street he made himself an easy target. And he had never been good with a gun. He glanced back at DeYoung, lit by light shining from the windows of the now-silent saloon. Why am I here, Drumwright thought. Why isn't DeYoung out risking his life instead? Perhaps the rain has driven me mad, as well.

He came to his own barbershop without seeing any movement on the street. Though he squinted and stared in the direction of the bank, he saw no signs of a body in front. Except for the rapidly darkening skies overhead and the hard rain, all seemed unremarkable. He stopped, listening and looking about, and then decided to fortify himself with another drink from his private supply.

He opened the door to his barbershop and his skin prickled. The air inside had changed. He held his breath, but nothing stirred. He tiptoed toward the back, holding his shotgun in front of him like a bayonet. As he crossed the threshold to the "operating room," he saw what was wrong. His surgical table had been toppled and lay tilted against one of the sawhorses that had supported it. The second sawhorse had fallen and lay under the table holding Pastor Charles's body. Otis the Frogboy was gone.

Drumwright, amazed, under his breath: "Maybe it's Otis, after all." He tried but couldn't imagine Otis the Frogboy hobbling to the stable, setting it on fire, and then gunning a man down in cold blood. He doubted that Otis would even have the sense to know he was in a gunfight. When the doctor had left him last, Otis had been having trouble even breathing, and Drumwright hadn't believed him capable of getting up, due to the severity of his burns. But he certainly had gotten up.

The doctor scratched his mustache and returned to his barbering room, where he opened his desk drawer to retrieve a vial of homemade applejack. When he did so, he noticed that his key ring was missing, and he stood up straight, now imagining Otis pilfering his keys and then. . . but what would he do with them? Otis had the intelligence of a slow eight year old. And yet. . . Drumwright searched all through his desk, felt his own pockets, but found no keys. He uncapped his little medical vial and took a long slow drink, and a sudden gust of wind blew his front door open and banged it against the inside wall. The doctor stowed the vial in his pants pocket and walked back out into the storm.

He called out Burns's name in a hoarse half-whisper several times but the sound died in the air. He looked back toward the inn, but he could no longer see DeYoung. As he drew closer to the bank, he still saw no dead body, and he became increasingly nervous thinking of Burns prowling around with a gun, and the Frogboy prowling around with a gun, and he wondered which one he would rather come upon suddenly. The thought of Otis with a gun particularly terrified him, since he knew from experience that it was impossible to predict what he might do. The doctor tried to remember a scenario from one of the Mexican War battles he had memorized that would help him, but the many hours he had spent re-imagining street scenes from that war seemed an utter waste of time now.

The doctor stopped in front of the telegraph office. He looked up and down the street, and noticed that the door to the marshal's office across the way seemed open. He thought about Jackson inside. He gave the bank a wide berth and hurried across the street.

Drumwright stood with his back against the outer wall and inched his way toward the marshal's doorway. Still nothing stirred. He sucked at his mustache and all at once, in a display of mock bravado, he stepped full into the doorway with his shotgun leveled, only to find empty space. He walked inside. It was dark. He waved his shotgun around.

"Jackson."

He tiptoed into the corridor, recoiling at the bright, acrid smell of urine, and saw that Jackson's cell door was ajar. He labored to fit this new piece into the puzzle. He walked back into the office and sat on the corner of the marshal's desk.

Otis the Frogboy had let Jackson out of prison and then set the stable on fire, and Jackson had killed Kerr and was robbing the bank? Where was Otis now? Where was Kerr's body? Perhaps Burns had killed Kerr and he was robbing the bank, and Jerry DeYoung was in cahoots with him, and the doctor had been sent out on a wild goose chase, or worse—sent out to get shot. Or maybe Kerr hadn't been shot at all, and Kerr had sprung Jackson and they were both in league with Burns and DeYoung. . . but that still left Otis, who certainly wasn't part of any scheme to rob a bank. The doctor opened his vial and took another long drink of applejack and decided that, whatever scheme was afoot, he could only be a booby in it. He opted to sit right there in the marshal's office until the posse returned.

He walked to the door and looked out on the street. The

gusting wind blew rain into the doorway. The emptiness of the street seemed eerie. He had never envisioned dying by a bullet, not even during the Quapatec raids on Rancho Mirabal twenty years before, but now the possibility seemed all too real, and the gun that would inscribe his headstone was wandering around invisible in the rain. He knelt down and held Jonathan's shotgun across his knees and drank some more.

The dense alcoholic mist in his mind was beginning to rival the mizzle outside. Hours seemed to pass. Or maybe just minutes. Or maybe no time at all. The doctor's pounding heart speeded time up, and his sodden mind slowed it down.

Finally, as if through a long tunnel of fear and desire, as if he had conjured it himself, he heard the fall of hoofbeats, and he brought his gun to his shoulder ready to shoot. The hoofbeats were followed by a pair of clipped whinnies. He turned toward the south and saw emerging like a vision the dozen or so men who had ridden out that morning. They rode up now leading the seven runaway horses, the last horse dragging a travois behind it.

Drumwright stood in the shadows of the marshal's doorway. As the posse drew even with the jail, he wondered if there might be gunplay right before his eyes, if Jackson and Kerr and maybe Burns and DeYoung might emerge from behind buildings with guns blazing and get the drop on Jonathan and his men. He raised his arm to wave, when Alberto Torres, at the head of the posse, cried out himself and spurred his horse forward. The rest of the horsemen followed suit, and soon the whole posse was hooting and galloping away toward the north end of town.

The doctor yelled, but his exclamation was drowned beneath a tremendous boom mingled with the sound of breaking glass, and the air was filled with a frightful, unnatural din. At first, Drumwright took the explosion for thunder, but he looked across the street and saw smoke in the broken windows of the bank. He froze in place, utterly drunk for the first time in decades, and confused, fearing for his life. He clamped his hat onto his head and set off running toward Jonathan, howling a weird, quavery, altogether wild yell down Main Street.

A Surprise Visitor

Diana was still standing in the bank's hallway with Moreno when the dynamite exploded. A deafening roar filled the bank. Windows shattered and objects clattered against one another and crashed to the floor. Smoke billowed down the hallway, and they smelled the light dry biting smell of gunpowder. They looked at one another in alarm and felt repercussions of muffled ringing in their ears, and they ran to see what had happened.

Loose sheets of paper were still drifting to the floor when they came to the main room. A gust blew through the broken windows, twisting the papers in mid-air. Smoke spiraled and plaited in curls, drifting into the corners and back out again toward the windows.

They found that the green partitions around the safe had been blown to shards, which now lay scattered around the room. The chair that the dynamite had rested upon had disappeared entirely.

It took a moment to find Jackson. He had ricocheted off a desk and landed torqued at the waist, his back flat on the floor and his legs turned almost all the way around. His torso had been ripped open and the bloody muscles of his chest could be seen beneath the singed remains of his shirt. His face was obscured by blood, which was flowing from seemingly every pore. Bits of Jackson hung in a spider web along the floorboards behind his body, and his blood had spattered streaks around the safe itself.

They turned from this grisly sight to the safe. The steel body of the cube had buckled in front and the door had crimped into itself. The combination dial was gone and the silver lever had blown off. There was a deep indentation where the lever had been.

Diana rushed to the safe and pulled at the stump that had been the lever. After some yanking up and down and side to side, she heard a scraping of metal against metal and the door budged. She gained a purchase on the corner and pulled with all her might. It jerked out a quarter of an inch, then another quarter of an inch, then it glided open without a sound.

Diana caught a wisp of smoke in her lungs as she bent to look inside. She choked and coughed and tears came to her eyes. Inside the safe, she saw six short stacks of bills, separated into bundles by brown paper bands. She snatched one and counted five hundred dollars in twenty dollar bills, and she grabbed another bundle and counted a thousand dollars in hundreds. A quick count of the rest of the bundles told that she and Moreno had appropriated more than five thousand dollars. There were other valuables in the safe, jewelry and documents. Diana held up a handful of fifties and looked at Moreno in triumph.

"That's how you open a safe."

Moreno looked at Jackson's mangled body. He too found his eyes watering, and he coughed and then heaved as if he would throw up. He breathed shallow little breaths while he waved away smoke, and he imagined his own body lying next to Jackson's, tattered with bullet holes.

Diana, slapping Moreno on the shoulder: "Come on. We gotta get outta here." Moreno didn't move. "I got two horses waitin' for us behind Doc Drumwright's." When Moreno still did not move, Diana pushed past him, grabbed her satchel from the floor and handed him Jonathan's Winchester. "If anybody comes through the door, shoot'em." She stuffed the money and jewelry into the satchel, then slung the bag over her shoulder and took her .32 pistol from the outer pocket of her mantle. When she stood upright again, Moreno still had not moved. "Let's go."

She shoved Moreno in front of her. He stumbled forward and roused himself enough to walk. The front door flew open. A man ran in and aimed a revolver at Moreno.

Moreno simply fell down out of the way, and before the man could draw a bead on either the falling Moreno or Diana beyond him, Diana squeezed off a round, which caught the man square in the chest. The man flopped backwards, and another man appeared in his place and Diana fired again. The second shot hit the second man in the shoulder and spun him back out of the doorway. Diana emptied another round into his back and he fell face down outside. Nothing else moved, and Diana rushed to close the door.

Moreno continued to lie on the floor. Diana ran to him and shook his shoulder. "Come on, we're this close to gettin' free. Just a short run to the barbershop, and we ride outta here forever."

He stood up, and Diana pulled him along after her toward the back hallway. When they crossed in front of a window, they heard shots and ricochets, and they crouched low.

Moreno felt as if he had entered a dream. He could not believe that people were shooting at him, trying to kill him. It was unreal. The wet air blowing into the bank prickled the bare skin of his neck. They crossed in front of another window and Diana fired a shot wildly out.

Diana had stopped thinking altogether and acted purely on impulse. For the first time in her life, she felt utterly free, and the more bodies that lay twisted around her, the freer she felt. Robert McKinley, dead in her room at the Coronado Inn, now seemed little more than a childish memory, and the thought of her own death, of the thudding pain of lead tearing into her flesh, vanished from her imagination. She heard only the gravelly noise of the rain and smelled only the biting scent of gunpowder and smoke. Her mind was no longer a dirty filter for hateful thoughts but encompassed her whole body, pure and clean. She saw everything, every edge of every windowpane, every crack between every board, the black pomaded hair falling across Moreno's forehead, with aching clarity.

They ran toward the back door. It was only when they were right upon it that they realized someone was outside, rattling the knob. Diana dropped her .32 into her mantle pocket and snatched the rifle away from Moreno. She blasted a round through the center of the door. They heard a cry and the doorknob went silent. Diana paused a beat, then unlocked the door and flung it wide.

Out in the open facing her stood three men with guns drawn. The body of a fourth lay in the mud. The three men were still looking at the unfortunate fourth man's body when they saw Diana's rifle and scattered to the left and right. Diana managed a single shot that flew harmlessly through the air before she slammed the door shut. She ducked down, locked the door again and scampered back up the hallway with Moreno in tow.

She was breathing hard. She looked back at Moreno and only now did she notice the cavernous loneliness in his eyes, and the exhaustion on his face. His lifelessness touched Diana, and she felt pity and disdain and an unfamiliar maternal rage all at once. She thought of killing him, and she thought of protecting him.

Diana seemed to Moreno like a demon, dilated eyes and

flared nostrils, and he no longer felt his own body hustling along the passageway. He felt like a rag doll. Everything he had once believed now seemed like the superstition of an extinct Indian religion. His mind was locked and empty, and he longer remembered the first link in this imprisoning chain of events, the first dark impulse that had led him to this moment: he seemed always to have been in this nightmare.

Diana stopped at a place where the main room met the hallway, a little corner from which they could see both entrances, where they had an open view of sky through two windows. She knelt down and dragged Moreno down beside her, then reloaded the .32 with bullets from her satchel.

Moreno: "You've killed me."

"You ain't even hurt."

"How many men do you think are out there? How many do you think you can shoot, out in the open, on the run? You've killed us both."

"With two of us shootin', we've at least got a chance. If you'd do some shootin'."

Spitefully: "You think they've left your horses out there, just waiting for you to ride away? You think there's anywhere to ride to? They'll wait outside the door. They'll use your horses as bait for an ambush. Every step is blocked."

"You can't predict the future, Moreno. That's what you said. You gotta act now and then make decisions as things change. That's what you said, right? So we've gotta take our shot now." Diana finished reloading. She snatched Kerr's pistol out of its holster on Moreno's waist and checked that it was fully loaded as well.

Moreno, blankly: "No. This is not what I said. This is not what I meant."

"Then what?"

Exasperated, but still wishing to clarify that he was absolutely not responsible for this disastrous turn of events, Moreno carefully articulated every syllable. "To risk something, you must be willing to improvise, you must take what fate offers you. That is improvisation, that is playing the odds, that is what I meant."

"And that's what we're doin'." She spun the chamber of Kerr's revolver, snapped it shut and forced it into Moreno's hands.

"No. Playing the odds means playing *favorable* odds, not stacking your chips on a bluff."

Diana pointed at Kerr's body. "Ask him if I'm bluffing."

Moreno looked at her with a contempt so angry his lip curled. He spit in her face. Diana's expression did not change as Moreno's spittle dribbled down her cheek, but she cocked her pistol and brought it up to his chest.

Moreno: "I have been gravely mistaken in you."

"I ain't to blame for your ideas about me. I ain't responsible for you at all, but if you wanna get outta this mess, I've got five thousand dollars that might do you some good. That was the point, wasn't it?"

Moreno stared into the eyes of Diana Clayborn and saw the debasement that he knew he should have seen all along. He wondered why he had never seen her clearly, why he had spoken to her at all that first day, what ill-conceived idea of her had driven him to formulate his plans in the first place. He was a fool. He was deeply embarrassed for caressing Diana's skin so tenderly, and with a rush of regret he hated himself for loving her. He saw that he had been betrayed by his inability to follow his own philosophy, that he had garbled the odds and miscalculated the chances and, worst of all, that he had been playing for phantom stakes, for a prize that had never existed. He could not decide if he was more disgusted with himself or Diana, but then purely out of self-defence he decided to hate

Diana, the scarlet dove, the murdering bitch, his ugly and vicious undoing.

Moreno: "I had the combination to the safe in my hand. It would have taken only another day to get that money, a single day, and no one would have been the wiser, and no one would have been hurt."

"You're mistaken about more than me, Moreno. You think you can lie and sneak your way through the world, like the world don't touch you. But you're as violent and mean as me, only worse, 'cause I have to be. You think stealin' don't hurt nobody?" Holding up the satchel: "Whose life savings you think this is? You think burnin' down buildings don't hurt nobody? The difference between you and me is I know what I am."

They stared into one another's eyes, each caught in the other's hate, each feeling the weight of the pistols in their hands and the cold sweat on their necks and the imminence of gunfire from outside. They felt each second as a new disadvantage in the coming fight, and yet they could not look away. But Diana's hate was more practiced and her patience shorter and she brought her pistol up to Moreno's face.

A cry came from out front, and they turned toward the door. Another cry, insensible, and then another, and they realized that a chorus of voices was yelling Oh Christ Oh Christ. Suddenly the cries coalesced into a name, and Diana recognized it not as the Christ's but the Frogboy's.

"Otis! Otis! Come back! Otis!" The front door swung open, and Moreno and Diana swung their guns toward the figure pushing through, but they did not fire. Standing before them, shirtless, with a length of bandage winding around his chest trailing behind him into the mud, was Otis the Frogboy. The cries from outside abruptly stopped.

Otis stepped inside. He grunted maniacally, a protracted low gurgling whooot that frightened Diana for the meaning it couldn't convey. The Frogboy saw Kerr's body on the floor and stopped grunting and then started over again, whooot whooot whooot, and when he was finished, he looked up.

Diana met Otis's eyes for the second time that afternoon, and she saw there a look of inchoate pain so deep that for a moment she felt it as her own. It was a Medusa's gaze. Diana froze in place and stopped breathing and stopped hating and just stopped. The idea of time wound down its own coil in her mind. The sound of rain stopped reverberating off the roof, and the gusting wind became still, and the last traces of smoke in the bank hung suspended as if in amber. Diana gazed involuntarily deeper into Otis's eyes, and she saw there, beyond his pain and confusion, a broken mirror reflecting not light but darkness, and the darkness reflected darkness, and at the very center of this house of mirrors of darkness was a nothingness that Diana felt as herself.

Otis brought his hands up to his face. He clapped them together and time started again. He took another step inside. A long trail of drool fell from his lips. Without knowing why, Diana crouched down below the level of the windows and ran to him.

Chaos and Confusion

When Jonathan Vega rode into Tres Cruces with the rest of the posse and the seven runaway horses and the body of the marshal dragging behind, he sensed that something had changed since he'd left. The quiet on the streets had a peculiar, pregnant quality, and Jonathan could not attribute this entirely to his own agitation at the marshal's death. It was Alberto Torres who first recognized the damage to his stable, and the posse spurred their horses forward, but before anyone could rightly appreciate this new development, the bank behind them exploded and Jonathan's horse reared up and Doc Drumwright came running from the jail wailing like a banshee. The horses stamped and reared in the street, and the riders turned them this way and that, unsure what to do. The horses from Rancho Cielito strained at their leads, snorting and whinnying in terror, and the street was utterly in chaos.

The drunken doctor, still afrighted at the explosion and the sight of the dead marshal, ran up to Jonathan. He blurted out his suspicions about Burns and DeYoung and Kerr and Jackson incoherently. Saul came limping up fast from the other direction, brandishing a pistol, and Jonathan turned to his nephew, who told a different story, and Alberto Torres ignored them all and spurred his horse on toward his stable. DeYoung ran up from the barbershop and said the stable was set fire, which Jonathan had already figured out, and the appaloosa from Rancho Cielito broke free and bolted, and two men rode after it. For a time, there was such confusion that no one could tell which detail belonged to whose story and they mixed them up in their minds, until the smoke issuing from the bank finally trumped everything else. Jonathan fired his revolver into the air, quieting the people but riling the horses still more. He told a couple of the hands to get the horses down to the stable, and everyone else dismounted and clustered around Saul and Drumwright.

At last, Jonathan understood that there had been some killing and that Jackson was loose, and it was already evident that the bank was being robbed. Jonathan sent three men with Hargis to the rear entrance of the bank, and Collins took a pair of men himself to attack the front. They all set off at a run through the street.

The first man through the bank's front door was a roper from Rancho Mirabal, and Diana gunned him down, and before Collins could think to hold up, he dashed into the doorway himself. Collins felt Diana's first bullet in his shoulder not as a pain but as an involuntary buckling of his mind, as if he were seeing a hole open in the air before his eyes, a hole without depth, and then he felt the pain as a heavy heat in his whole arm, as if someone had thrown a burning blanket over his shoulder. He twisted and heard another shot but didn't feel it enter his back between his shoulder blades, and then he was on the ground with mud in his mouth.

Hargis ran unsteadily around the Panaderia Jimenez. He had fired guns before only for sport and he felt unsteady and cowardly, and angry that he had been selected to lead other men. When he and the three men in his charge reached the rear of the bank, Hargis motioned for a cowhand from Rancho Cielito to open the door, and this man turned the knob and threw himself into the door several times before a shot came from inside, and the door was riven open in the center and the cowhand fell backwards to the ground. The door opened and Hargis saw Diana with a rifle, and he dove out of the way. The two men with him followed his lead, and a single shot whirred into the air, and the door closed again. Hargis ran away, as fast as his feet would take him, in the direction of the telegraph office, and the other two men hid along the side of the bank.

When Jonathan and Doc Drumwright and Saul and Jerry DeYoung saw Collins gunned down, they came up short, and Jonathan led them at a sprint across the street. When they had reached the eaves of the marshal's office, they crouched down and huddled together. That's when they heard the shots from the rear of the bank, and they saw Hargis cross between the bank and the panaderia in full flight, and then there was silence.

Jonathan: "It ain't no use throwin' ourselves in front of their guns. How did Jackson get out?" No one answered. "What happened to Alberto's stable?" No one answered.

Drumwright, to Jerry: "Where's Burns?"

"I don't know."

"Where's Kerr?"

Jerry: "Dead."

Drumwright: "If you're in on this, we'll hang you, boy. By God!"

Jerry, protesting ardently: "I swear!"

Jonathan: "There wasn't no dynamite in Tres Cruces except what you brought, and somebody just blew the safe."

"My hand to god, we saw Kerr dead and that's all I know. Doc! Saul! Me and Burns was down at the stable along with you all. We couldn'ta done it."

"So where's Burns?"

"I don't know."

Jonathan: "Well, this ain't what I call cover. Let's get inside." They retreated into the marshal's office and remained just inside the doorway, peering out. No one moved and no shots were fired. Jonathan was rankled and furious. "They ain't comin' out, but we ain't gettin' in, either." He looked at each of the others in turn. "The goddamn stupidest thing I ever heard of."

A few long moments passed and no one had any ideas. The doctor pulled out his bottle and finished off his applejack and then tossed the bottle to the floor, while Jonathan looked at him contemptuously.

Drumwright: "What happened to the marshal?"

"Hell if I know."

"And the horses?"

"We found'em a few miles south, near the sand marshes at the edge of the Fortuna. The marshal face down, holding property deeds to Cielito."

"Property deeds?"

"And a love letter."

Drumwright tried to put this information together with the marshal's telegram, but he was too addled to make all the points line up. "Was he shot?"

"No."

"Broke his neck?"

"Not from the looks of it."

"Drowned?"

"Nobody knows. Dead."

There was another long silence, and Saul shifted his pistol from one hand to the other and fanned his shooting hand in the air in a vain attempt to dry the sweat from it. He looked suspiciously at DeYoung and saw from Drumwright's face that the doctor was drunk beyond help and maddened with some internal demon.

They saw a movement in the window of the Panaderia Jimenez, and the door to the bakery opened and a figure stepped into the street. Jonathan chambered a shell in his rifle and got a bead on the man, but as he stared hard through sheets of falling gray rain, he made out that it was Otis the Frogboy, half-dressed, slightly bent at the waist, eating at something in his hands. Otis staggered this way and that, tossed whatever he was eating aside, and then clomped clumsily along the walkway toward the bank.

Saul: "What's he doin' out there?"

They watched as Otis progressed in baby steps toward the bodies in front of the bank, and when he stood over them, he raised his hands in front of his face and clapped. He stepped around Collins's body, grasped the doorknob, pushed the door open and went into the bank. He stood in the doorway for a long time, and every moment they feared he'd be shot down. Finally, Otis took another step in and the door closed behind him.

"What in the name of. . .?"

Jonathan stood up straight and walked out under the eaves of the jail, and the rest joined him there. Lightning cracked and the thunder that followed thudded an extra beat into their hearts.

Still no sign came from the bank. Jonathan noticed a man from Cielito, huddled against the side of the bank, waving to him. The man spread his arms, hunched his shoulders and turned his palms upward, asking what to do. Jonathan held one hand palm outward and waved the other hand toward the ground, as if patting a dog on the head, and the man across the way nodded and crouched back down where he was.

Through the murky wet afternoon gloom, they saw a light flash in one of the bank windows, and the light wavered and went out and then grew brighter, as if someone had lit a lamp. Drumwright: "What the hell does Otis have to do with those scoundrels?"

Jonathan: "What the hell does Otis have to do with anything?"

The light moved below the window and then stayed still for a long moment, and then the door to the bank opened. There was some frantic movement in the doorway, and some figures low to the floor dodged out of sight, and then Otis stood there alone. He held a brown leather satchel out in front of him. He looked to his left, back inside the bank, and then he looked directly at Jonathan and the others. A female voice cried out unintelligibly, and the lamplight grew brighter and the Frogboy stepped out. He limped around Collins into the street.

Jonathan: "That was a woman's voice."

DeYoung: "You think they got a hostage?"

Jonathan thought of Diana and of the stranger Calderon from San Juan. He thought of the dead marshal and of Jackson and of the scene in his tavern when Pastor Charles was shot. He thought of shooting Otis down.

The Frogboy continued across the street toward them, taking labored steps, the bandages around his chest unfurling in the wind and rain. Otis's face seemed frozen in a clown's laugh.

DeYoung: "What's he got in the bag?"

Drumwright: "Maybe it's a message. Maybe they want to surrender."

Saul: "Maybe it's the money from the safe, as a peace offering."

Jonathan: "Maybe it's a decoy. Maybe they're gettin' away out the back." He looked over at the man from Rancho Cielito, crouched at the side of the bank, but the man hadn't budged, and there was no other sign of movement on the street but Otis teetering toward them.

As Otis drew closer, they could hear him grunting like a

dreaming dog, grunts like sobs, and Drumwright instinctively started out to meet him, to help him, but Jonathan barred the way with his rifle.

"No sense givin'em a clean shot, Doc."

The four men watched Otis's awkward approach with bated breath, until the sound of his grunts became pitiful and his misshapen face grew painful to behold. They discerned, in between the splattering of raindrops on the overhang above them and the splashing of water running off the roof and Otis's animal sobs, a peculiar, steady, barely audible hissing that seemed to come from Otis himself. The Frogboy had nearly gained the marshal's office when the satchel he held in front of him exploded.

A Mad Dash

When they heard the explosion, Diana and Moreno burst through the bank's back door with guns drawn, but no one appeared to challenge them. Moreno held Kerr's revolver and Diana carried her .32 in her left hand and Jonathan's Winchester rifle tucked under her right arm. She had taken the money and jewelry from the satchel and stuffed it underneath her clothing, and the extra ammunition in her mantle pockets flopped and banged against her hips.

They ran toward the barbershop, and as they crossed between the bank and the panaderia, they heard a shot and a bullet whined past them. They turned to face a cowboy, who fired again and missed. Diana shot twice in return and clipped the man in the right ankle. He cried out and fell, and Diana fired two more shots and missed. From behind, they heard another shot, and they turned to face another cowhand running from the other side of the bank. Diana stopped, steadied her aim, and squeezed off a round, and the man fired two more shots on the run and kept coming. Moreno cried out as if hit, but still he did not return fire, and Diana shot again and the man's legs came out from under him and he fell splayed. His body slid in the mud.

Diana: "Are you hit?" Blood ran down Moreno's arm and she saw a patch of raw red on his neck, where a bullet had nicked him. "Let's go!"

She ran and felt her boots catching at the hem of her dress, so that she almost stumbled, and she cursed her dress and cursed herself for being a woman. Moreno remained standing there and put his hand up to his neck, and when he saw his own blood on his fingers, he cried out and chased after Diana at a sprint.

They passed behind the telegraph office and saw the two horses still waiting for them where Diana had tied them behind the barbershop. Moreno's body burned with pure fear and he overtook Diana. He outraced her to the first horse and untied it. As he did so, David Burns stepped out from the far side of Drumwright's shop with his shotgun trained on Moreno.

Diana called a warning, but she couldn't get a clean angle for a shot around Moreno and the horses, and she stopped in her tracks. Moreno stood with his revolver pointed at the ground, his arm stiff, the horse's lead in his left hand.

Burns: "I figured y'all might be wantin' these horses."

Diana, screaming: "Shoot him, Moreno! Shoot him!" She looked over her shoulder to see another man coming around the corner of the panaderia.

Moreno stood unmoving, as if his feet were foundation stones and his head a rusted out weathervane blowing with the wind. The double-barrels of Hector Alvarado's shotgun in Burns's hands stared at Moreno like the devil's own vacant eyes.

"Nobody plays David Burns for a fool." He squeezed the shotgun's trigger and the hammer clacked against steel, and Burns took a comic step forward when the gun failed to recoil. He panicked and pulled the hammer back on the second barrel.

Diana ran around the horses. "Shoot him!"

Burns pulled the second trigger and again nothing happened and he realized he was carrying an empty gun. His heart beat wildly, and he felt a surge in his chest and he ran forward, grasping the shotgun by its barrel. As Burns approached, Moreno finally brought his revolver up, but his finger seemed frozen on the trigger, and he looked at the hateful face of David Burns rushing to kill him and still he could not pull the trigger.

Burns swung the butt end of his shotgun at Moreno's head, and the edge of it split Moreno's upper lip and broke his front teeth. Moreno's head snapped back and he fell. He felt as if his whole face had been rammed into his eyes. Blood gushed into his nose and he could not breathe and the world became a field of fiery green dots. He forced his eyes open, but the dots did not go away, and all Moreno could see was blackness shot through with bright green pinpoints of light, each one a pulsing shrill pain. The world spun.

Burns lifted his shotgun to deliver another blow to Moreno's prone body. Diana shot him flush in the back of the head with her rifle, and blood sprayed over Moreno as Burns's heavy body fell across him.

The man running up from the bank fired a volley of shots, and Diana returned fire. The man took cover around the side of the barbershop. Diana spent the rest of her bullets at him methodically, shooting into the corner of the building to keep him down. She ran over to Burns and Moreno lying in the same heap and took Kerr's revolver from Moreno's hand. The cowboy fired from around the barbershop, and the front leg of the horse nearest Diana collapsed and the horse cried awfully. Diana untied and mounted her own auburn mustang, and kicked it toward the Coronado Inn.

Shots followed her, but she did not turn to look or exchange fire. She bent low over the saddlehorn and kicked the horse viciously, and the terrified animal surged between her legs and found his stride and raced into the pouring rain and wind.

Diana cleared the Coronado Inn and gained the road east

toward the place where the ferry used to be. For a long moment, the gunfire stopped. As she topped the rise east of town, she heard a pair of shots, and she looked back to find Alberto Torres, riding alone, giving chase.

Torres whipped his horse and fired wildly with a pistol, but Diana's stolen mount was fresher by far and she quickly outdistanced him, and he receded behind her.

Diana's horse liked the mud and kicked up huge clumps and charged through pools. Diana felt the rain as hard pellets against her face. She blinked hard and squinted and then gave up on seeing anything but a gray green brown blur, and she trusted her horse to carry her to the river.

Rio Fuerte. She had thought about it and thought about it, but she had never come up with a better plan than charging into it and taking her chances. As the countryside raced by, she had time to contemplate the river, but there was nothing new to consider. Moreno had been right: there really was no way across it, except to fling yourself into its roiling currents and hope for the best, and the best seemed a quick death by collision or injury, better than the slow death of drowning. As Diana pictured herself leaping with this auburn quarterhorse into the water and sweeping downstream and fighting across the current, she tried to feel the peace of her impending death, which at least would not be at the hands of another.

If Moreno had never talked to her, she thought, none of this would have happened. If the storm had never come. . . If the ferry on the Fuerte had never been swept away. . . If Burns hadn't. . . If Jonathan had never. . . If her own mother, whom she'd never seen, had just. . . If there really had been a Wilfredo Calderon. . . But there was no single stroke of fate she could think of that explained why she was galloping out of Tres Cruces, leaving its streets strewn with bodies, no reason she could think of for Moreno's stupid scheme to begin with, no real reason for Jackson to have shot that preacher. She was a thirty-four year old whore for no reason she could think of, and she angrily recognized that Moreno had been right about that, too. There were no reasons. She kicked her horse on, and she decided that, when she came to the river, she would ride into it without stopping.

THE LAST DESPERATE ACT

When Diana reached Rio Fuerte, her horse lathered and foaming, the river was a wide roiling brown tumult whose rushings and crashings mixed with the heavy thudding of clear silvery water falling from the clouds, until all the air was filled with the sound of water and the smell of water and the feel of water, and the earth was sodden with water, and nothing moved upon the face of the waters but Diana and her horse. Diana urged her horse into the river at a gallop, but the horse slowed and balked, lunged to the side and reared up, nearly throwing her from the saddle. She reined the horse in and told him that no harm would come to him if he went into the river. She kicked but again he balked.

Diana looked at the opposite shore, probably two hundred yards away, and she saw the white foam of the brackish brown water as it swept around boulders. She saw flotsam and debris washing by, and she told herself that she would make it across, though in her secret heart of hearts she did not believe that she would. She believed that she would be swept away by the river and drowned and that her body would be torn to shreds by the current and the rocks, and that she would be eaten by scavenger birds downstream, and part of her wished she had been killed by a bullet, and part of her wished she had never been born, and part of her wished she had burned down every building in Tres Cruces and shot every last son of a bitch the length and breadth of the town.

She trotted a little way downriver, trying to judge the speed of the current, trying to imagine at what point she would strike the opposite side if she entered the river just here, just there. But no place looked any better than another, and finally she just closed her eyes and willed her horse with special force and love for his innocent sacrifice to jump into the river with her. She kicked him again, and this time the horse leapt into the river and almost immediately was in up to his neck and they were floundering. Diana clung to the horse's neck, and he turned his head downstream and found his footing and then struggled through the slop and mud and out onto the bank again, and labored up out of the water. Diana's left foot was twisted in the stirrup, and she wrangled her leg against the saddle and against the horse and when she finally righted herself, she felt tired and scared and defeated. She was facing away from the river, and now she saw something that amazed her.

Alberto Torres was loping up through the storm, still waving his pistol in a marathon pantomime of rage. Torres fired his pistol wildly, though he was out of range.

Diana dismounted and noticed how much heavier her dress had become since her foray into the river. She was utterly sodden. It hadn't occurred to her that she would sink like a stone with yards of waterlogged cloth draped around her body, and for just a moment she remembered what Moreno had said about her intelligence, and she felt genuinely stupid.

She cast off her mantle and took a moment to shoot at Torres, who was bearing down on her. In a stroke of sheer luck, she hit Torres' horse, and Torres jumped out from under it and rolled several times in the mud.

Diana untied the back of her dress and tore at it until it loosened. She struggled out of it and let it fall to the ground. A bundle of bills fell with it, and she picked the money up and stuffed it into the waistband of her underwear, and she dropped more bills into her camisole, so that her belly bulged with money. As Torres stood up and came at her again, she spent the remaining rounds in Kerr's revolver in vain, and then turned and looked toward the river. She ran and threw herself in.

She was swept violently downstream and her knees scraped something on the riverbed. Her head went under, and she pushed off from the bottom and kicked and paddled. The water was surprisingly cool, and she was thrown down a cascade as the river fell along the rocky terrain. She heard a gunshot. She tried to look back, but she could not see her horse or Torres or either shore but only a tiny sliver of horizon where the sky met the river and, below that, turbulent brown water.

She paddled with all her might and made some progress toward the center. She swallowed a great mouthful of water, and for a moment she could not breathe, and then she was gasping and her arms felt heavy. She dog-paddled to keep her head above water, and the river swept her sideways, and pulled her head under anyway. She was choking underwater. Dynamic competing currents in the river tugged her arms and legs at strange angles away from one another. She could not find a rhythm for her strokes. She gulped water. The river felt like solid flowing ribbons of force, fast and powerful, and no matter how she fought them or in which direction, they pulled against her.

The water spit her up to the surface and she gasped and coughed. She did not recognize the landscape sweeping by. She was in the exact middle of the river, and her arms felt heavy and she seemed to have no control over her legs at all, and she saw all at once that the banks of the river dipped suddenly, and she was underwater.

She got caught in a rip current below a boulder in the center of a waterfall, and she looked up through the crashing water with her eyes wide and tried to push free, but she saw only flowing murky darkness and the current held her down. All at once she felt buoyant and she broke the surface and saw foaming white water, and the boulder right above her, and she took a gasping lungful of air and was sucked under again. She flailed her arms and fought, but the current held her down and she felt her toes sucked into a crevice where the boulder met the riverbed, and just as she thought her lungs would burst, the river spit her up to the surface again, and again she took in a lungful of air, and she breathed water up her nose and felt strangled.

Diana gave up hope. Unable to struggle any more and unable to keep herself from gasping water, she resigned herself to death, and as she did so, her body rolled out from under the boulder and she found herself downstream, slapping at the water with her arms, gasping staccato bursts of air. She hit her head against something in the river and a tree branch slid past her. She grabbed at it, but it was too small to support her weight, and she went under holding it and then came back up with her hair plastered across her eyes, trailing across her nose and into her mouth, as heavy as a bit. She gagged and tried to spit it out and she was underwater again.

When she surfaced, only her shoulders and neck responded when she commanded. She was exhausted. By sheer force of will, she made a few strokes, but she was unsure now which direction she was facing, and the banks of the river merged with the river itself into one long dirty brown horizon in nauseating motion. She told her legs to kick. She breathed a mouthful of water and went under again.

As she sank, she stopped feeling the motion of the current and became one with the river. She was dark motion and all around her was dark motion, and there was no light any more. For a long time, longer than she would have thought possible, she was conscious but her consciousness consisted entirely of coursing fluid blackness, womb-like but for its turbulence, and she began to feel quite peaceful and comfortable, and then, to her annoyance, she felt a disruption in her peace, as if a ray of light had found her across an ocean of darkness. She felt a strange thudding that seemed to come not from her own body, but from somewhere very far away, as if she were feeling someone else's sensations, and then she felt a pain in her chest and her head banged against something hard, and she realized that she was above the surface of the current again, and that she had stopped moving.

She coughed and sputtered and gagged out a string of clear slime, then she heaved and spit up more slime and coughed some more. Her right wrist hurt. She did not understand. Water still rushed all around her, over her, but somehow she was stable and she lay halfway out of the river.

After several minutes of just lying and breathing, she lifted her head. She found herself splayed across a shelf of rock, the water cascading over her body through half a dozen cataracts in a wall of stones above her, her ribs smarting against the rock and her right arm behind her back in an awkward position.

It took some time for Diana to realize that she was still alive, stranded somehow in the Fuerte. The shelf she lay across was slick and slippery and the current strong, and she could see over the lip of the shelf to the waterfall plummeting three or four feet down below. She moved her head gingerly back and forth, and after several minutes of fearful, delicate, and difficult repositionings, she was able to get up on her elbows. Every so often the current would shift slightly, and her hand would slide and she would lose her balance and almost fall crashing over the waterfall, and she would have to regain her equilibrium ever so carefully. She felt weak and soggy and defeated. At last, she steadied herself and looked toward the shore.

The first thing she saw surprised her no end: the sinewy green branch of a palo verde tree, the very end of which was no more than three feet from her. She followed the branch down and saw that she was merely ten feet from the riverbank, next to a clump of palo verde trees whose bases were obscured below the flood. She looked downriver. Beyond the waterfall below her was a little pool, and then another little fall, and then a stretch of relatively placid water just a few feet from land. If she could somehow manage this little stretch of falls, or if she could summon the strength to jump to the clump of palo verdes, she would have reached the other side.

The rain was falling steadily straight down now, lighter than it had been, and it seemed warmer than it had earlier in the afternoon. She tried to imagine herself leaping for the palo verde branch, but the rock beneath her was slippery and she felt sick and weak. She imagined jumping into the falls below and being sucked under by another rip current, and she felt even weaker and wasn't sure she could escape again.

After a long time of balancing unsteadily on the little shelf of rock, Diana tried to position herself for a jump at the nearest branch, but it quickly became apparent that the rock was simply too slick and the current too strong, that she would be swept away if she tried it; so she looked down at the cascade below and picked a spot where the current seemed weakest. She readied herself. She breathed deeply and looked longingly at the riverbank and at the pale green and brown of the palo verdes and the mud clumps of land.

She could not bring herself to push off from the rock. Twice she counted to three but remained stone still, until a tree branch swept over the rock wall behind her and dislodged a stone that rolled past her, and the branch nearly knocked her into the water. She shoved off toward the trees.

Her hand slipped out from the rock and her breast scraped across the stone and she found herself sideways in the water and then upside down and falling, head first, and she was deep underwater. Her hand struck something, and she pushed off of it, and her body tumbled so that her heels were above her head. She righted herself, and then she was falling through water again. She became disoriented and pushed herself accidentally toward the bottom, and then felt lightheaded and weak and topsy-turvy. Instinctively, through some deep animal memory, she curled herself into a ball and rolled up to the surface.

When her head broke the water, she saw a bank jutting out into the water and a little pool behind it, just a few feet away. With her last dregs of energy and will, she smacked the water with uncoordinated, ungainly strokes and let the current carry her into the reverse eddies of the pool, and suddenly she found herself in a calm. The current of the water pushed her up against the sod, trying to roll her back into the body of the river.

She scrabbled frantically at the earth and her fingers found a root to cling to, and she dug her nails into the muck and held on fast. She let her body float then for a minute, saving up the will to heave herself out of the water. She pulled herself out to her waist and thought she wouldn't have the strength to make it, and then she pulled herself out a little more, and then fell back into the river, holding onto the palo verde root with numbed red fingers. After another abortive attempt, she realized that she would have to pull herself out at that very moment or lose her grip and be swept down river, and she felt a surge of rage in her chest. Yelling from deep in her abdomen as she pulled, she lifted her torso up onto land and beached herself on a spit of sod.

She had made it across.

It took her the rest of the afternoon to struggle up away from the river, to a muddy spot a few feet away under a palo verde tree. All of the money and jewelry from the bank was gone. Her underwear was torn and her chest and shoulders bruised, and her face and arms scratched. Her right wrist was swollen and she had a knot on her left knee. She wasn't sure exactly where she was along the river or how far it was to the nearest town.

She flopped down on her back and drifted in and out of an exhausted and world-weary sleep. Heavy clouds drowned out the light, and when the sun set beneath a black veil of rain, Diana listened to the regular patter of the raindrops and the irregular plunk-plunk-plunk from the branches of the tree above her and the rushing whorl of the river below.

She was free.

DRUMWRIGHT REMEMBERS

After the first volley of shots from the bank, Hargis had run as fast as his legs would carry him to El Charro, where he hid behind a pantry cabinet in the kitchen, within view of the back door. He held his pistol out in front of him, equally ready to shoot or to flee. He felt as frightened and small and defenseless as a field mouse and felt no shame at all for his cowardice. He wished only that the shooting would stop and that he could remain out of harm's way.

Hargis heard the explosion of the dynamite in Otis's bag, and he saw Diana ride by and Alberto Torres after her, and then a tense calm enveloped the air around him and the shooting did stop. There was no sound but his own exaggeratedly shallow breathing and the relentless crashing of the rain. Still, he remained crouched in El Charro's kitchen till he saw Alberto Torres ride back into town, this time on Diana's quarterhorse. Hargis stood cautiously, stepped out the door and walked back into the wet and muck.

The first thing he saw as he emerged was even more gunfire: Alberto Torres dismounted and stood over the wounded mustang lying in the mud behind Doc Drumwright's barbershop. Torres emptied two slugs from his .44 Remington into the horse's skull. Torres then turned his attention to the body of David Burns.

Hargis walked toward him. As he approached, Torres suddenly whirled and dropped to one knee and raised his pistol, ready to shoot. Hargis stared into the wide barrel of the .44 and cried out in surprise. He realized that he was carelessly pointing his own gun at Torres, and he flung the gun away and threw his hands up over his head. His boot heel slipped, and he fell down on his tailbone in the mud. Torres lowered the hammer of his pistol slowly back into its cradle and stood up straight, scowling.

Torres spat: "That whore. That bitch."

Hargis, trying to sound poised: "You catch her?"

"She jumped into the river."

Hargis looked a question, but Torres dismissed it with a dour shake of his head. Torres pointed at Burns's body and then raised his hand in exasperation and let it slap hard against his thigh. "That bitch. Did you see my stable?"

Hargis wallowed out of the mud and got to his feet, and now they heard Doc Drumwright's voice shouting urgent commands from the other side of the building. Torres motioned for Hargis to follow him around the barbershop.

Drumwright was standing before the door of his shop, waving his right arm in a wild windmill motion. A pair of cowboys from Rancho Mirabal approached carrying Saul's unconscious body. Saul's left arm was bleeding where a scraggled shard of glass stuck out of it, and there was so much blood on his face that he was difficult to look at for long: he had nasty abrasions across his cheeks and nose, part of which seemed to be missing. The doctor himself sported cuts around both eyes and his spectacles were gone.

Drumwright: "You all hurt?" Hargis and Torres shook their heads no. "Then give me a hand."

They followed Drumwright into the barbershop, and the whole company gasped in unison. On the floor in front of them, seated slumped with his back against the medicine cabinet, lay Moreno. His chin and chest were covered with blood and his body was caked in so much mud that he looked like a clay figure; his front teeth were missing, his upper lip was torn, but, more disturbingly to the doctor, he was surrounded by half a dozen empty bottles and vials.

The doctor rushed over and examined the little containers and threw up his hands. He felt for a pulse in Moreno's neck.

"Dead?"

"Soon enough." Holding up vials: "He ate up all my laudanum and opium. It looks like he swallowed half the drugs in the chest." Motioning for the cowboys to take Saul's body into the operating room: "So much for anesthetic."

Drumwright told Hargis and Torres to reconstruct his operating tables and to lay the body of Pastor Charles on the floor in the back. When they were finished, the doctor sent them back into the street to find everyone who was injured and bring them in.

As Hargis and Torres were leaving, Saul suddenly regained consciousness with a start and a scream. The doctor tried to calm him, but Saul kept screaming. His eyes grew as wide as egg cups, and the doctor finally determined that Saul couldn't hear, that the blast of dynamite had deafened him. The doctor yelled at Hargis and Torres to go on out, and they left Drumwright and the two ranch hands struggling to keep Saul still on the makeshift operating table.

Hargis and Torres found bodies lying twisted all around the bank, some with men or women hovering over them, some as lonely and heaped into themselves as fallen scarecrows. The marshal's porch had completely collapsed, and Hargis noticed Jerry DeYoung sitting in front of it with eyes as glazy as spun sugar. Jerry was rocking himself ever so slightly and cupping his left elbow with his right hand, which was dripping blood.

Hargis: "You all right?"

"I guess so."

"You wanna have the doctor look at that?"

Jerry appeared not to understand the question, so Hargis pointed at his elbow, and Jerry looked down as if seeing it for the first time. He took his hand away. The bone above Jerry's elbow was broken and poking through his skin, and Hargis felt like vomiting. He coaxed Jerry to his feet and helped him walk to the barbershop.

* * * * *

By the time Drumwright was finished that night, he had practiced nearly every stitching, extracting, bone-setting, tourniqueting and salving technique he had ever read about in his journals, and he had invented a few of his own. Though there were relatively few gunshot victims who survived long enough for Drumwright to treat them, the ones who did had multiple injuries of a wide variety, including not just bullet holes and slugs lodged in flesh but sprains and broken bones from odd twists and falls and shock from blood loss, and Drumwright was forced to work with no painkiller besides liquor. On top of that, when the sun set, he was reduced to cauterizing and sewing and setting by lamplight, and there was a great deal of moaning and yelling, and Drumwright was exhausted by the strain of the work, both physical and mental. He turned his entire shop and Hargis's telegraph office into makeshift hospital wards. Despite his effort, when he was finished, he still tallied ten corpses and a few more hopeless cases. It wasn't until after midnight when he finally staggered down to the Coronado Saloon, sat down at the bar and poured himself a very large glass of redeye.

In the lamplight, Drumwright looked at his haggard reflection in the mirror of the walnut backbar. He knew he was lucky even to have his eyesight, the way his spectacle lenses had shattered in the dynamite blast that had killed Jonathan and Otis. He saw the streaky scabby cuts around his eye sockets and knew that he would be scarred, that his flesh was too old to heal neatly. He drank.

"So. Diana."

Drumwright recalled the knife cut to Diana's shoulder, the cut that he had treated only that morning, a morning that now seemed like long years past, and he thought of Jonathan's hot and rancorous temper. He was amazed that he hadn't deduced Diana's involvement in all these calamities from the start. It was so clear in hindsight, yet he still had difficulty reconciling himself to the idea that Diana was capable of such viciousness. When had it come to this? he wondered. Such a lot of damage wrought by such a small woman. He gingerly touched a cut above his right eye and winced through the whisky.

He tried to imagine what had brought Diana to such desperation. Had she gone mad in the rain? Had Jonathan finally struck one blow too many? Though he had known Diana since she was nine years old, he could not remember her clearly as a child; he thought of her only and always as a cynical, embittered, tired woman. Yet, as far as he knew, Diana had never lifted a finger to harm anyone before, not even in her own defense. She had never had a truly violent bone in her body. When had it come to this?

He remembered Diana naked, in his operating room, as he treated her for cuts and bruises or body lice, or the effects of the miscarriages she induced. He remembered her in a lemon-yellow Mother Hubbard dress, with her hair up in a chatelaine twist, drunk to the gills, flitting around the Coronado Saloon after the Rodriguez Vein had first been struck, bantering with a packed house of miners, her voice spiked with sarcasm. He remembered Diana riding into town in the back of a buckboard wagon, exhausted and stupefied, after a "business" trip to the

Crutchfield Camp on the Fortuna, where they were panning for gold. "A baker's dozen of corpses by tomorrow morning."

Diana hadn't had an easy life—but who had? He reached for the bottle and poured himself another redeye. In the dim, flattened reflection in the mirror, the bottleneck pointed directly at his chin and the spout of amber liquor fell in a wavering line down his Adam's apple. The bottle gugged. He turned it back upright and looked into the whisky he had just poured as if supplicating an oracle. "Was it really this bad, Diana? This bad?"

He took another deep drink. He breathed in the sharp chiles-and-molasses of the redeye and stared at his mirrored face as if it were someone else's and listened unconsciously to the hard rain, the racket of which now seemed eternal and necessary. As his head sank into his folded arms on the bar and he succumbed to sleep, Drumwright for a single split second recalled another Diana, as if in a dream, a Diana lost to the world: he remembered her as a little girl, in a moment of sunshine and dry air, the blithe optimism of a fine spring day. She wore a pretty blue dress and sprinted across a field above Rio Fuerte, trailing a bright red Chinese kite on a string, laughing over her shoulder at the kite-tail bobbing above the heather.

The Uneventful Disappearance
of Alexia Bauza

No one had thought to record exactly which day the storm had started. When it finally relented and the clouds with their towering black pillars of rain rolled away across the Menodoc Plateau toward Holguin and left the skies over Tres Cruces shimmery blue, no one knew how long the ordeal had lasted. Some said forty days and forty nights, though some said more and some said less; but whatever the exact length of time, when the storm was over, no rainbow arched above Tres Cruces, and no one spoke of covenants or promises.

At first, the townspeople celebrated the break in the weather by sitting out sunning themselves or taking long walks through the muddy fields beyond town. Occasionally, as they sat by the banks of the agitated Fuerte or the roaring torrent of the Fortuna, they encountered a drover from one of the local ranches riding the opposite banks and they shouted bits and pieces of news at one another. In this way, they learned that Potterville was now nothing more than splinters and mud and that most of the temporary Indian villages that routinely drifted to and fro across the flats had disappeared. The ruin of crops in the flood promised hardship and hunger for the coming winter. Telegraph lines were down as far away as Algodones. The entire length and breadth of the flats was in disarray. But the most urgent reports that reached them came from Rancho Cielito, where a search had been underway for several weeks for Alexia Bauza, youngest daughter of Jesús Bauza, the ranch's patriarch.

Alexia was the wealthiest and most prominent among many who were missing in the wake of the floods, and men from Rancho Cielito came and hollered inquiries across the Fortuna, first about her and then about the marshal. The townsfolk told the men that the marshal was dead, and the ranchers took this news grimly.

Both the Fuerte and the Fortuna remained unpassable for nearly two weeks after the rain stopped, and in that time the food in Tres Cruces finally gave out and everyone was reduced to daily half-pint rations of beans. The mood in town returned to its former bleakness, and now their wagging bellies and the relentless heat of the naked sun convinced the townsfolk that they had gone from bad to worse. They took to lying in their beds all day or skulking in the common rooms and taverns once again. The whisky was the last thing used up, and Mr. and Mrs. Mathers noted with consternation just how much of it there must have been in Tres Cruces all along. Doc Drumwright finally drank the last drop of alcohol in town and shortly thereafter lay incapacitated on his bed for several days, sweating and screaming with delirium tremens. Finally, a handful of men from Rancho Cielito, led by Jesús Bauza himself, forded the Fortuna and rode into town.

They dismounted at the Coronado Inn, and Jesús Bauza dismissed the weak backslapping and handclapping and cheering of the gaunt disheveled townspeople with a somber, businesslike demand to see the marshal's effects. When this request met only silence, Bauza asked for Jonathan Vega. This request also cast a pall. Bauza noticed the tourniquet on Jerry DeYoung's arm and the disfigurement of Saul's face and the funereal air beneath the celebration of his arrival.

Bauza: "Then it's true? It's all true, the story I heard?"

Hargis, stepping forward: "Jonathan and the marshal and

a dozen others."

"All dead?" Searching their faces: "And Alexia, my daughter?"

The crowd in front of the Coronado Inn looked one to another, and when they shook their heads no, Bauza turned to his men with his heart in his throat, beseeching with his eyes, but they too had nothing to offer him. Bauza, yelling: "Is my daughter among the dead?"

Alberto Torres: "Your daughter has not been seen in Tres Cruces, señor." He offered a terse narration of the events surrounding the seven horses from Rancho Cielito, which were now stabled across the street in Torres' burned-out barn; and he recounted the marshal's fate and the property deeds found on the marshal's body, and told of the letter the marshal was carrying, signed by Alexia. Bauza demanded the letter, but Torres informed him that it had been destroyed in an explosion. He gave Bauza a brief, accurate account of the fires and the bank robbery and the blast that had killed Jonathan, and said that Jonathan had been carrying Alexia's letter with him at the time of the explosion, and only shreds of it remained.

Bauza looked around him as if seeing Tres Cruces for the first time. He saw the damage to Torres' stable, and to the marshal's office and the bank. "Then it was all true? And no one has seen my daughter?"

The crowd murmured no and averted their eyes, and Bauza asked if the doctor had not survived. They told him that Drumwright had in fact survived, and that he was lying in a fit of tremors and madness in his barbershop, and, in any event, that he was no more competent to comment on Alexia's whereabouts than anyone else. "And no one has seen my daughter?" He repeated the question as if too stunned to receive the true answer, hoping that enough repetitions would elicit the response he needed.

They led Bauza into the saloon, poured him a glass of water and finally coaxed out of him an account of Alexia's disappearance. It was uneventful and the more disturbing to Jesús Bauza for its lack of drama: one day, shortly after the rains had begun, she had vanished from Rancho Cielito. As far as they could tell, she had taken no personal effects, no money that they knew of, and she had left no trail for anyone to follow. They had discovered the disappearance of the seven horses at this same time, and they had been inclined to believe that the one disappearance had something to do with the other. They feared that Alexia had been kidnapped or killed by rustlers.

However, in the course of examining Alexia's belongings, Bauza had found a single letter folded neatly in her Bible, a confession of love from the marshal, and he had thereafter assumed that the marshal was responsible for spiriting her away. Bauza had formed search parties and combed the flats from Holguin all the way to Santa Elena through the worst gales and tempests; but after weeks of searching and discovering not even a footprint, they had given up and sat agitatedly waiting all this time to cross into Tres Cruces and demand an explanation from the marshal. They had thought to find Alexia herself stranded here with the rest of them.

Hargis again told the story of the telegram that the marshal had sent to San Luis as the storm had begun, and he again recited the contents of the telegram from memory; but this information baffled Jesús Bauza and the men of Rancho Cielito as much it had everyone else. No one had ever heard of a Señora Repilado of San Luis or of a Repilado family anywhere on the flats. Jesús Bauza's face became wooden and blank, and the light left his eyes.

After a few vain attempts to console Bauza, and after a few halfhearted efforts at explaining the marshal's mysterious telegram, which had wearied the people of Tres Cruces for weeks, an awkward silence descended on the tavern and everyone shifted their weight and cleared their throats and tried not to look at Bauza. Finally, their stomachs demanded action. Now that the Fortuna was passable, Hargis suggested that a party be formed to ride to Holguin and see if the people there had fared any better in the storm, and to bring back supplies. The Coronado Saloon returned to life and movement, and men retired to their rooms to gather clothing and equipment for the trip. Hargis and Torres and DeYoung sympathetically shook the hands and squeezed the shoulders of the men from Cielito. Mr. and Mrs. Mathers tried to comfort Bauza with sighs and doleful looks.

After many weeks of despair, the people of Tres Cruces were once again filled with hope, and they moved with purpose and discussed in covetous tones the items they wished to bring back from Holguin. They cautiously looked forward to real meals and regular contact with the outside world, a return to normalcy and forgetting.

But Jesús Bauza just sat with his men, at the very table where Jackson had gunned down Pastor Charles, an island of stillness and silence in the sudden swell of activity. No one had seen his favorite daughter.

EPILOGUE
THREE YEARS LATER

A Measure of Justice

The streets of San Luis were paved with cobblestones, and the mills on the Verde River to the east of town churned loudly day and night. The buildings of downtown San Luis reverberated with whining scraping brakes, clanging bells and the whooshing steam of the trains traveling across the plains, the trains that huffed implacably east or west toward the oceans or southwest across the monotonous desert flats to the Gulf. San Luis was a cosmopolitan city, with old established families who had lived there since it was the northern jewel of Mexico, since it was a tiny piece of Spain, a far-flung outpost of old France. There were even some criollos of Quapatec descent whose ancestors had occupied the Verde Valley before Europeans had set foot in North America. Living among these descendants of the valley's rich past were Chinese, Japanese, Irish and Hungarian laborers, and African blacks—former slaves—all struggling to find their place in the voracious Manifest Destiny of America. The valley's rich mud and clay now bricked the factories, apartments and massive buttresses of the train station of San Luis, which gave the city a nostalgic European ambiance, despite the dusty wide-openness of the surrounding plains, and despite the unsettled matter of the renegade Pichua Indians to the northwest. San Luis hosted the country's most popular literary figures on their lecture tours, attracted renowned opera singers and entertainers, and was becoming one of the most important and influential of the rising Western metropolises.

The name San Luis was regularly on the tongues of politicians and tycoons in New York, Washington and sometimes even London. It was a city of bulk and progress, a stepping-stone from the bustling crowded east to the burgeoning wide open loneliness and brimming promise of the west.

When Diana had arrived in San Luis, she was insensible of the luck that had guided her, in a meandering line, across the Menodoc Plateau to this city. Her main concerns after dragging herself out of Rio Fuerte had been the coyotes that howled at her just after sunset, and the bands of horsemen that crossed and recrossed her trail, and the fits of shivering and fever she developed from malnutrition, thirst and exposure. She ate mesquite bark and grass and cactus pads, and she pricked her flesh with countless brushy golden needles. She watched lightning strike too near too many times, and her legs often gave out as she traversed the flats, her hair tangled and matted. The effort to leave Tres Cruces had been trivial compared to the effort of lifting one leg after another, tramping through hostile Indian country toward an unknown destination and an unknowable fate. It was only through force of will and spite for Tres Cruces that she kept going and finally came to a well-marked trail, where she simply lay down in exhaustion and hoped against hope that the next travelers through would be decent folk rather than Indians or cowboys or drifters, who might rape and kill her just for sport.

As it happened, Diana lay on that nameless trail only half a day before Cyriack Kanakaredes, a recent immigrant from Greece, discovered her; Kanakaredes lifted her into the saddle of his horse and rode her to his home in San Luis, where his wife Ena fed Diana chicken broth. They bathed her, bundled her into bed and attended to her constantly until she responded to their cooing inquiries. When she understood that she had arrived in San Luis safe and sound, Diana claimed amnesia and took great care never to mention her real name, or Tres Cruces, or the Coronado Saloon, or the names Vega, Drumwright or Mathers. She claimed no kinfolk and no knowledge of how she had arrived there, where she had come from, or what she had been doing on the forbidding Menodoc Plateau alone. Ena Kanakaredes and all of her friends from the tiny Greek community of San Luis tsk-tsked and fawned over Diana and grew indignant toward Diana's fate on her behalf, and Diana pretended confusion and concern and despair at her lost identity; but in reality she could not have been happier to have drowned her past in the roiling Rio Fuerte.

Since she claimed not even to remember her own name, the Greek women named her Zoe, which means life, because they said that only someone with an abundance of life could have survived out on the flats alone, injured, starving and nearly naked. While Diana practiced calling herself Zoe over and over again every day in the mirror, the Greek women included her in their company, and she learned who her new friends were and what she needed to do to remain among them.

Ena Kanakaredes helped Zoe get a job carding wool in a factory, and for several months Zoe gave all of her money to the Kanakaredes family in gratitude for saving her and helping her. She slept in their common room on a pallet made of rag rugs and worn blankets. She learned Greek and accompanied Ena to Saturday coffee klatches and Greek Orthodox church services. After nine months had passed, she began setting money aside for herself and walking through the tenements of San Luis looking for a room to rent.

Beyond her hatred of the smell of wool and the chemicals used to process it, Zoe felt utterly indifferent about her job. Though she was unused to labor and resented her fatigue at the end of every day, at least the job was not humiliating, and she found that her abhorrence of her own body relaxed somewhat. She was able to take some pleasure in the simple efforts of daily life; but she had not escaped sexual servitude in Tres Cruces to become a wool carder in the tiny, clannish Greek community of San Luis, and on bad days the urge to flee the alien women who surrounded her and their strange language and volatile emotions swelled in her chest. This life was not what she had imagined, not what she wanted, not what she would settle for.

She continued carding wool for another year, and she continued surveying the tenement buildings and shotgun houses near the Verde River, poking her head into other factories and shops nearby. Despite her reluctance to embrace the community of Greek women, Diana thought of herself more and more as Zoe Kanakaredes, and she cooked lamb and cheese pastries, made yogurt sauces, and tossed salads with spinach and walnuts and olive oil. Her own reticence notwithstanding, she felt accepted by this strange extended family. She remained supremely untroubled by the murders she had committed and the destruction she had wrought: her conscience did not bother her, and she did not dream of Tres Cruces. To Zoe, Diana's acts were not crimes but balancing weights in the scales of justice, and the fact that she had murdered innocent people did not trouble her, since she considered none of those among the dead to be genuinely innocent.

After two years of living with the Kanakaredes, Zoe took a room of her own in the house of Maricela Hernandez, the widow of a prosperous industrialist. Maricela's late husband had made his fortune manufacturing cement during one of San Luis's regular building booms, and she lived in a single-story brick house whose property sloped down to the Verde River. It was through Maricela that Zoe got a job in the industrial laundry near the cement factory, washing hospital sheets, hotel bedding and table linens from railroad dining cars. Though

Zoe's economic station did not improve with the job, she felt herself one step further removed from her old identity—from Tres Cruces and from whoring—and despite the long monotonous hours and the special harshness of the lye, she took satisfaction in making the dirty things of the world clean again.

Through the laundry, Zoe found the position she had always wanted but had never known she wanted: as she washed and sorted bedsheets and linens, Zoe came into regular contact with women from the local hospitals and charitable organizations. She became interested in the orphanages of San Luis, in the plight of the children she heard about, who had no families, no homes and no prospects. Their stories reminded her of her own. She began volunteering at Casita Santa Teresa, a home for orphaned girls, and she found discussing everyday things with the girls astonishingly cathartic. She could relive her own traumas and humiliations at a safe remove and turn them into comfort and understanding for the frightened young girls.

Her dedication while volunteering was so unflagging, and her enthusiasm for even the most tedious tasks so great, that she eventually won a regular position as a House Sister at Casita Santa Teresa. Though the pay varied between little and nothing, depending upon the philanthropic contributions that came into the orphanage, Zoe felt that the life she had led as a prostitute in Tres Cruces, its debasements and terrors and despair, had finally been redeemed. Her sadness at the irrevocable waste of her own life up to that point was ameliorated by the idea that she could save others from a similar fate, and she enjoyed the innocence that still flourished in some of the girls. Their naiveté allowed Zoe a measure of simplicity and peace herself, and she settled in at Casita Santa Teresa and made the orphanage her home.

* * * * *

In the three years since the flood, Doc Drumwright had watched the decline of Tres Cruces accelerate. As long as Rancho Cielito and Rancho Mirabal remained prosperous, Tres Cruces would never completely die, but it was becoming more a way station than a town, an emergency supply depot for the ranchers. The Hidalgo Trust Bank did not reopen after the robbery, and the residents of Tres Cruces were forced to keep their money and valuables in Holguin, Santa Elena or in their mattresses; and when the old marshal was replaced, the new marshal established his main office in Holguin and passed through Tres Cruces only on routine checks or during crises.

Saul, whose hearing partially returned in the months following the dynamite blast but whose face remained permanently disfigured, took over the Coronado Inn, but he didn't even try to replace Diana: thus, the principal reason for local ranch hands to visit the Coronado disappeared and Saul's business suffered. The residents of Tres Cruces became resigned to their moribund fate.

The only business that continued to prosper was the telegraph station, which was rebuilt promptly and remained the only quick form of communication between the ranches and the outside world; but the business of the station was not enough to occupy Hargis full time. He developed the habit of drinking tequila with Doc Drumwright at all hours of the day, and they sat together in the telegraph office or the barbershop, playing chess distractedly and listening to each other's tedious narratives.

As he always had, Drumwright continued to make semi-annual trips to San Luis for medical supplies and books, to see cabarets and plays, and to drink a better variety of alcohol than he could afford regularly in Tres Cruces. Most of these trips ended in drunken squalor, and this was true of his visit to San Luis three years after Diana fled.

In San Luis, Doc Drumwright almost never ventured down to the Verde River: it was the city's industrial area, a section of factories, dilapidated tenements and convalescent homes. Whenever Drumwright was confronted with an entire sanatorium filled with consumptive patients or other hopeless cases, or he saw poor ragged immigrants huddled together on stoops with yellow eyes and wan expressions, he felt more like a barber than a doctor. At those times, he viewed the medical profession with distaste and longed for his barbershop, where his authority was unquestioned and his time invaluable, and where real suffering remained relatively rare. However, on this particular trip, Drumwright heard of a new riverboat with an especially racy cabaret, and he heard that the boat was docked at a pier near the industrial section, near a long row of mills, soup kitchens and orphanages. Always eager to explore fresh opportunities for drink and gambling, the doctor found himself walking one evening in a drunken haze through the poorer section of town, toward the new riverboat cabaret.

His hat pulled low over his brow, he affected cosmopolitan indifference to the unfortunates around him. He waved away beggars with the same fluttering of his hand he used on horseflies; but as he came upon a block of run-down row houses, he noticed the slight figure of a woman who was strangely familiar to him. Something in her gait, the angle of her head as she listened, the expressive motions of her hands reminded him of someone he knew, and Drumwright lingered in the street to observe her.

She was strolling slowly, conversing with another woman. They both wore long dresses and short-brimmed cloth hats, and they were speaking with an intensity and conviction that belied their casual postures. Drumwright approached cautiously, eavesdropping, and he found that even the tone of the woman's voice was familiar, as was the cadence of her speech. Through his alcoholic stupor, he suddenly recognized Diana. At first, he could not believe his eyes, and he stared at her as if he were seeing a ghost. He felt the weight of the dead bodies of three years before in his arms. He saw the blood and mangled flesh before him, as if it were all happening right then. He had assumed, as all the residents of Tres Cruces had, that Diana had drowned, but here she was standing before him in the flesh: the last scarlet dove of Tres Cruces, the murderer and bank robber, the mythologized and demonized bitch who had killed more men in a single afternoon than had died in the last war with the Pichuas.

Drumwright listened to her conversation more intently. The two women were discussing women's suffrage, and the woman with Diana was holding out a pamphlet when she noticed Drumwright's fixed gaze. She took him for a common drunk, and she motioned Diana away. When Diana turned and recognized Drumwright, her heart leapt into her throat, and she grabbed the suffragette by the arm and pulled her briskly up the street.

Drumwright ran after them and grabbed Diana by the elbow. "Wait! Diana! Stop! I want a word with you."

"I'm afraid you've mistaken me for someone else."

"No, it's no mistake." Drumwright's face flushed, and his grip on Diana's elbow tightened. "Diana, some people in Tres Cruces will be very interested to speak with you."

"Sir, I'm afraid you've mistaken me for someone else. My name is not Diana." Jerking her arm violently out of Drumwright's grip. "Please leave me alone."

The suffragette: "If you don't leave us alone, sir, we'll call for a constable."

Drumwright: "Perhaps you should, ma'am. I'm sure a constable would be interested to hear what I have to say."

The suffragette: "Sir, you're obviously drunk. Leave us alone."

Drumwright looked hard into Diana's eyes, which burned with cold fire. She yanked her elbow out of his grip, then turned and whispered something he couldn't hear into the suffragette's ear. The suffragette nodded. Diana then turned back to Drumwright with sudden aggression, pushing and shoving him with surprising force. He stumbled back on his heels several feet, reeling, and Diana pushed him again and again, until he finally recovered his balance and stood firm, and Diana's face came close to his.

Diana, loudly, theatrically: "Sir, you need help, and I'm going to direct you to a Christian shelter for drunks and invalids." Now whispering viciously: "Doc, you get this straight: Diana's dead. She died three years ago. Unless you want to join her, you'll go back where you came from and never mention her name again." She loudly and demonstratively pointed the way to a mission, then turned briskly on her heels. She rejoined the suffragette, and they hurried down the street without looking back.

Drumwright stood there for a long time. He could hardly believe that he had just found Diana Clayborn in this most unlikely, industrial, impoverished section of San Luis. He was supremely rankled, not just at the surprise of it, not just because he thought Diana owed the town of Tres Cruces restitution, and not just because she owed him personally for the scars he still bore on his face. He was rankled because his sense of justice was offended, that anyone could commit such dastardly crimes and get away scot free! The very principle of justice demanded that she be punished. As he stood watching the two women hurry away, he considered which authorities he might turn to for satisfaction; but as Diana turned the corner a block away, she shot Drumwright a look so icy, ruthless and calculating that his mind froze in mid-thought, and she was gone.

He took out his flask and drank deeply of the scotch he had just purchased. He thought about the lives destroyed by Diana's hand, the corpses that he personally had buried. He drank again, quite openly and carelessly in front of passersby, though this was a crime in San Luis.

Drumwright's disgust grew with his cowardice. He hated Diana because she was still alive, and he feared her, and he believed that it would be possible for her to kill him, or to have him killed, even if she was put behind bars. There would be a trial, and a waiting period, and she would be allowed visitors, and there would be time for her to make good her threat. Was he willing to risk everything for her capture, he asked himself, willing to risk his own life to bring her back to Tres Cruces from beyond the grave? As far as the town knew, she was dead and there was no longer any question of justice. Was he willing to take such a chance—to sacrifice himself, potentially—for the *principle* of justice?

He stood in the street, waiting until he was sure that Diana was far away. Then he walked in a state of increasing agitation to the new riverboat cabaret, vowing, as he boarded, to buy half a dozen whores that night and to extract a measure of justice from each of them.